Species of Feeling

DONIGAN MERRITT

Novels by Donigan Merritt

One Easy Piece
My Sister's Keeper
Hatch's Island
Hatch's Conspiracy
Hatch's Mission
Possessed by Shadows
The Common Bond
Blossom
The Love Story of Paul Collins
The Last Island (digital only)
Species of Feeling

Species of Feeling

A novel by
Donigan Merritt

Bb
B & b Books
Boulder, Colorado, USA
2013

Species of Feeling is the original version, extensively revised and updated, of *Hatch's Island*, published in different form by Bantam Books, NY, 1983.

Bb
B & b Books
Boulder, Colorado, USA

Copyright © 2013 Donigan Merritt
ISBN: 978-0615622941

Cover & frontispiece, original art by David Voss
Cover design: Jcartworks

Grateful acknowledgment is made for permission to quote from *The Magus* by John Fowles. Copyright © 1965, 1977, by J. R. Fowles Ltd. Reprinted by permission of Little, Brown, and Co.

It is not only species of animal that die out, but whole species of feeling. And if you are wise you will never pity the past for what it did not know, but pity yourself for what it did.

-- John Fowles, The Magus

The agony of death may be said to meander. It goes, comes, advances toward the grave, and returns toward life. There is some groping in the act of dying.

-- Victor Hugo, Les Misérables

For Holly: Always and forever, the love of my life

War leaves its debris: the human jetsam of horror. Even its good and honorable survivors will carry at a depth and with a weight, considerate to each, the ember of war. For some this ember is cool enough to be held, displayed for the interest and edification of the fortunately uninitiated; in others it is an unsettling, submerged heat trapped within the private soul; in yet others – and we give thanks to one or another of our various gods if we are not among them, these derelicts of war – the white phosphorous heat burns with such devastating intensity that it reduces the entirety of their lives to pale ashes. I would like to tell you the story of such a man, a warrior gone to ashes.

the author
Tuva, Olowalu Islands, 18 February, 2010

1

Tuva was not an easy place to find. In those days only the desperate, the crazy, or the committed vagabond were apt to stumble across it, much less propose to seek it out. Not that Tuva, one of the largest of a half-dozen consequential and lesser atolls in the Olowalu Group, was unappealing or inhospitable, for it was, as these islands often are, quite a beautiful place.

Maybe Tuva was a bit more lost. In the middle of nowhere, abandoned to itself in the incomparable vastness of the world's emptiest place, the wide harbor beyond Tuva's long jetty was located on the apex of latitude 19° 20' south by longitude 145° 10' west, resting disguised from the common world, two-hundred-seventy-five miles east-southeast of Tahiti, and an immense twenty-six-hundred miles of blue on blue from both Honolulu and Auckland.

Tuvans were officially Polynesians, although at the farthest fringe of what on charts is known as French Polynesia, but the Olowalu Atolls did not belong to the French. They ended up in the essentially disinterested hands of the Australian government at the end of the Great Pacific War, while France kept the more popular ones.

Tuva covered a mountainous thirty-eight square miles, something less than ten percent the size of Tahiti. It was the second largest of the Olowalu Islands. Completely encircled by a coral reef, there were only two openings wide enough and deep enough for boats with much keel to pass inside, and then only at the slim high tide. One of those openings led into the harbor of Tuva town. The other faced Napuku, a village on the opposite side of the island, which could only be reached by boat or on foot over the island's dominating dragon-shaped mountain, Kilohana.

Tuva's population of some two thousand included a mostly static, quite small, motley assortment of odd castaways, typical of the human flotsam drifting around the world's oceans, who now and then washed up on some far beach like ours; I among them.

There was an English painter, who thought himself Gauguin reincarnated, who ran out of paint, canvas, and money, sometime in about 1968; he tended bar at Papa Jack's. There was a lively homosexual fellow named Jolly Malcolm, who was once headmaster – claiming the pun as his own – of an exclusive boys academy in Sydney. Mr. Jolly, as he liked to be called, was the Australian government's bureaucratic representative, the Governor you might say, for all of Olowalu, although he chose to live on Tuva for reasons of his own, the nature of which I am not inclined to speculate. His assistants, they did come and go, were always posted back at the provincial headquarters in Tama Tama, the capitol town of Olowalu Island.

Among we castaways were only a few women, and Jenny Hunt was the only American woman. She came with the Peace Corps and stayed. For many years she was simply called the *haole wahine kumu* – the foreign woman teacher. She married Tioni Makani, son of Kamuela Makani, the island's traditional chief and wealthiest resident.

I was the only other American for quite a long time, until the man known only as Hatch appeared. I managed the copra factory. That's a long and boring story; here's enough of it:

As you know, copra is the extracted dried flesh of the coconut, one natural resource Tuva had in some abundance. Mainly, copra is processed into oil for a variety of food products, but it is also used in cosmetics, particularly skin care items, moisturizers, suntan lotions, and the like. Our factory was only the first stage of the process. We shipped fat and lumpy burlap bags of dried copra to Olowalu, and then on to Papeete. If you have ever used *monoi de Tahiti* skin care products, some of it started with Tuvan coconuts.

Originally, the Australian government owned the copra plant. They sold out to an American agribusiness conglomerate that kept me as the on-site manager. The Americans sold out a few years later to a group of businessmen from Tahiti. I just stayed on. Of course, by then I had married a Tuvan girl, who turned out to be something of a natural baby factory.

There were quite a few Orientals. They individually ran the two general stores, all three grocery stores, the two bars, and everything else that could be considered a business, except the fish market, which was traditionally part of the community as a whole, and ran itself in some spontaneous way. The farmers' market operated independently in a government-provided location – a grassy, palm-lined park next to the street behind the Government House.

There were a few Hindi men in Tuva town, who took native wives and lived adequately as purveyors of bananas, coconuts, and notably potent marijuana they sold to occasionally passing yachtsmen.

We bought the majority of our coconuts from a consortium of these East Asians., not a one of whom I could say I liked or trusted all that much.

Besides the copra factory, there was no other industry and very little tourism. There was not, in those days, even a hotel, although Mr. Lee offered rooms with breakfast on the second floor above his emporium. Since virtually all of Tuva's visitors came on yachts and slept aboard, those rooms saw almost no use. This suited his daughter very well, since it was she who had to clean the room and prepare and serve the breakfast.

Once there was guano to sell. The harvest and sale

of bird droppings was lucrative, but that was before an accidental mongoose influx annihilated most of the island's bird population within one generation. Eventually we ate all the mongooses, or mongeese, whichever it might be. Too late for the birds.

Most of what money there was came from the Australian government, and much of that could be considered more or less welfare.

Everything was self-contained and self-sustaining on Tuva, and most people lived simply by fishing and vegetable farming, by working in the copra factory or one of the small businesses, or by doing some bureaucratic chore for the Australian government.

An infrequent government freighter brought mail-order goods. Sears reached Tuva by catalog many years ago, much to the distress of Mr. Fukumitsu and Mr. Lee, who individually owned Tuva's two main and intensely competitive general stores. When Mr. Lee won the Sears catalog business, Mr. Fukumitsu, screaming racial epithets regarding the Chinese in general and Mr. Lee in particular, made one awkward attempt to run down Mr. Lee with his motor scooter. Mr. Lee, a decidedly slight man, as bent and tiny as a bonsai, retaliated by hiring one of the frequently stoned Hindu men to burn down Mr. Fukumitsu's store. Mr. Fukumitsu foiled the attempt by offering the Hindu arsonist a bolt of tapa cloth for his wife if he would instead go back across the street and burn down Mr. Lee's Emporium. Mr. Lee then offered the profiteering Hindu a pretty strand of large simulated pearls to go back to Mr. Fukumitsu's store with the torch. This continued back and forth, to the gossipy amusement of the entire town, until the two merchants, realizing that murder and arson seemed to profit only the ever-smiling Hindu, made up and shared Sears.

Between semi-annual freighter visits, a few yachts came across the island – not always on purpose – and tied up briefly at Tuva's dilapidated wharf. There being no airport, that was the only way, other than seaplane, to get to Tuva. Their crews drank, took photographs, womanized, and sneaked out at dawn a day or two later, after promising marriage to various local girls. Tuva lay south of the usual routes between Tahiti and the Tuamotus, so such visits were rare; sometimes a year or more passed when only the supply freighter arrived.

It was on such a sailing yacht that the man called Hatch arrived in the rainy season that year.

He appeared on the wobbling wharf early one morning during a quick rain squall, standing out in the tropical wet as if a good cleansing was just what he needed. He had no papers, but no one paid much attention to Australian laws in those days, or these days, for that matter. Besides, who could have known he was going to stay?

The yacht's captain said that he added him as crew in Singapore, and that the man he knew only as Hatch was a good worker during the six months he was aboard. "I'm sure he told me his name, but I probably forgot it." Before that, the captain could only speculate: "I think maybe he was in Indonesia, or it could have been Malaysia. He doesn't talk a hell of a lot. But he seems to possess experience of these places. Good man, though. Never a problem."

Tuvans, being natural gossips, and with a limited variety of entertainments, enjoyed the telling of Hatch stories. During those early years no one came to know him well; frankly, we can say no one knew anything whatsoever about him, until the terrible event that made Hatch's story worth the telling.

Rumors abounded. Outrageous things were claimed: he was an escaped murderer, he was a failed minister, he was a spy hiding from Russians or Americans, or maybe the Chinese, he was just a washed-up derelict, just another boat bum, or maybe a deserter from the war in Vietnam, or maybe some other one.

After a few years, the Hatch stories made the rounds so many times that people tired of them; the gossip simply faded away. Hatch was eventually accepted as another of the crazy whites such faraway islands had always attracted.

He was not an unusually large man, not by Polynesian standards, but he possessed a kind of virulent look about him. An inch under six feet and weighing around one-eighty, he had the build of a distance swimmer, and was indeed frequently seen swimming in the lagoon off his beach.

It seemed to me that no matter what the rest of his face was up to, his eyes remained vacant, the look of a man who had seen all he wanted to see and had lost any interest in the future. Eventually we would learn about this, although few were capable of even imagining such things, especially because they were true.

He lived that first decade on Tuva quietly and peacefully, although tolerating no molestations of his privacy. He built a house on the island during those first few months after casting up on our shores. Let's call it what it was: a shack. He built it on a coastal coral flat trapped between the sea and the jungle, about a mile and a half from the edge of Tuva town. He constructed it entirely by himself from the remains of an abandoned lumber warehouse; a single-wall box with a pitched roof of corrugated tin, deeply rusted. It was a solid enough house, and it squatted, bleeding rust down its sides, like a brown fat Buddha.

There was a narrow and sparkling white beach in front and wrapping around one side of the shack; the rear butted into the jungle. A short jetty collapsed in a storm and he never repaired it. The remaining support posts resembled the bones of a beached whale. A palm grove approached the high tide line and its fallen coconuts washed up onto the beach like abandoned brown monkey heads. Bananas, guavas, and mangoes grew out back. Around the house, twisted koa trees, pandanus grass, wet ferns, bougainvillea bushes, ginger, and plumeria grew wild. Off to one side there was an impenetrable stand of bamboo. Vines sneaked up the unpainted plank walls like kelp.

Hatch, the land and his house, were as isolated as the leper colony on the atoll of Kamalo – a fact noted more than once by the preacher at Ho'okahi Pentecostal Church, who made one probing visit to Hatch's place in the name of the Lord, and was quietly but firmly rebuffed. That was the only try; the rest of the proselytizers probably knew better from the start.

The house could be seen from only two positions – from straight out to sea, just barely appearing, possibly a phantasm, through a narrow space framed by a gap in a grove of bent, swaying coconut palms, and from the topmost and endmost part of Kaiwi Point, a stark, black lava promontory that effectively cut off Hatch's shack from the harbor of Tuva town, on the other side.

It seemed that one day the jungle would consume the shack, encase it in the green, lost to all but archeology.

He had almost no visitors and rarely cleaned or straightened up the place. There were a few books, a stack of ancient, molding magazines, a fisherman's relics: broken-tipped rod, spare and broken reels, unproductive lures awaiting an overhaul, coils of monofilament line, smaller coils of steel leader wire, a cigar box and a shoe box filled with a variety of hooks, a pile of fishing net waiting to be repaired, a few amber glass fishing net floats he picked up on the beach, and hanging over two long nails near the door, his snorkel gear.

Nothing decorated the walls, there were no curtains over the louvered jalousie windows; his bed was a camping cot, although the wicker two-cushion sofa would probably have been more comfortable. He had a couple of chairs, one of which he used at the desk he made from an abandoned door nailed into one corner of the room, the other chair stayed in the kitchen area, where he ate at the plain counter. He wrote in spiral-bound Japanese school notebooks at the desk, but mainly used it as a platform for working on his fishing gear. There was a utilitarian kitchen and the toilet was outside. He could shower in fresh water beneath the rain cistern. The house had no electricity, but there was a small propane tank that fueled a countertop two-burner cooker.

Most nights, he sat at the table, and by the light of a Coleman lantern he read or wrote, smoked and drank whisky. He read mostly about fishing because that topic dominated his small collection, and sometimes from two fat collections of essays he had sent away for – Montaigne and Emerson. He couldn't sleep until he was drunk, and sometimes not even then, or only for a few hours. He would be up through the rest of the dark. If he could not sleep, or felt unsure of it coming, he would go out to the narrow lanai and sit listening to the sea urging itself against the reef.

He told me once that he felt compelled to go outside in storms, walk out to the beach and let the salt spray pummel him, the wind's roar deafen him. In a place without seasons, in limitless summer where the only possibility of change was the rain whipping the palms, one could easily suppose that storms were a reminder of power, of anonymous threat. They were to me, so maybe I am only extrapolating.

Hatch made a modest income from selling fish and bartering. Sometimes he sold to passing yachtsmen exotic seashells he gathered while diving from his outrigger canoe inside the reef. One might not see him for a month or more, then he would appear out of the jungle to trade for food or a little cash, varying with his need. When he came into town on those rare days, he would inhabit Papa Jack's Bar, staying all of a day, and sometimes a night, too, then disappearing again. He drank cheap Japanese whisky and warm Foster's from fat blue cans. When the bar closed to get swept out, he might be found asleep on the edge of the wharf; probably he was too drunk to make the long walk back to his shack.

Sometimes, purely plastered, he prowled Papa Jack's like a caged wild animal, talking anxiously and with lavish gestures, waving his arms, spouting like some raving lunatic of a Hyde Park philosopher, not usually making much sense. In those moments, people were a bit afraid of him.

I must emphasize how rare this was, lest it seem I make too much of it. Usually Hatch kept to himself and stayed out of both the bar and the town. Yet, a man, even one inclined toward intense solitude, could bear only so much time entirely alone before it compressed into the black hole of loneliness, which I myself had known a time or two.

He was amiable with the other fishermen and they would occasionally sit together on the jetty, talking late into the night about the size, although never the exact location, of their catches. Hatch mostly listened as he watched small, tide-trapped sharks trying to work their way out of the spare lagoon and back to the open, unlimited cafeteria of the sea. These men apparently liked his company and thought they knew him a little; he was a fisherman and they were fishermen, a fraternity of occupation. But they did not know him. Hatch always only talked about fishing, weather, and matters regarding boats, while the other men gossiped, talked about friends and family. Even after years, Hatch was a pastless, futureless creature, an ephemeral and even temporary presence in their lives, just as likely to disappear forever as to reappear next week.

I had no reason to believe he might have been celibate, nor would I have had any more reason to think him profligate. He had women sometimes, so people said, but the visits by those women were even more rare than his own ghostly appearances beyond his shack. They worked the trade, and there were only a few such women on Tuva; one of them became somewhat regular, making the long and not easy walk from town to Hatch's shack once or twice a month, going on nearly four years. Eventually she went away with a Filipino deckhand on a long-line trawler.

Maybe she was the one who knew Hatch best, although she said that he was unaffected by the comings and goings of her or the others. Kalena, that was her name, happened to be there on more than one occasion when he screamed from a nightmare. She said Hatch woke with a start, hands in front of his face as if reading his palms, crying out with a sound like a deep guttural moan. He had sweated through his gray tee-shirt and shorts, and through the bottom bed sheet. He brought the palms of his hands close to his face as if expecting to see them bloody. He stared at his palms in the faint glow of dawn coming through the open window behind the bed. There was nothing on his hands but sweat, she said; still, he wiped them frantically on the sheet. He got up and had a drink, then crawled into the bed and seemed to fall back into a restless sleep.

Kalena did not talk about this, except to her sister, A'ala, who was not herself a woman of light spirit. It was A'ala, a friend of my wife, who told us what Kalena had said about Hatch and his nightmares, and this was long after Kalena had gone away.

What Hatch told Kalena on one of those bad nights, was that he had abandoned all expectations, all hope for the future, on a steaming morning in the Laotian jungle. He was just waiting to die, but not brave enough to hasten that end.

A'ala explained that she did not understand everything Kalena told her, there were big words not common to her or anyone she knew, ideas anyone would find strange. One terrible thing, she continued, that he told Kalena, is that there is only one question important enough to spend any time with – deciding to live or to die, to persist in existence or abandon it with ultimate finality. Everything else is just the game of temporary animated molecules. I explained animation and molecules for her, and said Laos was a country in Southeast Asia. A'ala was not impressed; she laughed at such a silly notion, even after I had helped her to understand it.

We often saw him walking quite long distances, as long a distance one can have on a small island, which was not large, even as such atolls go – not quite seven miles long by just under six miles wide, shaped like an oval with a chip missing from one edge, the missing chip forming Tuva's gently-curving harbor. He was often seen walking alone in places where there was no likely destination.

Now and then I met him at Papa Jack's, and being compatriots, or at least born in the same country, we would talk about matters of no consequence to anyone, passing the evening hours. I came to know a little about him in bits and pieces acquired over ten years of those occasional evenings in the bar.

Hatch had been living on Tuva for five years before I learned that he was once upon a time a student at a California university, studying about the most esoteric thing I could imagine: Classical Literature. He happened to mention this when I made a comment about how he knew so many words in Greek and Latin, which occasionally peppered his more drunken speeches. A couple of years later, after hearing A'ala's story, I asked if he had been in the Vietnam War and he answered, "Not exactly." He had a distinct way of cutting off a conversation when he was ready to end it – he ordered another round and asked some question about you.

Once – I had known him for only a year then – I happened to ask what he wanted to do when he decided to stay on Tuva and build a house? I had thought of possibly asking if he would like a job at the copra factory, since he clearly had very little money; Americans sticking together, you might say. He downed his beer, clanked the empty can on the bar, put one hand on my shoulder, and said this in as plain and direct a voice you could imagine: "My friend, all I want is to be left, just like that shack of mine, to rot and rust on this island in the middle of nowhere. I want to fish, to drink, and if I am lucky, to die in peace. That's pretty much it, Don. Let's have another drink, and you can tell me why you stay here?"

And so Hatch might have gotten his wish, had not the American yacht, Hard Wind, driven by an offshore storm, sought shelter in Tuva Bay, ten years to the month after Hatch arrived in the same manner.

2

On that morning, as the Hard Wind glided through the reef, Hatch left his bed – if you can call a cot a bed – lit an oil lamp, and went outside to the toilet shed to relieve himself. Then he sat on a stump by the front of his shack and split the top of a green coconut to drink its thin, sweet milk, waiting for the sun appear above the eastern ridge. He drained the coconut, ate a few chunks of its meat, then walked into the flat water of the lagoon and swam out to the reef and back. He rinsed the salt from his skin beneath the rainwater cistern behind the shack.

Breakfast consisted of a mango, some red onion, and opakapaka fish, all marinated together in lime juice. He dressed in ragged jeans faded almost bone white, a sleeveless denim shirt faded slightly less, and torn canvas shoes, adding his sheathed K-bar knife to the belt and putting a small flashlight into his pocket.

He intended to cross the lower northern ridges of Kilohana, to the village of Napuku on the opposite side of the island, where he hoped to trade a shovel, and if necessary, his best pocket flashlight, for a new propeller for his Johnson fifteen-horse outboard motor. He could get Mr. Lee to order a new prop, but it would take six months, or even a year, and the engine was necessary for working beyond the reef. The fishermen in Napuku were by necessity hoarders and Hatch hoped one of them needed a shovel more than a spare Johnson prop.

It would take a three hours to make his way up and over the island's residual volcanic spine through Rotava Valley and down the windward cliffs to

Napuku. He figured that bargaining would take another hour or two. If he returned by way of the shorter but more rugged trail through Poki Valley to the south, he could get back to Tuva town in time to pick up some supplies and have a drink at Papa Jack's. Had his prop not bent on a clump of brain coral the day before, when he stupidly, or drunkenly, tried to pass over the reef on a falling tide, he could simply have motored around the atoll within the protection of the reef and made it to Napuku in less than an hour. Of course, then there would be no need.

It was nearly noon when Hatch reached Napuku. Because of increasing wind kicking up ten-foot walls of spray where the sea contacted the reef, the Napukuan fishermen had not gone out. Some tended nets on the beach, and some did small repair jobs on their outrigger skiffs. Others slept in the shade or stood in clumps, talking story. Children, dozens of them, ranging in age from toddlers to early teens, played along the beach. A few of the older boys, who would have been fishing with their fathers had the weather allowed, tossed a rugby ball around on the village's only street, a dirt and crushed coral lane running the entire length of the village and parallel to the beach. Two girls doing the family laundry stooped over a tin tub between two frame houses; clothes hanging from lines strung between palm trees flapped in the wind like prayer flags.

Some five hundred people lived in Napuku, the only other settlement on the island large enough to be called a town. Napuku was separated from Tuva town by the dragon-tail hump of Kilohana mountain, all that remained of the volcano that formed the island however many millions of years ago. Ridges dropping down from the collapsed cone of Kilohana split the island in half. The actual distance between the two towns amounted to less than five miles, but it took half a day to walk from one to the other because of the thick interior jungle and jagged cliffs dropping precipitously to the sea.

There were only two small food stores and one bar. The only shop in Napuku sold fishing and boat supplies, along with odds and ends of hardware. Most of the simple houses were thatched, although a few had wooden walls and tin roofs. Further down the coast, where in one valley there was a bit of flat land, farmers worked small hard-won clearings below the rich, rain-sodden, windward slope of Kilohana.

Because of their relative isolation, the people of Napuku tended to hoard. It was not an easy trip to load an outrigger with supplies and navigate the shoals around the ragged, jutting outcropping of Kaiwi Point. During the few years of required schooling, the children of Napuku were boarded with friends or relatives in Tuva town. But many children did not go to school. Mandatory education was, like all the Australian laws, easily ignored. Napukuan families did not like being separated from their children, even if they were only five miles away. To them, Tuva was a city – a place with more than two thousand residents, with two schools, four churches, a storefront sort of Buddhist temple, three general stores, four bars, and a public building, the government house, which showed movies on Saturdays. They did not want their children exposed to the paganism of the Anglican or Catholic or Pentecostal Churches, nor to the sloth induced by the bars. The people of Napuku kept to the old ways, conceding only to outboard motors and erratic electrical power from the new generator booster located near the mountaintop.

Hatch often said that he preferred the style of Napuku to Tuva, and regretted not having built his house on the windward side of the island. Sometimes he thought of tearing down the house, it was really no more than a small single-wall shack, and hauling it in chunks around the island on his outrigger skiff. He told me once he just might get around to it someday, and I took him seriously.

He walked down the dirt street toward the house of Apalama, Kamuela Makani's uncle, and by royal heritage the mayor of Napuku. Apalama was also the best Tuvan fisherman, which would have given him the status of mayor regardless of being descended from Tuvan royalty. Hatch crossed to the upland side of the street to avoid the wildly-kicked rugby ball, and headed to Apalama's house.

The old man greeted Hatch and stepped into the sun. Apalama's skin was wrinkled to the texture and color of a sea cucumber. He had once been tall, although not as tall as his nephew; age had stooped him considerably. His teeth were nicotine stained. He motioned for Hatch to follow him around to the side of the house, to a pair of wicker chairs set up at the edge of his wife's vegetable garden. Apalama was known for his formality.

"Some beer?" Apalama asked in English. Hatch spoke a little Tuvan, but they both knew English would be faster, and certainly more intelligible.

"Beer would be very good, Apalama. Thank you. After the mountain. It is hot even in high places today."

"Lahela," Apalama called out to his wife, who was visible in the open window ten feet away. "Two cold beers, and bring Chesterfield." Returning his attention to Hatch, "So, you come over the mountain? The sea is great today, mad like a wife."

"Yes, over the mountain. The sea is indeed rough, whether like a wife I cannot say."

Hatch stood politely when Lahela came out with the bottles of beer and Apalama's prized Chesterfield cigarettes.

Lahela Makani – an overstuffed woman with a handsome face, who was fifteen years younger than her husband's sixty-one years – nodded to Hatch and handed both beers to Apalama, who in turn handed one to Hatch. Then she took a single cigarette from the pack before handing it over to her husband. Hatch quickly took a match from his pocket and lit Lahela's cigarette.

"Mahalo," she said, thanking him. She took a deep drag from the cigarette and blew a cloud into the air on her way back inside, smoke trailing her like steam from a burdened locomotive.

"She has her blood now," Apalama said by way of explaining his wife's rude behavior in taking a cigarette from her husband's pack and smoking it in front of a guest. "A man wishes for old times, when women had their own house for this event." Apalama drank from his beer and waited for Hatch to do the same. After Hatch drank, Apalama again welcomed him to his home.

"Mahalo," Hatch said. He found himself rather wishing he had a woman who could have stood living with him for twenty-five years; he would let her take a cigarette anytime.

According to custom, the two men shared their cigarettes in silence, observant, attentive to the scene around them: a stiff breeze fluttering the palms, the omnipresent rumbling of the sea smashing into the reef, the high, happy voices of children, clanking noises from the open kitchen window, pigs rooting, chickens clucking, dogs barking, someone singing on the beach.

Hatch smoked the expensive cigarette to the butt, then handed it over to his host to extinguish and save. By the end of a pack, the old man would have saved enough tobacco to roll one extra cigarette.

"If I was not so old," Apalama broke their silence, squeezing out the ember and shaking the remaining tobacco into the cellophane of the package, "I would take that woman to Tuva town and leave her for the Kahuna to tame. Alas, I need her useful services."

"You are not so old you cannot go to the sea and control it."

"Better the sea, better the sea," Apalama said, giggling.

"Apalama, I bent the propeller on my Johnson outboard and cannot fish beyond the reef until I get a new one."

"I see. This is a problem."

"I have come to ask if you know any man in Napuku who might have such a propeller to trade."

Apalama studied the matter, tilting his head to stare into the palm fronds that shaded them, rubbing both temples with his index fingers.

Hatch continued. "I have brought with me a very fine shovel, made from American steel."

Apalama looked at it lying beside Hatch's chair. Hatch reached down and picked up the shovel, handing it over to Apalama.

Apalama flicked a fingernail against the steel edge of the shovel. "It is very good steel. This is excellent hardwood of the handle, and a good long handle it is, as high as a man's chest from the ground."

"The blade is the strongest steel made in America, and will hold an edge even in lava."

"Umm. You say this will dig in lava?"

"I have tried it. Yes. It will dig in lava. I mean the a'a kind, not laupahoehoe. Of course, it can dig into the soil for planting potatoes, or any other crop, as if the earth is like poi."

"Dig a burial place?"

"With this shovel a man can dig a fine and deep place of rest, where the spirit in a man's bones may sleep in peace throughout time, not disturbed by man or animal. But surely you, Apalama, are not … ?"

"No, not me. That woman never let me die. For another."

"I see. Also, Apalama, you have a good garden here. With a shovel like this one you could more easily plant vegetables as fine as these."

"This is Lahela's garden. Lahela got already da kine."

"My compliments to Lahela for such a fine garden. In that case, I would like to ask if you know of any man in Napuku who needs a shovel like this one, and who might have the kind of propeller I need?"

"Johnson kind?"

"Yes, fifteen-horse."

"Sam Pakilua could need such shovel, and he have da kine same motor."

"Could you please go with me to see Sam Pakilua? I do not know him."

"Another beer, then we go."

"Ah, thank you. Your beer is very cold." Hatch thoughtfully let Apalama know that he knew how proud the old man was of the new electrical feeder line to his house, running the reefer he had waited a year to get through Mr. Lee's mail order.

"Lahela," Apalama called out to his wife. Her head appeared in the window. "Two beers."

They shared the beers and had one more cigarette. Apalama liked Chesterfields because he liked saying the name, and because it was the first American cigarette he had ever tasted. To have shared two with Hatch was a sign of respect. Whatever else Hatch might have been, Apalama knew him to be a good fisherman and a respectful man.

They talked about fishing. Apalama mentioned the unusually strong wind and said it portended at least two more days of bad water. They inquired about one another's health.

When the cigarettes were finished, Apalama stood and said it was time to go to Sam Pakilua's house. He picked up the shovel and started off. Hatch took an unopened pack of Chesterfields from his shirt pocket and left it on the round table between the two chairs, then waved farewell to Lahela, who watched from the kitchen window.

It was a hundred yards between the two houses, and when they reached their destination, Apalama went inside with the shovel. Hatch waited by the street. He could hear their voices coming from inside the single-wall frame house; it felt like eavesdropping, even though, because they spoke Tuvan, he couldn't understand much of it. He walked toward the beach, until their voices disappeared beneath the surf sound, and stood with his back to the house, watching a man repairing a casting net. Four boys, chasing one another with sticks, toyed dangerously close to running into the widely-arched net. The fisherman ignored them, knowing they wouldn't dare. Ten minutes passed while Hatch squatted on his haunches and drew circles in the sand with a stick. When the door opened behind him, Hatch stood and walked back toward the house.

Apalama and Sam Pakilua, who looked many years older than Apalama, came into the yard. The shovel was in Sam Pakilua's hand, the propeller in Apalama's. Hatch approached and offered to shake the old man's hand.

"Mahalo, mahalo nui loa," Hatch thanked him profusely. "It is the best shovel I have ever seen, it will do good work for you."

Sam nodded and returned silently to his house, leaving the shovel leaning against the outside wall. Apalama handed the propeller to Hatch.

"This is exactly what I need," Hatch said.

"Sam Pakilua need da kine."

"Does he have land to clear?" Hatch was only making conversation as they walked back toward Apalama's house.

"He is to die soon. His boys will make a grave for him with your shovel, da kine you say go into lava."

"I see." Hatch looked at the propeller. It was not new but in good shape. He held it behind his back the rest of the way.

They stopped by the front door and shook hands. When Apalama went inside, Hatch continued across the garden path. Lahela was sitting in one of the chairs, puffing happily on a Chesterfield, the pack Hatch left nowhere in sight. Lahela looked at Hatch and smiled, patting the bulging pocket of her apron.

"Take," she said, pointing toward a small package wrapped in a taro leaf.

Hatch picked up the package, nodded to Lahela, and departed. He opened the package on the trail and found six sweet, fat, sugar cookies.

3

The speck of the ketch's sail on the western horizon appeared motionless after being first spotted by a man harvesting coconuts from the taller trees along the shoreline. Word spread quickly through the village. By the time the ketch came near enough to be recognized as a two-master, forty people had gathered on the wharf, and all the way back to the long, warped-plank lanai in front of Papa Jack's Bar, which faced the wide harbor.

Mr. Jolly Malcolm sent one of the schoolboys aloft with his binoculars. The boy scampered up the tallest object on the shore, a coconut palm, and with his legs grasping the rough trunk to leave his hands free, watched the yacht's approach. When she made the turn to line up with the narrow passage through the encircling reef, the boy called down, "American, Mr. Jolly. I can see the flag."

"Good boy, Keolo," Mr. Jolly replied in his lilting voice. "Now you get right down before you hurt yourself."

The boy slung the binoculars over his back and descended the curving tree with experienced grace and speed.

By the time the ketch dropped her reefed mainsail and turned downwind under a storm jib, there were maybe a hundred people on the wharf. Outside Hua Pala passage, the crew could now be seen moving about on deck, furling and bagging sails. The ketch cleared the reef under power and came alongside the wharf in a graceful sidelong drift, snuggling tight against the car tire dock fenders. Small, brown, barefooted boys ran to accept the mooring lines tossed to them by crewmen. The ketch secured, the helmsman shut off the engine and tipped his white skipper's cap to the gathered crowd. Women giggled, blushed, turned away. Men moved closer, preparing to hawk wares, or just to satisfy their curiosity. Two crewmen pitched bright coins into the clear water for the dock urchins to dive after.

It was the first boat to appear in Tuva Bay in five months, the second that year.

Across her stern we could read – Hard Wind, and below that – San Diego. The crew clearly relished the attention paid to them by the crowd on the pier. Nothing, the captain admitted later, like Papeete, their last port, where they were ignored by everyone but the whores, hustlers, and port police. The crew went about the business of docking with the air of actors on a floating stage, the Tuvans their audience. The captain, we learned his foul name in due course, shouted orders to the other three men, while simultaneously checking out the younger women on the pier.

It was obvious, the one he wanted. Caught in his gaze, she demurely lowered her eyes and turned to leave. But her two companions, much braver girls, playfully held her back. The captain tipped his cap and smiled. Her friends giggled and prodded her forward. When the captain stepped off the boat and approached, she pulled away from her friends and disappeared into the crowd.

"Don't be scared, my shy beauty," the captain called out, although by then she was nearly out of sight.

"I am no scared of nothing," one of her friends said, standing in front of the captain and blocking his path. "That one is no girl for you, Mr. boat captain."

That girl, Kukana Pele Makani, was the only daughter of Kamuela Makani, the chief and most powerful man on Tuva. Uncharacteristically shy for an island girl of seventeen, an advanced age for young women living in the moist sensuality of tropical islands, she had not been allowed the same freedoms and experiences of her friends. They could go for night walks with boys, during which, of course, they often made love. Even if allowed, everyone believed that Kukana would not have been interested.

My own daughters ... that's another story.

Kukana – although, to my mind, not the most beautiful young woman on Tuva – was abundantly pretty. Her coconut-oiled black hair had never been significantly cut, only ragged ends trimmed from time to time; it hung so far down her back that she had to flip it aside to keep from sitting on it. She had the height, but not all of it, of course, from her six-foot-seven father, and a compelling figure from her mother.

Sadly, her mother died when Kukana was seven years old. Emma, Kukana's mother, was an exceptional woman, and Tuva mourned her passing for well more than the official year. Kukana had Polynesian skin that, after childhood blemishes faded, could be favorably compared with the color of polished bronze. Because of her height, just a thin hair short of six feet, and her mother's gift of early full breasts, she looked well older than seventeen years.

From where did her shyness, her flagrant naïveté come? Of course her father was protective, and evidently more so after her mother died, but many fathers are like that, while unfortunately their daughters do not take to the lessons. My oldest daughter, Mia, was pregnant at fifteen, and got married last year when she was the same age as Kukana Makani. (Mia and Kukana were friends since childhood, and she was one of the girls with Kukana on the wharf that fateful day, but, at least, I can say, not the one who came on so blatantly with the yacht captain. That was Rosie Lau.) My hopes for her, my struggle to instill at least some modicum of responsibility into her head, came to nothing in the end. Though I love her mightily, regardless.

I digress. A habit of isolation, I'm sure.

Kukana had completed her compulsory eight years of education on Tuva, but possessed a natural intellectual curiosity that extended well beyond what our educational system required or could provide. She was the most regular visitor to the small library in an annex wing of the Government House, and Mr. Jolly claimed Kukana had probably read every book in the room, her favorites more than once. She could work arithmetic problems, had a basic idea of geometry, and spoke both English and French quite well. She was more widely traveled than any of her friends, having been with her father, mother, and brother to the Olowalu provincial headquarters at Tama Tama, to Tahiti, to Fiji, and once when she was seven years old to the cities of Sydney and Canberra, where likely on that trip her mother picked up the virus that killed her.

In spite of all that, she was reticent beyond what could be called shyness. It might have been her mother's death at such a sensitive age, or maybe just her nature, a dewdrop blossom awaiting the sun, if you will pardon my vain attempt at something a bit purplish.

At any rate, Mr. Jolly Malcolm approached the captain to ask for his passport and the yacht's papers. I tagged along, curious to meet these Americans. Meanwhile, Mia and Rosie went looking for Kukana.

With nothing much left to watch, most of the Tuvans departed, returning to whatever they were doing when the yacht came into view. Two old men, who always spent their mornings fishing for amberjack from a low platform on one side of the wharf, fastened their rods to posts and walked alongside the rather large ketch, as if inspecting her for purchase.

It was almost lunch time, a stiff breeze blew from the mountain and funneled through the valley into the village. It was hot now. The idea of a nap in the shade of a loulu palm attracted some, others returned to work at the copra factory, back to the shops, or for the lucky, to Papa Jack's or the Lotus Bar for an afternoon's libations. A few others remained on the wharf, and some of those followed the captain on his quest for supplies.

Mia and Rosie caught up with Kukana, and somehow convinced her to go with them to Papa Jack's.

In Papa Jack's, where sandwiches were available, Kukana sat across a small round table from Bill Byron. That was the captain's name. She watched him devour a tuna sandwich, a hardboiled egg, and a slab of fried Spam with a pineapple ring on top. Two other members of the yacht's crew were also in Papa Jack's. The fourth crewman, David Byron, Bill's younger brother, remained on the boat for security. Mia and Rosie were at the next table with the other crewmen.

Kukana thought Bill Byron had the lightest hair and beard she had ever seen – nearly white, with a bit of yellow in it, like a white plumeria. The only other time she had seen hair that white was on the wife of a government agent, who came during one of the regular freighter visits a dozen years ago, when Kukana was five years old. She was on the wharf in Mr. Jolly's care when the woman disembarked from the ship's tender and made her ungainly way toward the street. Kukana ran up and asked if she could touch her hair. The woman bent down to allow the "cute little dark child" access to her platinum hair. Kukana thought it felt like dried out and stuck together strips of pandanus grass, and said so.

Later, Mr. Jolly explained to Kukana that the woman's hair wasn't natural, that she bleached it in a way similar to how Tuvans bleached clumps of dead coral to turn them white and remove the foul odor of dying polyps and crustaceans. After that, Kukana thought that white hair was something bleached to kill an awful odor.

It took Kukana a while to become comfortable enough with the yacht captain to ask about his hair, which did not smell bad at all. Finally, helped by the rum he was on the semi-sly mixing with the cola in her glass, she asked if she might touch it.

"It's real," Byron told her. "Go ahead and grab yourself some. Check it out."

Tentatively Kukana reached up and ran her fingers through his thick, yellow-white hair. "It's not sticky," she said with unhidden surprise.

"I do wash it now and then," he joked, laughing at her wide-eyed expression. He lifted her hand and put it back on his hair. "You can play with my hair as much as you like, honey."

Kukana touched his hair again, then put both hands back into her lap. "I think you have pretty hair," she said. "It is like the color of the plumeria."

"You don't know what pretty is until you have my view," Bill patted her thigh. When he didn't remove his hand, Kukana moved it for him, then scooted her chair a few inches away to make the point. "You're the prettiest girl I've seen in these islands, and baby, I've seen a whole lot of them."

"Have you sailed all the ocean everywhere?" She leaned a few more inches away from his roaming hand, and glanced over her shoulder toward the door, nervously expecting her father to show up and catch her sitting in the bar with this haole man.

Bill took a drink from his glass of rum and lit a cigarette. "I tell you, Koo – ?"

"Kukana."

"Oh yeah, Kukana."

"My friend Mia's father, he is also an American, he says my name is the same like Susan in English." Kukana glanced at the table where Mia and Rosie sat with the other crew members, but they weren't paying attention to her.

"Well, I've known a lot of Susans, but none pretty as you."

"How far have you sailed to come here?"

"We left San Diego sixteen months ago. We've been kicked out of ports from Apia to Nuku'alofa."

He tried adding more rum to Kukana's Coke, but she put her hand over the top and stopped him.

"You said you live in Hollywood?" Kukana moved her leg farther away from his hand.

"More or less."

"Are all the girls in Hollywood pretty, like in movies?"

"Nothing compared to you, honey. A girl like you could write her own ticket in the States."

"Write my ticket?"

"Have anything you want."

"Oh. I see. Have a ticket to get anything I want. But I have already anything I want," she lied a little. Kukana had many unfulfilled dreams, dreams difficult or impossible to fulfill on Tuva. "Maybe I will go to America one time."

"If you want to see America, baby, you can just hop on my boat and sail away with me."

Kukana laughed. "Hah, that is a silly thing to say."

"Why silly?"

"My father is the chief of Tuva, a very important man in all Olowalu."

"So that makes you like a princess."

"Yes," Kukana answered, taking him seriously. It was the most natural thing in her world. "I am a princess here. Chief is like the king in America."

"We don't have kings in America, honey, but maybe we ought to, if we get princesses like yourself." He scooted his chair closer to hers, the sides of their legs then touching.

Kukana blushed. "I flew one time on an airplane," she added proudly. "I flew on the airplane from Tahiti to Sydney; that is in the country of Australia. I don't remember much, though, because I was only seven years old."

"In America you fly everywhere, all the time. In California you can see airplanes coming and going, like every minute, the sky as full of them as birds. We have more airplanes in America than you have palm trees. Would you like to see that?"

"But they must run into each other, yes? So many? Like birds? But really, I don't like airplanes. One time when we were close to land, the airplane turned on its side like a frigate bird diving for a fish," she demonstrated a banking turn with her hand, "and I felt myself being a little afraid. I did not understand how the airplane will not fall to the ground and be smashed. Tahiti looked like a rock in the water. Tuva must be smaller even than that."

"In America, you can fly all day and see nothing but land."

"There must be as much land in America as there is water in our ocean. Australia looked like that."

"Absolutely. In America there are specks of water on the land – ponds and lakes, things like that. Here there are specks of land on the water."

Kukana smiled at the image, but was starting to worry that the captain was getting drunk. His leg kept touching hers and his hand kept going back to her leg even after she removed it. She was flattered by the yacht captain's attention, but she was also worried about her father, whose hopes for her made him especially strict, although that was also his nature. He would never approve of such a thing, not anywhere, and certainly not in Papa Jack's Bar. It was the wrong thing to do, and she knew it.

Most island girls were sexually experienced by the time they were in their mid-teens, but Kukana was the daughter of a man who a few short generations ago would have been a demigod; she lived by a different set of mores. It was certainly not proper for Kukana to be in Papa Jack's with an American sailor, drinking Coke from a glass into which he kept pouring rum. Now she was feeling a little afraid of him, but trapped by having chosen to be there in the first place.

The English bartender, Dennis Lindsay, came around and sat on a bar stool with his guitar, hoping to generate a few tips in the brandy glass he set on the bar. The only songs he knew were English and Irish folks songs. While Kukana listened to the bartender's tunes, moving her head naturally with the rhythm, Bill Byron rested his hand on her thigh and stroked the soft, warm, golden skin at the edge of her red, flower-print dress.

Maybe it wouldn't be so bad if he only touched her there and did not try to do any more than that. That was as brave as she could allow herself to be. The rum buzzed in her head and she found herself rather enjoying the electrical tingling feel of his teasing fingertips.

She had read many romantic books; she enjoyed the excitement of being treated as special by the American, who laughed so easily and made everything sound like fun. After his ship sailed away, all of Kukana's friends would probe her for stories. She would be inclined to maybe make up a few for entertainment. Nobody would believe her anyway.

Then she noticed. She had no idea how long it had been there, but suddenly she realized that the captain's hand had pushed up the hem of her dress and lay on the highest reach of her thigh, his fingers hardly the width of a hand away from her most private spot. Kukana scooted back her chair and knocked his hand away as if one of the fuzzy banana spiders had fallen on her.

Indignantly, she cried, "What are you doing?"

"We both know what I'm doing, darling. All we need to determine is how much it's going to cost me to explore a little further up this valley to paradise."

Bill reached over and touched her shoulder, but she

shoved him away and stood, pointing to Hattie, the fat woman in a red muumuu at the bar, saying, "You can go see her if that's what you want."

Kukana turned and ran out the door.

Bill Byron looked over at Hattie. She returned his glance with a wide, tooth-gapped, beckoning smile.

"Christ!" Bill muttered, tossing some cash on the table and heading for the door after Kukana. The other two men from the Hard Wind's crew shouted after him: "Go get her, Billy. Don't let her get away." Their laughter followed him to the street.

His footsteps creaked on the plank sidewalk; Kukana wasn't far ahead. He caught up just as she turned off the street toward the Government House and fell into step beside her. She refused to look at him.

"Hey," he shouted to stop her, but she continued ignoring him. He reached out and took her arm. She shrugged him off with a hot glare. In reality, she was scared nearly to death.

"Suit yourself," Bill Byron said, and turned to walk back to the bar, muttering along the way. He was overheard by Mr. Fukumitsu, who was standing on the sidewalk outside his store: "Fucking little tease."

Kukana turned around after he left and walked to the Government House Library, where she could sit among the books, her favorite distraction. She sat there half an hour, reading randomly. Her sister-in-law Jenny was responsible for most of the book purchases; it was also the school's library. Most were textbooks, although there were a couple of hundred novels, almost all reflecting Jenny's tastes, and that meant romances and detective mysteries. The books Mr. Jolly ordered were Kukana's favorites. Before leaving, Kukana went to Mr. Jolly's office to ask if he would order some more by Mr. Graham Greene. He told her she should try a Russian next, and he would put the book of Mr. Chekov's stories on the shelf as soon as he finished it.

4

Hatch entered Poki Valley late in the afternoon, after working his way through the underbrush and undulated laupahoehoe lava on the craggy leeward slope of Kilohana. Nearing the southern edge of Tuva town, he heard unusual noises not far off one side of the trail. The jungle foliage was too thick at that point to see any distance beyond the narrow path.

There was a tin-walled tool shed used by banana workers over there, and the noises, human noises, came from it.

He put down the propeller and marked its location with a stick poked through the shaft hole. then crept into the tall elephant grass alongside the footpath toward the shed. It could have been workers, but something wasn't right about the sounds. Besides, it was nearly dark, and nobody worked in the spider land of the banana grove after dark.

The sun now behind Kilohana, the canopy of trees blocking much of what daylight lingered. He pushed aside a clump of grass and moved cautiously toward the shed. The door was half open, a light, like from a flashlight, darted around the otherwise dark interior.

A man's voice commanded: "Be still, damn it!"

Muffled sobbing.

Hatch stopped instantly. At first he thought the voice had been directed at him. He pulled the knife from its sheath.

Through the door opening, he could just make out three men. One stood aside, his pants dropped to his ankles, his ass shining wet like a skinned pig's. Another man stood near the corner of the shed, where a simple shelf had been knocked down, spilling cans and tools and rags onto the packed dirt floor. He heard another voice but could not see him. They were strangers, one of them with such blond hair that it appeared white, virtually glowing in the near-dark room.

Hatch moved silently into the doorway, where he noticed the girl lying on her side, curled into a fetal position, naked. He couldn't see her face because her long black hair spread over it. The third man, now visible in the corner, held a flashlight pointed at the girl, illuminating the scrapes and bruises on her arms.

"Come on, Davy. Do her, for Chrissakes!" the man with the white hair said to the one holding the flashlight, who didn't seem much older than a teenager.

One of the men reached down and began pulling up his khaki shorts. "Jesus fucking Christ! Don't be such a pussy, kid."

"How am I supposed to fuck her while she's crying like that? Come on. Let's just go."

David Byron, holding the flashlight, started to turn, and when he did the beam angled toward the door.

"Hey!" Hatch shouted, startling the men.

"Get that light out of my face," Hatch told the boy. The light caught the glint of the K-bar blade before the kid turned the flashlight toward the floor.

"Who the hell are you?" Bill Byron said, taking a step toward Hatch.

"Don't move," Hatch ordered. "Don't any of you move."

"Don't get carried away here, friend. This isn't what it looks like," one of them said.

"You three move into the corner and stay put. I am really good with this thing," Hatch said, holding the knife out.

When they were in the corner, Hatch approached the girl on the ground and reached down to touch her shoulder. Her entire body tensed from his touch. He could see clearly now the cuts and bruises all over her arms, the backs of her thighs. There were spots of blood in the dirt. She must have fought like hell, Hatch thought.

"You are safe now," Hatch told her, making his voice as soothing as he could. He repeated it in Tuvan: "palekana, malu." He touched her shoulder. "I want you to get up. Stand up, go, hele mai."

The girl turned her face up and with one shaking hand moved some of the hair away from her eyes.

Hatch recognized her. Who wouldn't? He didn't remember her name, but knew the girl was the daughter of Kamuela Makani.

"Oh man," Hatch said. "You guys are seriously fucked up now."

Her face exposed, Hatch saw a gag stuffed into her mouth. He reached back with his free hand and pulled the gag out. It was her panties wadded into a ball. Sensing movement, Hatch turned his attention back to the men standing only a few feet away.

"If you make any kind of move, it will be your last. Killing is easy, and I don't mind it." Then he turned back to the girl and said, "It's all right now. Get dressed." He dropped the panties next to her hand.

Kukana Makani sat up and scooted backwards, stopping only when her back hit the tin wall. She was crying and struggling to speak, pointing frantically in the direction of the three men who attacked her.

Hatch pulled the penlight from his pocket and shined it toward her: both eyes were swollen almost closed, her lower lip split open and oozing blood, and there were raw scratches around her neck.

"He … they … ," Kukana tried to speak through the sobbing. "He said he will kill me … ."

"I know," Hatch said, calming his voice for her. "You don't have to worry now. They won't hurt you anymore. But you need to put your clothes on, please."

Kukana stayed backed up against the wall,

pointing repeatedly toward the three men. She gurgled words in Tuvan, not all of which Hatch understood.

He turned his attention to the men, who looked as if they were about to make a move against him. "If you think I won't kill you, just move one time. Don't think you have any chance against me with this. Do we understand each other?"

David Byron acknowledged by nodding his head. One crewman still had his pants around his ankles. Bill Byron only glared.

Hatch glanced back toward Kukana. "Where are your clothes?"

Kukana was sobbing and shaking, clutching her panties to her chest with one hand and pointing at her attacker with the other. "They … they … he … ."

"This is such bullshit," Bill Byron said in mock defense. "She brought us up here. She wanted it, man. We paid her a helluva lot of money … ."

"No!" Kukana cried.

David jerked his head toward his brother and started to say something, but Bill pointed his finger at David's face and said, "You just shut up."

"Where are her clothes?" Hatch demanded.

"God damn it, I don't know. The bitch wasn't wearing nothing but a skimpy dress and those panties."

"I didn't ask you what."

"Over there someplace, I guess." He inclined his head toward the mess where the work shelf had collapsed.

Hatch looked in that direction and noticed a piece of red and white cloth. "Stay put," he ordered, then went over to retrieve the cloth, Kukana's now torn dress.

"Listen to me," Hatch said to Kukana in a firm voice. "None of these men are going to hurt you, and I am not going to hurt you. That's over now. You are all right. Palekana. So put on your underpants and your dress."

Mutely, Kukana pulled the dress over her head; the panties remained clutched in her hand.

"Good. That's good."

"Look man, this isn't what you think. Come on. You're making a helluva mistake," Byron said.

"If I have to tell you to shut the fuck up one more time, I'm just going to have to cut off your tongue. Do you understand that?"

Byron nodded, hardening his glare.

Hatch wasn't sure what he ought to do next. He could not give his attention to the girl without taking his eyes off her rapists, and if they did in fact come at him at the same time, he might not be able to stop all three. But he couldn't just leave her sitting on the ground naked. They had done a lot of damage to the girl's face; Hatch was inclined to just kill the sons of bitches and be done with it. Three less assholes in the world, he thought.

It was rapidly getting darker. Hatch still had his small flashlight, and that would be enough to illuminate the path around the back of the banana grove until reaching the lights at the church.

"Pull up your pants. You look stupid," Hatch told the crewman, who complied immediately.

"You," he said to David. "Toss me your light."

Hatch put his own flashlight between his teeth and caught the other one in his free hand. He handed it to Kukana and told her to go, right now. The light seemed to calm her. "Go home," Hatch told her. "And when you get to town, send some men back here. Go. Come on, you can go now." He raised his voice to the pitch of an order and repeated in Tuvan: "Hele mai!"

Kukana stared at him as she had not heard, a curious, but still frightened look on her face.

"You're okay. Now just get up and walk outside to the path. You know where you are."

Kukana stood, then stumbled until she felt confidence in her legs. The flashlight beam scattered around the inside of the shed.

"Remember, tell your father to send some men back up here," Hatch called after her as she disappeared through door.

"Okay, my friend," Byron said, sensing an opening now that the object of their violence had left. "She's gone. We can be reasonable about this. What do you want to do now?"

"You really don't want to know what I'd like to do now."

"Money? Look, we don't have a lot, but there's some back on the boat, down in the harbor. A little dope, maybe? Bet you never see high quality Burmese coke out here. Just name it. I don't want any hassles, all right?"

"Who the fuck *are* you?"

"What difference does that make? We're only passing through, just here to let the storm blow by."

Like the captain he was, Bill Byron was doing all the talking.

"I don't like you, any of you," Hatch said, as if making a remark about nothing of particular interest.

"Did I suggest we get married?"

"I think I'll just cut your balls off and be done with this mess," Hatch announced dispassionately, moving a step closer.

"God *damn*, man! Are you fucking crazy?" Byron said. "We didn't do shit to you, dude."

Hatch was stalling so he could figure out what to do next, how to get these three men down the hill in the pitch dark.

"Look, my friend … ."

"Call me friend one more time and I'll slice your dick off and put it in your big mouth. Clear?"

"Yes *sir*," Byron replied mockingly.

"Now let's just take a little walk back to town and see what the girl's family wants to do with you. It won't be pretty, you can bet on that."

Hatch did not hear the fourth crew member at the door until the man was already on top of him. He had only an instant of awareness before a club bashed into his skull, dropping him to his knees. A foot smashed into his face and another kicked his ribs. He tried to roll away, but one of the men landed on his back. He felt the electrical heat of a knife blade slicing at his back and shoulder. Before losing consciousness, he wondered if the girl had even made it home.

The last thing he heard, before the comforting finality of unconsciousness was the sound of voices shouting in Tuvan.

5

"He ought to be in a hospital," Mr. Jolly told Kamuela Makani.

"We can take the Americans' boat and go to Papeete," Kamuela responded with the authority of a man used to deciding the way things would be. "They will not need it again."

"Except that it would take three days to get there, Kamuela. He won't live three days, in my opinion. And I don't think we should try to move him now that the bleeding is contained. If he starts bleeding again, well ... ," Mr. Jolly stroked his chin in thought.

"Do you say he will die anyway, we go or we do not go?"

"My goodness, how should I know? I'm no physician."

"Then stop talking like you know something."

"You asked for my opinion, I might remind you."

"You are the director of government."

"What has that got to do with the price of gin?"

Jenny Hunt Makani came from Kukana's bedroom down the hall. "Will you two stop arguing, or at least take it outside. I finally got her to sleep."

Mr. Jolly shrugged apologetically. Kamuela went to Jenny and took her hand in both of his, asking about his daughter.

"Sleeping now. I gave her just a very little bit of morphine so she would sleep. I don't think she has any serious injuries, at least physical ones; mostly just bruises and scratches. Don't worry, Kamuela. She's going to be all right."

Jenny's voice was tired. She was not aging well on Tuva. She was a pretty twenty-two year old when she came with the Peace Corps in 1966, a petite woman with long auburn hair, big emerald eyes, and a patch of freckles across her nose and cheeks. She had since gained forty pounds, the freckles became a splotch, and her skin had wrinkled deeply from salt air and tropical sun.

Kamuela walked across the hall to see his daughter. Jenny approached Kamuela's huge bed, where Hatch lay, still unconscious. He had been that way since the men carried him from the banana grove shed. Jenny did the best she could with his wounds, using the medical supplies the government doctor left behind during one of his bi-annual visits. She bent over Hatch and checked the compresses on his back.

"I think his injuries are quite serious," Mr. Jolly commented. He bobbed slightly back and forth when he bent over to look at Hatch's face. "Isn't he a hard-looking man, though."

"Hard-looking?" Jenny wondered.

"Maybe more like strong and self-contained. I wonder what it felt like when those goons pulverized him? I remember one time when I was a schoolboy, some of the lads took me into an alley … ."

"I have no doubt that if he were conscious it would hurt like holy hell," Jenny interrupted.

"I fear it would have killed a soul such as I."

"I'm surprised it didn't kill him."

"Well … yet."

Kamuela returned and approached the bed. In a somber tone, deep with emotion, Kamuela announced: "Hear what I say. This man will not die in my house. I, Kamuela Nakaloloa Makani, owe to this man a great debt – the life of my daughter – and he will live for me to pay it. This man will not die here, not this night, not in my house."

"That should do it," Mr. Jolly whispered sarcastically to Jenny.

To Kamuela, Jenny said, "I don't know how much blood he lost, but it must be a lot. Look how pale he is." She felt his brow with the back of her hand. "And how hot he is. I am not trained for things like this. I can put on some iodine, give out aspirin, clean cuts, put on bandages, and the like, but God, Kamuela, I can't handle anything like this. I don't know if he has broken bones, and I couldn't set them anyway. Look how his wrists are bent and crushed. He could have a concussion and may be bleeding internally, and I wouldn't know what to do about it."

"Are you saying he will die?" Kamuela bellowed.

"Don't shout at me. I don't know, but yes, I do think he's dying, and there's nothing I can do."

"But a doctor can save him?"

"I don't know. I'm just saying that I can't. Don't put this responsibility on me, please."

"We will have a doctor for him," Kamuela announced.

"That's fine," Jenny said. "But the nearest doctor is in Papeete, and the fastest anyone can get there is two and a half days in a fast boat. I don't think he can survive a trip like that."

"The doctor can come here by airplane and land in the lagoon. This was done many times during the war years."

Mr. Jolly interrupted. "How do you propose to get in touch with the doctor so he can fly here? I must say now, Kamuela, if you had listened to me when I wanted to get that shortwave radio … ."

"Quiet." Kamuela turned his back and stood motionless, staring out the French doors, across the balcony and down to the bay.

Mr. Jolly shrugged and walked closer to the bed to look at Hatch. Jenny started to walk back to Kukana's room.

Suddenly Kamuela turned around and grabbed Jenny's arm. "Would not a boat like that one in the harbor have such a radio?"

"Why yes, of course," Jenny answered.

"Great idea, Kamuela. I am sure it would," Mr.

Jolly agreed. "But, not to put a damper on things, it isn't likely to have the necessary range. It is over three hundred miles to Tahiti. Now if I had that shortwave radio set you said we didn't need … ."

"Yes, but it might be possible to get a relay from a ship, or even a passing aircraft," Jenny said.

"You know how to work a radio?" Kamuela asked Mr. Jolly.

"More or less, yes."

"We will go use this radio now," Kamuela announced, and without waiting another moment, strode from the bedroom and out of the house, with Mr. Jolly rushing to keep up, chasing Kamuela breathlessly down the hill to the harbor.

There were three radios on the ketch. One Mr. Jolly recognized as a low-range citizens band of the kind outback ranchers used for communication between a vehicle and the house, useless at any distance. There was a ship-shore VHF radio with a possible range of one hundred and fifty miles. There was also a single-sideband *ham* radio set, but Mr. Jolly didn't know how it worked. He pointed all this out to Kamuela, who was not interested in such details. "Just call," he ordered. "Call until somebody answers."

Mr. Jolly elected to try the VHF in hopes of reaching a ship and getting a relay. He knew that the international distress channel was number sixteen; if that didn't work, maybe they could go to the government house, where the crew members were being held prisoner, and ask one of them for help.

"No power," Mr. Jolly said, getting nothing after turning on the radio.

"Is it broken?"

"It's probably all right, I think the batteries need to be turned on, wherever that might be." Mr. Jolly began searching the instrument panel. He located the navigator's panel and a row of toggles, thankfully labeled. When he flipped the battery switch, the radio crackled to life.

"Bully!" He cried, as excited as a child. "Damn well, I say."

A piercing beeping noise came through the speaker and it stopped as soon as Mr. Jolly punched in the number sixteen and it appeared in the LED readout. "Now we're in business."

"Say something," Kamuela ordered.

Mr. Jolly took the microphone, cleared his throat dramatically, and lowered his voice an octave to give it an important sound. "Ah ... mayday. This is Tuva calling anybody. Mayday. Mayday from the island of Tuva." He released the transmit button and waited.

"Talk louder," Kamuela said.

"A radio transmits at the same level, no matter what the incoming volume is set for." Mr. Jolly was pleased knowing something Kamuela did not. He keyed the microphone again and repeated mayday three more times, adding, "This is Mr. Jolly Malcolm on the island of Tuva calling. Anyone out there?"

The instant he released the button, a voice came through the speaker so loudly and distinctly that Kamuela leaned away from it.

"We have your mayday, Tuva. This is Qantas 676 responding to Tuva's mayday. Go ahead, Tuva."

Mr. Jolly looked incredulously at Kamuela and sputtered, "It's a bloody airliner, for Chrissakes! We got an answer from a damn bloody airplane."

"Go ahead, Tuva. We have your mayday," the pilot's voice erupted from the speaker again.

"They're Aussies," Mr. Jolly bubbled. He keyed the mike and responded. "I say, Qantas, good of you lot to be up there at the moment. My name is Julius Malcolm, previously of Bonds Boys School, Sydney."

Kamuela hit Mr. Jolly hard on the shoulder and Mr. Jolly almost dropped the microphone. Rubbing his arm, he said, "That damn well hurt, Kamuela."

"Just tell them to call for the doctor in Papeete," Kamuela scowled.

"Well of course, I was coming to that." Mr. Jolly keyed the mike again. "Our mayday concerns a desperately injured man here on Tuva, an American chap. We are in dire need for a doctor to come over from Tahiti by seaplanc. Could you possibly help us out?"

"Tuva, Qantas 676 back. We will shortly be out of your range, please repeat your need."

Mr. Jolly repeated the request, emphasizing the necessity of coming by seaplane and landing in the lagoon. "It is urgent, Qantas. Life or death."

"Tuva, Qantas. Can do. I presume the authorities in Tahiti know where Tuva is?"

"Of course they know," Mr. Jolly shot back. Turning to Kamuela, he added, "Bloody idiot."

"Roger that, Tuva. This bloody idiot will relay your request to the authorities in Papeete. Good luck down there. This is Qantas 676, out."

"He *heard* me!" Mr. Jolly cried, dropping the microphone as if he had bitten him. "And I gave him my name. Christ!"

"This radio is a good thing," Kamuela said, putting his hand on the radio panel as if anointing it. "We will have one at the Government House."

The pilot's accent left Mr. Jolly agonizingly homesick. He kept the radio on for a little while after Kamuela left the yacht, hoping someone might call. Later, walking off the wharf, he remembered that Kamuela had promised a radio for the Government House. He could call anytime then. Smiling broadly, he shuffled down the street to Papa Jack's and bought a bottle of gin. Then he headed back to the Government House to see how the cute young man in the tight white shorts was getting along as a prisoner.

Word of the violation of Kukana Makani, her rescue by the man called Hatch, and the violent attack against him, spread through the village as if borne on the storm winds that blew the yacht into their bay only

44

yesterday. By evening, nearly everyone in Tuva knew that Hatch was dying in Kamuela Makani's house, and that his attackers had been captured and were now locked in the storage room in the Government House.

Curious villagers gathered at the Government house to see what would happen next. Papa Jack's and the Lotus Bar were filled to capacity and doing a boisterous business. All the bar chatter concerned the men from the American yacht and the heroism of Hatch, the strange American living all these years like a hermit at Kaiwi Point.

Soon, many villagers had worked themselves into a vengeful fury. A hundred men converged on the Government House, carrying flashlights and torches, knives, hoes, and banana machetes.

Mr. Jolly was in the large meeting room talking with the two guards when he heard chanting from the approaching mob.

"Listen to that," Mr. Jolly said to the already nervous guards. "Almost sounds like they intend to harm those blokes," he said, indicating the men behind the locked storeroom door.

One of the guards went to the window, then turned back to his companion and said, "Hele mai! Le's go, bruddah. Dey coming for get dem kanes."

"They are *what*?" Mr. Jolly shouted.

"Dey coming for dem men, Mr. Jolly," the guard repeated, grabbing his shirt from the back of a chair and heading for the back door, the other guard already ahead.

"Wait! Hey!" Mr. Jolly gave chase. "You boys stay right here. Don't you dare run away."

But the guards had already run away, disappearing out the back door.

"Well, I say, that's just bloody damn brave of you," Mr. Jolly shouted at them. He had no idea what to do next, so he picked up the flask of gin from his desk and took a long, thoughtful, pull at it.

"Christ," he muttered, going to the window. There

was indeed a mob. When they saw Mr. Jolly's face, voices shouted out for him to release the yacht's crew into their hands.

"Peace, my friends," Mr. Jolly said drunkenly. He leaned from the window and stretched out his arms to the mob. "Go home. Go home to your families," he shouted. Soon he was laughing at the image from an old cowboy movie, where the sheriff turns back a lynch mob. Absorbed by the image, he shouted: "I'm the law in these parts." Then he backed away from the window in a fit of giggles.

That was an essentially true claim. As the Australian government's representative, he was the symbol of the Australian legal system, such as he, or any of us, understood it. That meant that he handled the paperwork involved in running the school, checked the papers of any visitors who showed up, and distributed paychecks when the mail boat stopped by; once in a while he got to usher around Australian bureaucrats on winter junkets. But it was also true that anything passing for crime on Tuva was handled by the *real* law: Kamuela Makani.

Mr. Jolly leaned into the window again and waved his arms at the crowd. "I am the law," he yelled. "Desist from this folly at once, do you hear?"

Although the crowd pointedly ignored him, Mr. Jolly felt proud of his stand, in spite of the fact that the crowd was about to force its way through the door. Mr. Jolly, albeit drunk, had stood his ground while the guards ran away.

"What are you doing there?" Mr. Jolly heard a voice from inside the room behind him. He jerked back from the window and saw Kamuela coming through the back door. "Move from the window," Kamuela ordered.

Mr. Jolly reluctantly surrendered his brave position at the window, replaced by Kamuela, who stuck his massive head and shoulders out and said, "Mahalo." The crowd began to calm down. "Mahalo," he repeated, thanking them for being quiet. He spoke in Tuvan. "You are right to want to see these men pay for their evil deeds. But I, father of Kukana Pele, have that right, and I do not give it away."

Responding to a shout from the crowd, Kamuela said, "Yes, it was a crime against our island and all our people. But it was first a crime against my daughter. Then it was a crime against the man who saved Kukana's life, who himself now lies gravely injured in my house. Revenge is my right first, and I do not give it up. Thank you." With that, he moved away from the window and turned around. The crowd noise diminished to a low rumble.

Mr. Jolly moved aside to let Kamuela pass, whispering behind his back: "Now *that's* a sheriff." Then in a louder voice added, "Well said, Kamuela. Well done. But I did warn you that something like this could happen tonight, with emotions so aroused." He offered the flask to Kamuela, who brushed it aside.

"So you did, Mr. Jolly. You have proven yourself right two times this day. I will send more men, better men, to guard our prisoners."

"Braver than the last, I hope."

"Not to guard against our people, but to guard the criminals against escape. Will you stay until the guards come? I have left Kukana and Hatch with only Jenny to be with them."

"Of course. Count on me." Mr. Jolly tipped up the flask and drank a substantial amount.

"I do count on you," Kamuela said as he checked the lock on the storeroom door. Then he exited the back door as quietly as he entered.

Mr. Jolly walked to the storeroom door and leaned against it. In a voice loud enough for the men inside to hear, he said, "You lot are in a bloody mess."

"Hey! Wait a minute," voice called out from behind the door. "Is that man's name Hatch?"

"The man you tried to kill, you mean?"

"You called him Hatch. Is that from Hatcher,

maybe?"

"It's just Hatch," Mr. Jolly said.

"Hey, just a minute. I want to ask you something," the voice continued.

Now that was a curious thing, Mr. Jolly said later. He pulled a chair close to the door and sat down to hear what the man had to say.

6

The Hard Wind's crew was kept isolated in the Government House all that night, brought only water and fruit. No one spoke to them and they were not allowed to speak with anyone outside the room. Mr. Jolly presumed this did not apply to him, and spent some time chatting with the men through the door.

Early the following morning the distant drone of a twin-engine seaplane could be heard approaching from the northwest. By the time the plane made a downwind pass over the lagoon, Kamuela Makani had walked down to the wharf and taken a skiff to meet the plane, which was too large to taxi close enough to the wharf to dock and unload. Village children, shouting gleefully, watched the plane skim the calm lagoon and splash down, casting a silver and rainbow-hazed spray in an aura around it. That was the first airplane any of the younger children had ever seen, except as occasional silver dots in the distant sky.

Kamuela received the French doctor and took him up the hill to the patient in his house.

The Makani house was the largest on the island, constructed during the big war from materials sometimes supplied by, and sometimes stolen from, the Australian Royal Navy. It sat at the rear of a manicured lawn, the path through the lawn marked by a row of evenly spaced, improbably tall, royal palms. The lane from town to the house stretched behind the Anglican Church up a steep slope for two hundred yards, then through a grove of bananas and stately breadfruit trees. From its position high on the slope, the view encompassed the entire leeward coastline of Tuva. The house was built on two levels, colonial French in style, with wide-open verandas accessible through French doors. It could have been transported whole from the New Orleans French Quarter.

Kamuela towered over the doctor. With a royal genetic heritage of extraordinarily large people, Kamuela was six feet, six inches tall, weighing a robust two-hundred-ninety pounds. His wife, who died from influenza ten years before, when Kukana was seven years old, had been small, even petite, by comparison. Kamuela was desperately in love with his wife, Emma. Their marriage changed him from a philandering, wild, often violent man, into a responsible, dedicated, patient leader of his people. After Emma's death, Kamuela transferred those emotions to Kukana. That the yacht's crew remained alive at this point was evidence of Kamuela's softening; what his daughter-in-law Jenny called, "the Emma effect." A younger Kamuela, before Emma, would have decapitated all of those men on the spot, then tossed their remains to his royal brothers, the sharks.

That afternoon, after a lavish lunch and substantial payment, the French doctor returned to the waiting plane, leaving behind detailed instructions with Jenny Hunt Makani for Hatch's on-going care. He said that Hatch would definitely never have survived the trip to Tahiti, but if there were no recurring infections, he would live. The knife blade cut no vital organs, the cuts were all slashes, not stabs, so they may not have intended to kill him. He suffered a cracked rib, and both wrists were severely broken; presumably they stomped on his hands. He had a concussion, but it's mild. The bones would mend, his body was replacing the lost blood. It would probably take a while, but he would recover.

"He's a lucky man," the doctor told Kamuela as they walked back to the pier. "He has been this lucky before, I'd say."

"The scars?" Kamuela supposed.

"Yes. Those are bullet scars, do you know? He has been shot once in his side and the bullet went through; there is another wound on his right thigh, and I see no evidence that the bullet was removed surgically, so we may assume he still carries it. As you request, I have no questions about what may have occurred in his past. But if I were you, I would want to know more about such a man living among your people."

"He is the hero of Tuva," Kamuela said. "That is all anyone needs to know about him."

As Kamuela and the doctor boarded the skiff for the ride out to the seaplane, some of the boys – pier urchins – had already swam ahead of them to the plane. The pilot allowed them to play on the pontoons until Kamuela helped the doctor aboard.

Kamuela shooed the children away so the pilot could start the engines, and they played in the spray from the propellers.

Returning to his house, Kamuela found Kukana asleep in a chair next to Hatch. Her head, spotted here and there with bandages, lay on the side of the bed, her hand resting on Hatch's arm at his elbow, above one of the new casts that reached from the tips of his fingers to just below his elbows.

7

The village was always quiet at that hour. I walked with Tioni, a big man like his father, bringing up the rear, Kamuela in front, with four of his cousins alongside. We passed Mr. Fukumitsu opening his store, and then Dennis, who was passed out on a bench on the lanai in front of Papa Jack's. Two old fishermen, Pono and Kaavanuii, who usually decorated the end of the pier as they waited for amberjack coming into the bay, did not turn to watch the odd procession on its way toward the foreign yacht, knowing it was not their business.

The Hard Wind's crew remained quiet. They may have believed they were being escorted to the boat and would be set free, their punishment being banishment. But I doubt it? Maybe they supposed it was punishment enough to have spent three days sleeping on the bare concrete floor of a hot, cramped storage room, with only a tiny window for light and nothing to eat but fruit, hard bread, and water. But I could have assured them that it was not.

Kamuela bunched his prisoners beside the boat and told Tioni to board first with the shotgun. After Tioni was in position, I also boarded, weaponless by choice. Then Kamuela told the prisoners to follow.

"Take them down and lock them somewhere," Kamuela told his cousins in Tuvan. He turned to Tioni and me, adding in English so the prisoners would understand, "If they try to come out, shoot them."

"Oh, come on. Don't do anything stupid," Bill Byron said.

"Tioni," Kamuela said to his son.

"Yes, Papa?"

"This one I don't like most. He talks again, put

your shotgun on his face and blow off his head."

"Happily, Papa."

They locked the Hard Wind's crew inside the forward cabin, the door guarded by Tioni and one of the cousins, who carried Kamuela's old automatic pistol. I joined Kamuela and the other two cousins on deck, where we prepared to get the ketch – it was quite a beautiful, even luxurious, yacht – underway.

I cannot claim that I did not know how this day would end, or that it would linger in my nightmares.

With Kamuela at the helm, the Hard Wind cleared the reef passage and headed north around Kaiwi Point in a steady breeze. Kamuela maintained a northerly course all morning. By mid-afternoon, we were forty miles from Tuva and ten miles from the nearest group of low, uninhabited atolls, most no larger than a football field, although two were a bit larger and were from time to time inhabited by wandering fishermen.

It was a beautiful day for a sail, with animal-shaped white clouds over the sea, more blue than the sky. I had not been on the open sea in a sailboat larger than an outrigger skiff in two decades. I was almost seasick, but not yet. I could guess what Kamuela intended to do with the men below, even though he had not said. He was going to dump them into the sea. I didn't know if they would be dead first.

Kamuela sent his cousins below to help Tioni escort the prisoners onto the deck. The ketch crashed through steep swells as Kamuela brought her into the wind in order to lower her sails, which I set about doing. When the prisoners were bunched together on the bow, along the port rail, there was no land in sight.

"Please, mister," the younger Byron pleaded. "You aren't going to kill us? That would be cold blooded murder."

"Shut up, Davy," his brother said harshly. "Don't give them the satisfaction." Byron turned his head and spat over the rail.

David held the rail to keep from slumping to the

deck, he was clearly so afraid. Byron kicked his foot and told him to act like a man.

"I didn't do nothing to you, or to your daughter. I never touched her," the crewman named Mel protested.

"You piece of shit," Byron said.

"Quiet!" Kamuela ordered. "I am not going to kill you. I am not a killer, not like you. You would have killed my daughter if Hatch did not stop you, and you tried to kill him. But I will not kill you."

David Byron sniffed back tears.

"If we wanted to kill the son of a bitch, he'd be dead," Bill Byron stated.

"Then what are you going to do?" the fourth crewman asked, the one we now know was Guns Harper. "I can promise that you'll never see me again if you let us go." Harper was the one who came up behind Hatch with the club. "Do you even know who he is, the man you call Hatch? Maybe you should know that first."

"All of you! No more talk! I hate the sound of your coward voices."

The mainsail luffed loudly and the ketch rolled lazily in the swells. Sea gulls found us, squawking overhead and swooping over the yacht, hoping for a meal. I felt as though the wallowing around was going to make me sick; the embarrassment in such a situation would be ... well, embarrassing.

"Yes, please just let us go," David pleaded again.

"They aren't going to let us go, you morons!" Byron said. "Go where? What are they going to do, give me my boat and swim back?"

"Untie them," Kamuela told his cousins.

To the prisoners, Kamuela said, "Look that way." He pointed aft. "That way lies Tuva. If you are ever seen in Tuva, you will be killed at that moment. Now look this way." He pointed forward. "There lies a refuge, a small atoll called Palm Reef. If you are strong and with favor from your God, you might reach its refuge in two or three days swimming."

"Swimming?" Byron was incredulous. "You must be out of your fucking mind."

"It is our tradition, and you are getting what you did not give," Kamuela said with surprising patience. "A choice, a chance to live. This is your choice. We will cut you into bait-size pieces and feed you to our brother sharks, or you may swim for the refuge and your life. If you make it to the refuge, your crime is forgiven, for it will be because the first God sees you as worthy of saving. If you die, it is because the God sees you as unworthy of life among decent men."

"Now that's just a great fucking choice, old man," Bill Byron spat the words.

Kamuela continued. "If you try to come back to Tuva, we will kill you, no matter what the God chooses."

David Byron was crying. Bill punched his kid brother's shoulder and told him to stop acting like a pussy.

"Swim with the sun to your left side at ninety degrees until darkness comes. Then replace the sun with the brightest star you see. Keep it always straight to your left side. If our shark brothers do not find you appetizing, in two or three days, if you keep moving, you will come to the atoll. You must listen for it; it is low and you will hear it long before you see it. Be watchful of the current; it pushes to the right as you swim. If you do not account for it, you will pass the atoll. It is two more days to the next one, and it is much smaller. From there, nothing until the ice."

That said, Kamuela nodded, and suddenly all four men were pushed over the railing and into the ragged sea.

I threw up over the side, then went to help with the sails.

8

The Makani houseman, Akamu Palani, welcomed Mr. Jolly and me as we came onto the lanai, as we were observed walking the long path between the royal palms from the edge of town. He led us to Kamuela's bedroom – the first time I'd been that far into the Makani house – where we found Kukana slicing fruit for her patient; there was no doubt from the moment he regained consciousness that he was her patient, Mr. Jolly had said on our walk up the hill.

"So how are we today?" Mr. Jolly inquired, approaching the bedside in what I thought was a quite familiar manner.

More reticent in that circumstance, I remained in the center of the truly gigantic room, admittedly shocked by the man I saw under a pale tan sheet in Kamuela Makani's equally gigantic bed.

"Hello, Hatch," I offered my greeting. "I suppose there's not much reason beyond courtesy to ask how you're feeling?"

"*We*," Hatch responded in a rather snarling tone, I thought, "would appreciate it very much if you can get this girl to stop feeding me like I'm *her doll*." That comment seemed to have used up all his breath, for he gasped.

Kukana simply shrugged and smiled angelically. She continued slicing golden mango into bite-size pieces.

Mr. Jolly giggled, patted her shoulder, then pulled close a wooden, cane-seat chair. "You look so much better awake than you did lying here like, well, like the dead man you almost were."

"That's some bedside manner, Mr. Jolly," I remarked.

"I felt better dead," Hatch said, nearly cracking a smile. "Hello, Don."

"And yourself, Hatch." I walked to the foot of the bed. I was uncomfortable in that situation, and had only agreed to come after Mr. Jolly convinced me that maybe Hatch would welcome a visit from one of his own, from an American. Hatch had never cared one way or the other if I was an American, or from Timbuktu. I always thought of him as state-less. Although once or twice we had engaged in lively debates about professional football teams: Hatch favored the Steelers, I the Raiders. Neither of us really cared; it was just passing time in the bar.

"Stay awhile and you can have the dubious thrill of watching a grown man being fed like a baby. At least she's stopped chewing it first."

"Oh how quaint," Mr. Jolly gushed, in his way. "Like a mama bird."

I said "ugh."

"Exactly, Don."

Hatch was covered to his chest by the sheet, both arms, cast from fingertips to well up his forearms, lay on top of the sheet. Both his eyes were an ugly shade of brownish yellow, and there was a white bandage around his head. Another bandage, consisting, it appeared, of a huge piece of gauze held in place by strips of adhesive tape, covered the entirety of his left shoulder all the way to his chest. Anything else was disguised below the sheet. The stench of medicinal alcohol and ripe mango together was almost too much.

Like a mama bird, I thought, looking at Kukana. No, that was not how she gazed at Hatch. She finished slicing the mango into a small wooden bowl. The scrapes and cuts on her forehead and upper right arm would have looked so much more dramatic if not in proximity with Hatch's more horrific wounds. Definitely not the gaze of any kind of mama.

"Well," Mr. Jolly said, standing and replacing the chair by the wall, "we see you are about to have your breakfast. We just wanted to stop by and check on the hero of Tuva."

"No more of this hero stuff, please."

"A man cannot deny what others wish to make of him," Mr. Jolly said. "There could be worse appellations. Trust me."

"Well, you must know, Hatch, that what you did was a damned heroic thing," I added.

Hatch squeezed his eyes closed, whether as an expression of pain or dismay I could not tell. Kukana took a piece of mango in her fingers and directed it toward his mouth. Hatch turned his face away.

"Please," Kukana said softly.

"Just a minute," Hatch said, opening his eyes and looking toward me. "I left an outboard motor propeller at the side of the trail, not far from the shed. It's marked by a stick through the shaft hole. Do you mind seeing if you can find it?"

"Of course," I answered.

"No need," Mr. Jolly interrupted. "Your propeller was found and, in fact, has already been delivered to your house; if I'm not mistaken, it has been installed on the motor."

"Thank you."

Mr. Jolly snorted a laugh. "Oh, I didn't do it. I believe you have Tioni to thank."

"Yes, it was my brother," Kukana said. Then she again pushed the mango toward his mouth and repeated, "Please."

Hatch accepted the bite and closed his eyes again.

"Now there's a good chap," Mr. Jolly said, almost reaching over to pat Hatch's good shoulder, but seemed unsure how good it might actually be and stayed back.

"Next time you're in Papa Jack's," I said by way of departure, "drinks on me."

"Thanks for coming all the way up here," Hatch said before Kukana put another piece of fruit into his mouth. His voice was terribly weak; coherent, but soft and tentative.

I had no doubt our visit had used up all the energy he had for such things. I think he was starting to fall asleep before we got to the door.

We walked down the long hallway back to the veranda. Kamuela Makani was waiting there. He stood from the round glass table and greeted us.

"Join me for tea," Kamuela offered, gesturing for us to sit at the table. "Would you prefer coffee, Don?"

I was surprised Kamuela remembered that I had no taste for tea.

"If it's not any trouble. I'm fine anyway."

"Americans." Mr. Jolly muttered. "Who else would throw good British tea into the harbor?"

Kamuela sent his cook, Twilla Pihi, to bring the pot of tea and a cup of coffee. I supposed it would be Nescafé, and it was. If that was all I could get, maybe I would have become a tea drinker.

"Our patient seems to be doing much better than I would have thought only a couple of days ago," Mr. Jolly said.

I nodded agreement, although it was the first time I had seen Hatch since the cruel events of that evening.

"He is quite a strong man," Mr. Jolly continued.

"Jenny agrees. She tells me that a week ago she was sure he would die, and now he eats, he even wants to get up and go home."

Mr. Jolly laughed.

The tea and my coffee arrived. Twilla told Kamuela that Hatch wants something more solid than fruit and water. What did he think? Kamuela said he would ask Jenny.

"His sleep is haunted," Kamuela said.

"What do you mean?" Mr. Jolly asked.

"Each night he cries out; what parts of him can move he … you have seen a wounded bird trying to fly. He does that. It is a terrible thing. The entire house awakens. Only Kukana's voice calms him, and then he sleeps again."

"Does he say anything in these nightmares?" I asked curiously.

"He says 'my.' But never says his what. Just 'my,' again and again, until Kukana runs to him and speaks into his ear, holding down his broken wings with her body. Then she sits in the chair beside him until he sleeps in peace again. I have found her still there come morning light; still in the chair, bent over with her head on the edge of the bed, herself also sleeping. I believe it is good Kukana has this to do. I think they heal each other."

"He never says my what? Even awake, does he know?" I wondered.

"He says he has no memory and tells us his apology for having disturbed everyone. I tell him nothing he could do except not get better can disturb us."

"We don't know anything about him before he arrived," I pointed out.

"We know about him now, and that is enough. But gentlemen, I want your opinion on another matter; you Mr. Jolly, as director of government, and you, Don, as an American businessman who carries some knowledge of the wider world."

"Of course," Mr. Jolly said, and I nodded agreement.

"We have an untroubled island," Kamuela began. "We are free of crimes against one another. We do not steal from our neighbor – not his property, not his wife, not his rights as a man. If we fight one another, it is only in the proper spirit and with respect for life. We do not murder. A man can sleep where he will, in safety, unmolested. No one here can go hungry or go without shelter. Are these things not all true?"

"Yes, I agree, Kamuela," Mr. Jolly said.

I nodded again, deciding not to point out the obvious exceptions to his pretty picture of life on Tuva, including the reason Hatch was lying bandaged like a mummy in his bedroom.

"I believe it is changing, what I just described. Even here in the middle of the greatest ocean, we are losing our peaceful isolation. We are found more often now by passing boats, and how many more will deliver into our lives bad men like those last ones?"

"God forbid," Mr. Jolly said.

"God does not allow or forbid. God waits to see what we do, then He judges. I think these men will come again; not, of course, those men we left in the ocean."

I was thinking that if it were one of my daughters, I wouldn't have had the patience to wait and let them spend days drowning, although I can see a bit of justice at work there. I probably would have shot them on the spot. That is the American way.

"But men like them. Tourists, as well. I have seen the results in Tahiti and Fiji, as well as smaller islands like our home. I have seen how people are made crazy with false needs. I have seen what men do to each other for greed and lust. That is why in those places – Tahiti, Fiji, even Olowalu, Puuloa, and Keokea – you will find the need for police, for some kind of jail. Isn't this true?"

"All too true, I'm afraid," Mr. Jolly agreed. "But Kamuela, you know that in all my years here, not until those bloody Americans, has anyone needed to be locked up on Tuva. No offense, Don."

"None taken. You notice I no longer live there."

"We think of you as Tuvan now," Kamuela said.

"Thank you, sir. As do I."

"You are saying what was in the past, Mr. Jolly. I am saying we must prepare for the future. I have decided that Tuva must be prepared for what will come."

"Who could disagree with being prepared for the future?" Mr. Jolly said, caught up in the spirit of the thing.

Then, abruptly, Kamuela said, "I am going to

make Hatch Tuva's magistrate of police."

"We don't have any police," I said, quite taken aback by this strange suggestion. It was not even a suggestion, it was a statement of fact, a done deal.

"Hatch will be the police," Kamuela said emphatically.

"Well, yes, I see," Mr. Jolly said. "Indeed he is a strong and courageous man; what one hopes to find in an officer of the law … ."

"Also honest and admirable."

"I suppose so," Mr. Jolly agreed in a cautious tone. "But it occurs to me, Kamuela, that outside of his admittedly heroic deed in saving Kukana from those vicious scoundrels, what do we know about him? He has lived among us all these years as a virtual stranger. He happened to be in the right place and did the right thing. Yes, at great cost to his person, but well, you know, sometimes I get the impression that maybe he wishes he had taken a different route that evening."

"Stop!" Kamuela banged the table and all our cups went flying. "I will hear nothing bad spoken about this man. He is the hero of Tuva."

Twilla appeared to the sound of the breaking cups and swept the pieces clear of the table.

"Bring the whisky and three glasses," Kamuela told her. "The one with a black label," he added.

I supposed then that my work day was going to be cut rather short, and also that Mr. Jolly had a point.

"I didn't mean it in a bad way about Hatch," Mr. Jolly corrected himself. "Just food for thought."

Twilla brought the bottle and glasses on a tray. Kamuela poured. We clinked glasses in toast and I appreciated the taste of whisky far better than I could afford on a regular basis at Papa Jack's.

"I didn't bring this up before, Kamuela," Mr. Jolly began. "I didn't see much point, and anyway, who can say how much veracity … ."

"What do you have to say?"

"One of those American men told me that he thinks he knows who Hatch is, or was, or used to be."

"Really?" I inquired with great curiosity. I had had unanswered questions about him for years.

"Go on," Kamuela said.

"Now, I am only repeating what I was told, so don't bang the table again, at least not until I have drained my glass of this truly fine Johnnie Walker."

"Mr. Jolly!"

"Right. One of those men claimed he recognized Hatch. He was the one who came in from behind and launched the attack. The others called him Guns, which I thought a fitting name for a brute. Anyway. I am getting to it. So this criminal bloke says Hatch's name is Frank Hatcher. Hatch was his nickname. This Guns fellow said he served in some sort of special forces thing back in Laos, or some such place in some such time. Long before Hatch showed up here. Of course the man he knew then was a lot younger, clean shaven, shorn hair, and all that military sort of stuff."

"Maybe this is true, maybe it is not. What does it matter?" Kamuela interrupted.

"I can see it," I added. "Him having been a military man. I asked him once about that knife he always carries ... ."

"Do you have a point?" Kamuela also interrupted me.

"Just saying ... ."

"That's not all the bastard told me, Kamuela."

"Go on, then."

"Well ... now don't bang the table. I am just repeating what he said"

"Damn it, Jolly Malcolm!"

"Well, then, he said that Hatch, or Frank Hatcher, or Captain Hatcher as he sometimes called him, is a deserter; that he disappeared after some ambush got his men, his team, killed."

None of we three spoke for some seconds. I processed this possibility and thought it was not entirely unlikely. I may have wished it false, but that wasn't enough to make it so. I don't know if it mattered much to me, since I was not exactly a fan of the Vietnam fiasco, using student deferments and an early and short-lived marriage to stay away from it myself. There but for fortune, as they say.

We were both looking at Kamuela, waiting. He held his drink at a point halfway up between the table and his mouth, as if unsure if he wanted to drink or to throw it down. I picked up my own glass, just in case; half the Scotch remained.

Then Kamuela put his glass back on the table and spoke. "This is not true. I will tell you why. First, those men would say anything hoping to save their lives, anything to distract us from where the evil truly lies. Second, and this is more important, Hatch is not such a man. So it is a lie."

I knew better than to ask Kamuela at that point how he could know Hatch was not such a man. I doubt they had spoken to one another ten times in the last ten years. Mr. Jolly and I exchanged glances and our eyes conveyed the same message – leave this be for now.

9

Kamuela ordered the finest carpenters on Tuva to gather materials and begin construction of the new magistrate of police house, to be built on land he donated near the bottom of his own expansive property, just up the hill from the rear of Ho'okahi Church.

I don't believe that by that point Kamuela had asked Hatch if he actually wanted to be the magistrate of police. Kamuela had no experience with people not doing what he asked of them. So as Hatch continued a rather miraculously fast recovery in the Makani house, the construction of his own new house was already well underway.

Kamuela had gotten his housekeeper, Twilla Pihi, to agree to become housekeeper for the new magistrate of police. At first, Twilla considered this something of a demotion, from housekeeper to the island's chief, to working for a policeman. But Kamuela put it to her another way, she would be housekeeper to the hero of Tuva. After that, Twilla was excited by the prospect, and not quiet about it. In a single day, everyone in Tuva town knew whose house was being constructed on the hillside behind the church and that Twilla Pihi would be taking care of Tuva's hero.

Mr. Jolly was ordered to "fix things with Canberra." Kamuela wanted Hatch's position to be official, with a salary from the Australian government.

Finally, Kamuela made it clear that the empty Cheoy Lee ketch, Hard Wind, still tied up at the far end of the wharf, now belonged to Hatch; spoils of war, one could suppose.

Mr. Jolly approached, following Sunday services,

and took me aside. We walked along the street in the general direction of the wharf, Mr. Jolly's arm through mine, as he was wont to do with anyone, regardless of gender, and no one took any implication from this common gesture of his.

I supposed that because we were rather like co-conspirators with Kamuela on this, having been taken into his confidence from the start, that was why Mr. Jolly came to me with the problem he faced.

"How am I supposed to make this official, Don? What name do I use? Simply, Hatch?"

"What are you planning to do?" I wondered.

"That's what I'm asking you. Might you consider approaching Hatch, I mean, once we can be sure he is on the path to full recovery, so to speak, and get a reading from him regarding this matter?"

"I suppose I could do that. But does he even know what's going on? Has Kamuela told him yet?"

"Not yet. Kamuela is waiting until Hatch is well. He wants it kept secret from him until he is ready to leave the Makani house."

"Then how would I be able to broach this subject without … well, you know."

We reached the wharf and turned around, strolling in the direction from which we had just come, occasionally exchanging friendly Sunday greetings with passersby.

"I thought you might work around the dilemma by taking a separate approach."

"Such as?"

"You might say, I mean in the context of a general visit inquiring about his health, something like your passport was going to expire soon and since you plan to live the rest of your days on Tuva, you were thinking of applying for an Australian passport. See what he might say to that. I mean, the talk of a passport."

"He doesn't have one?"

"I don't know. It never came up in those days

when he first arrived, and there has been no reason to wonder about it since."

I stopped and loosed his arm from around mine, turned to face him. "Mr. Jolly, tell me. Do you believe what that man said about Hatch?"

"Well, how could I know? For sure, I mean."

I waited.

"Yes, I do. Some of it, anyway."

"So do I."

Mr. Jolly laughed. "We have a bit of a sticky wicket here, Don."

At that same time, whether or not to talk with Hatch about the official position Kamuela intended for him was about to become moot.

A crew of ten men worked daily on the new house, including Sundays, after services of course. There were no plans, but Kamuela had sketched a set of drawings to indicate how it was to look. It would have a peaked roof of red tiles, a foundation sunk three feet into the earth, and solid walls. There would be glass in the windows. Most of the materials were scrounged from old and abandoned buildings; the roof tiles were from the old copra warehouse office, which we stopped using three years ago and never got around to tearing down.

That Sunday, the same as last Sunday, well more than a hundred townspeople showed up to picnic and watch the construction of the new house for the hero of Tuva. Also that Sunday, four outriggers came around from the Napuku side, bringing another twenty-five people to join the construction site picnic.

Guitars and drums appeared. A man from Napuku had written a song in celebration of the hero of Tuva, and after he sang it through only three times, everyone there knew the words and began singing in chorus. Mr. Jolly and I could hear it clearly all the way from the middle of town, so we walked up the hill together.

Kamuela Makani, Twilla Pihi, and Akamu Palani

strolled down from their house to join the picnic. I saw my wife and daughters and walked over to join them, telling Mr. Jolly we should meet that evening for a drink at Papa Jack's and decide the best course of action, although naturally, in spite of some natural curiosity, I did not want to be involved in this.

Meanwhile, the music could be clearly heard in Kamuela's bedroom, where Hatch slept. Kukana had gone to stand by the window, from where the construction site and the now continually expanding post-church picnic crowd was visible far down the hill.

Hatch stirred and opened his eyes. Kukana turned from the window and saw him awake.

"It's about you," she said. "Can you understand the words?"

Hatch lifted himself slightly to lean against the headboard, blinking away the residue of sleep.

"Would you like for me to open the window?" Kukana asked.

"It's nice music. Sure."

Hatch began to understand some of the words.

"Now they are singing about me," Kukana said. "What a pretty song. It is music from the church, but new special words."

Hatch closed his eyes and slumped back to the bed again.

"They call you the hero of all Tuva, even on Napuku side."

"Oh, please," Hatch sighed.

Hatch squeezed his eyes so tightly closed that it wrinkled his face.

"Do you not like your song?"

"I am not a hero, Kukana. I just want to be left alone."

"Hah," Kukana said, as if she knew a secret, which she did, and one she was about to reveal. "But you are a hero. Would there be a song about you if this were not true? Would Papa be building that house for you if it were not true?"

Hatch opened his eyes. "What house? What house for me?"

"Oh no," Kukana cried, "I have ruined the surprise. I was not supposed to say about your house. Papa wants to tell you." Her shoulders slumped in dismay.

"I don't understand what you mean about a house for me."

"Never mind anyway. There are many people down there. It is like a festival. Maybe everybody from after the service at Ho'okahi."

"What goddamn house?!"

It was the loudest voice she had ever heard him use. When she turned around from the window, Hatch was struggling to raise himself from the bed.

"No! You must stay in bed," she pleaded. "Jenny says you must stay in bed. If you fall I cannot pick you up." She held out her arms as if she could block him, but Hatch already had his legs over the side and was trying to push up with the casts over his forearms.

"I am so sorry I told you about your house. Please stay on the bed."

Hatch pushed himself awkwardly up to a wobbly stance.

"Please, please don't. You will fall."

Hatch was already up, using the wall for support. He moved slowly along the wall toward the window. Kukana rushed to his side and tried to support him. Even after all the weight lost as he recovered from the attack, he still outweighed her by fifty pounds. When he reached the window, he leaned against the sill, propped against the edges of his casts. He felt dizzy, not used to the feeling of his body weight. He could see the crowd gathered at the end of the slope across the wide lawn, the excavation, the piles of building materials.

"What is this?" he asked.

"Papa wanted to tell you, when you are feeling

better. He will be so angry with me now; I am such a stupid girl."

"Why did you say this house is for me?"

"Papa says you need a new house. A house more suitable for … oh, that is also a surprise. I am so stupid. I almost told that one too."

"This is crazy."

Hatch must have turned around too quickly, because his brain was unable to coordinate where he intended his body to go, and he fell forward, hitting the wall with his head.

"Oh no, oh no, oh no," Kukana cried repeatedly as she dropped to the floor next to him. She cradled his head looking for blood, but there was none. She tried to pull him back to the bed, but he was too heavy for her. Panicked, certain he was dying and it was her fault, she ran hysterically from the house and down the hill to find her father.

10

Kamuela stood on the lanai with Jenny, facing down the hill.

"You were too hard on her, Kamuela. I think she was taking care of things pretty well here, especially when you consider what happened to her. Let's not forget that during our concern for him."

"You cannot deny that she let him fall."

"Oh, please. If I had been here, do you think I could have stopped him from getting up if he wanted to? What about you? What would you have done? Tied him to the bed?"

Kamuela ignored the charge. "Where is Kukana? Where did she go?"

"I think she is with friends. Or maybe she needs to be alone for a little while to work this out for herself. I don't know where she is, but I am sure she is all right. Considering how you treated her. In your zeal to honor the man who saved Kukana from those pigs, have you forgotten what she also went through that day?"

"I have *not* forgotten," Kamuela responded with a snap.

"I'm sorry, Kamuela. I know you haven't. Kukana is a sensitive girl, she always has been. Her emotions are barely below the skin, but that is who she is and always has been."

"I will find her and bring her home."

"Wait." Jenny put her hand on his huge forearm. "Let me bring her home. I think it would be better if I talked to her first, woman to woman, you might say."

"Maybe you are right."

"I also think you should let her continue caring for Hatch until he is capable of leaving this house on his own, and I don't think that time is too far away. In fact, it's probably a good thing if he gets out of bed and tries to walk around a bit more. I think the reason he got dizzy and fell was because his muscles have atrophied. He can't stay in bed all the time."

"What means atrophied?"

"Being useless. The point is, I can't stay away from my classes to monitor our patient all the time. And I really do believe it is good for Kukana to focus her attention on his health, and not think about what happened to her."

"Maybe you are right, Jenny. Okay, you go and bring Kukana home. I will let her sit with him, bring his food, and help make him no atrophied to be."

"That is the right thing to do."

Kamuela put his arm around Jenny and hugged her with a strength that never failed to surprise her.

"I am glad, Jenny Makani, that you decided to stay with us, that you married my son, that you are my other daughter." He brushed her cheek with a quick kiss.

"Kamuela, you are such a pushover."

Jenny could not find Kukana anywhere in town. It grew dark and no one had seen her. By then Jenny – remembering from her own youth in Virginia the times it seemed important to run away, at least for a little while – began to worry that Kukana may have done something foolish. She was so naïve and sensitive that it was hard to predict how her mind would process all this. Maybe everybody was focused too much on her savior and not enough on the victim.

She checked Alii Street once more before becoming worried enough to drag her husband Tioni away from his friends and send him off to check the beaches. Somebody had to have seen her. Everyone on the island knew Kukana Makani. If Kamuela realized that Jenny had not by that time been able to find his daughter, he would have roused the entire population to search for her. Jenny did not think it had come to that point quite yet.

Kukana, as we know now, had gone to Hatch's shack at Kaiwi Point, where she only sat on the steps of his cracked and thin lanai and watched the eternal water coming and going, paralyzed with dread and remorse.

Now, our young lady was on her way back to town, through the jungle that divided the beach at Kaiwi Point from the town of Tuva. It had gotten dark. She felt invisible, moving along the black trail by touch and instinct, the feel of vines and high grass alongside the path guiding her back to town. Sometimes a sound she didn't immediately recognize, or the surprising touch of a limb she had not seen, startled her. Then the lights of town appeared.

The first person Kukana saw as she came off the path and walked onto the end of Alii Street, where it terminated by the old copra warehouse, was Jenny, striding toward her with her hands stuck with determination on her abundant hips.

"Where the devil have you been?"

"I cannot even go for a walk without everybody being mad at me?"

"Your brother and Charlie Mahi, and who knows who else by now, are out looking for you." Jenny was not able to maintain the stern tone with which she began because she was so thankful to have Kukana standing safe and sound in front of her. But she also did not intend to let her off too easily. "I have been everywhere there is to go on this side of the island, and was about ready to head over to Napuku ... ."

Kukana smiled. "What?" Jenny said. "You think I cannot walk over that mountain? I was walking over that mountain when you were still crawling. Besides, don't distract me. Where *were* you, Kukana?"

Jenny kept herself parked squarely in front of her niece as if to block her from disappearing again, thrusting out her hip to accentuate her anger, which actually had already dissipated.

"Walking," Kukana repeated, then mimicked Jenny's thrust out hip.

"I had to keep your father from launching a full-scale search party, so you can stop mocking me, *dear*."

Jenny looped her arm through Kukana's and held her forearm.

"We need to go find Tioni and tell him Little Bo Peep has come home."

As they walked along, Jenny said, "Your father treated you unfairly. I told him so, and I am sure he understands. Darling, I really don't blame you for wanting to get away from it all for a little while. You just need to tell somebody where you're going."

"Is he … ?"

"Your patient is fine. He didn't hurt himself any worse, if that's what you mean, and it was not … do you understand me? Listen, Kukana. It was *not* your fault."

Kukana remained silent and they walked alongside the harbor. Eventually they found Tioni and as soon as he began to chastise his sister, Jenny stopped him. Tioni and Charlie went back to repairing nets, while Jenny and Kukana continued through town.

"Is Papa mad at me, too?" Kukana asked after Tioni left.

"He wasn't mad at you, honey. His frustration was misdirected. Your father has worked himself up into such a feeling of responsibility toward that man that it clouds his thinking sometimes. Do you understand?"

Kukana nodded, but Jenny had the feeling that she wasn't interested in understanding right then. They continued along the plank sidewalk toward the church. Jenny, who always persisted in wearing shoes, made clicking sounds on the boards.

They offered a greeting to Dennis Lindsay, who was propped on the long bench outside Papa Jack's, drunk, strumming chords on his cracked guitar. Attempting a formal bow to the ladies, and he called every woman over the age of about ten a lady, Dennis tripped over his own feet and dropped the guitar for another crack.

"Oh Dennis," Jenny said, and pulled Kukana along.

Before the church, they turned up the lane that led to the next street.

"Where are we going?" Kukana asked.

"Would you like some tea?" Jenny asked.

Kukana could see they were going to the house Jenny had shared with her brother since their marriage.

It was a small house, at least relative to the Makani house another quarter mile up the hill, but both large and stylish compared with most other houses on the island, as befits the house of a chief's son. Tioni didn't much like the chief aspect of his life; he both acted like and thought of himself as a fisherman. Jenny loved that about him, because he could if he chose do nothing at all and live the same way.

They went into the kitchen through the back door and Kukana sat at the round breakfast table while Jenny lit the stove. "There is a bit of cake leftover, only a day old. Would you like some?"

"No, thank you. Tea is okay."

Jenny stood at the sink preparing a teapot and looked out the window, her favorite view from the kitchen. The jalousie slats were wide open and a palm frond had worked a tip through the opening between two glass slats. A drying line strung between two palm trees in the yard still had sheets and pillowcases hanging. That is what Jenny liked about the view, clothes drying on a line; it reminded her, when she needed to be reminded, of her childhood in northern Virginia. Kukana watched her aunt watching the flapping sheets.

"Do you miss America?" Kukana asked when Jenny brought the pot, sugar cubes, milk, and two cups.

"Yes, of course. Only sometimes, though. As you would miss Tuva if you ever lived somewhere else."

"I will never live somewhere else," Kukana whispered.

Having not heard the remark, Jenny continued. "I miss changing seasons. I miss drive-in movies and convertibles on the open road. I miss the golden arches of McDonald's, not to mention the Big Mac. It's all silly stuff, really. My parents are dead and my friends are scattered to the four winds. This is my home now, and it always will be."

Jenny took one of Kukana's hands between both of hers. "You know that because it is impossible for Tioni and I to have children, you and Kamuela and Tioni are my family. After Emma died … you know I think of you as my daughter."

"I know," Kukana said, but her eyes were probing the inside of the teacup from which she had not drunk. "Do you think he misses America? Isn't he American like you?"

"Hatch, you mean. Yes, that's what they say. His accent is American, I mean, not Australian or British, like that. He is definitely a strange one. I can't say what goes on in his head. I don't think that before this happened I ever had a conversation with the man."

"I wonder if he has a wife or a family in America?"

Jenny shrugged. "You like him, don't you?"

It came to Jenny all at once, when Kukana did not answer and did not lift her eyes from the teacup. How could she have missed it? For nearly three weeks she had hardly left the room where Hatch lay abed. Often Jenny had come to visit and found Kukana asleep in the chair by the bed. Kamuela and Akamu had to make her leave the room so they could bathe him. She would come back immediately and take up her chair.

She read to him even when he was unconscious. She fed him; the first few really desperate days Jenny had seen her chew bits of fruit first and then put the mush into his mouth. It was obvious, Jenny realized; how could she have not understood this already and stopped it in the beginning?

"Oh, darling, you do like him, don't you?"

"I honor him," Kukana said.

"Kukana, my darling, Hatch is most definitely not the man for you. You cannot let yourself think for one moment that he is."

"Are you saying he is a bad man?"

"No, I am not saying he is a bad man. But he must be forty years old, or more. He is old enough to be your father. It is totally understandable that you might feel a kind of respect, a kind of affection, for him, but it would be terribly, terribly wrong for you to confuse those natural feelings with love."

"You are older than Tioni. Six years more."

"Five and a half, but that's not the point. I was twenty-five years old when I married your brother. You are only seventeen."

"Tioni was nineteen, and it was all right for you to marry him."

"Jesus, Kukana. In the first place, I hope we aren't even having a conversation about marriage. My God!"

"I have friends younger than me who are married and already have babies."

"And your friends are not the only daughter of Kamuela Makani, who raised you to be educated, thoughtful, *smart*. Besides, your friends are not married to someone forty years old."

"How do you know he is forty?"

"I don't know how old he is. I don't know *anything at all* about him."

"Why do you criticize Hatch? What has he done to you?"

Exasperated by then, Jenny tried to put patience back into her tone. "Darling, please understand. I certainly do not dislike the man. I have enormous respect for what he did for you. I just want you to see that it is not healthy, it just wouldn't be right, for you to confuse gratitude with love. Not right for either one of you. Why does an American man come way out here to live … ?"

"You are an American and you decided to live here. Mia's father is an American and he stays here."

"I don't mean to sound like I'm attacking … ."

Kukana stood abruptly, the tea in her cup still untouched and now cold. "I don't care what you say. I am going home now, and don't worry, I won't get lost."

"Shit," Jenny swore as Kukana went out the back door, passing between the fresh sheets, and heading up the steep hill home.

11

The remaining days of Hatch's confinement in the Makani house passed quickly. Hatch was apparently used to urging his body to heal. One day he could walk around the bedroom unaided; the next he walked outside and sat with Kamuela on the lanai, from where he could see the continuing construction project of the magistrate of police house. A week after that, Tioni sawed off the casts. The following day, Hatch declared he was going home.

The day before, when Kukana knew Hatch's casts were coming off the next day, she went back to his house at Kaiwi Point. When she was there a few weeks before, she thought it looked like a trash dumping place. The area around the house was littered with bottles, cans, odds and ends of fishing paraphernalia. She was shocked to find it just as bad inside.

She had already decided to clean it for his homecoming, but she could see it would take all day, not the hour or two she had first imagined.

She immediately encountered an insurmountable problem: what to do with the trash? By the time she had picked all of it up from around the house, there was a mound to her knees. By the time she added all the trash from inside, the little mountain of debris was almost to her waist. Had he taken nothing to the landfill since he arrived? It would be impossible for her to haul it away now, and certainly not alone. She had no choice but to leave the trash hill where it was and get Akamu to help her later. Maybe if she asked nicely, Akamu and Tioni would do it themselves.

Hot and sweaty from her labors, Kukana removed her clothes and lay them over the lanai railing, then walked to the lagoon to cool off. She did not swim, much too tired already. She lay at the water's edge and let the sea lap over her legs. She didn't want to get her hair wet; it took hours to dry. Then she let the sun dry her body and took a last walk through Hatch's shack to survey her work.

She had noticed the notebooks laying on the table in the corner; she put them into a neat stack. Now she opened the one on top and flipped through the pages. Every one was filled with an almost unreadable scrawl. It would not be polite to read it without his permission. She closed that notebook and hoped he would not assume she had invaded his privacy because she had seen these notebooks.

She was naked. In his house. A house she had just cleaned like a wife would. She stood just inside the open door and looked around. It really was a dump. Why did he live like this? It was quite obvious how much Hatch needed her in his life. He would know this when he saw what she had done, that she could do a wife's work, even if she was the daughter of a chief.

She lay on his bed, which she had so carefully made up from the twisted mess of sheets that were on it before.

Naked. In his house. On his bed.

She put her hands between her legs. Then she was so embarrassed she began to cry.

She smoothed her wrinkles from the sheet, dressed, and walked home.

Hatch and her father were seated in the wide-back wicker chairs on the lanai when Kukana walked along the lane. She came up the steps and offered casual greetings.

"We wondered about you," Hatch said.

That he wondered about her was thrilling. She smiled enigmatically, and as she walked past them into the house, she said, "I went swimming."

"Your hair is not wet, Kukana," her father noted,

although by then she was inside.

That evening, Hatch, his casts just removed, could join the others for dinner at the long koa wood dining table. As Twilla went around pouring wine, Kamuela announced what everyone already knew, that Hatch would leave the next day, adding that he would return to his house at Kaiwi Point. He was now well enough to care for himself.

Twilla stopped pouring and asked, "But what about his new house, the policeman's house?" Obviously Twilla was looking forward to living in the new house and having only one man to take care of, especially since that man was the hero of Tuva.

Kamuela had not yet told anyone about his discussion with Hatch earlier, that Hatch had refused, albeit graciously, all of Kamuela's offers: house, job, and the yacht.

Hatch started to speak, but Kamuela interrupted and said, "He wants to think about it."

"You are not going to be the Tuva policeman?" Twilla asked, abashed anyone would turn down such an honor, especially the house that goes with it.

"No, I'm not," Hatch answered. "Although I am flattered by the offer … for everything. I am deeply grateful for all you've done for me, all of you – Akamu, Kamuela, Jenny, Twilla – for the food that healed me so quickly, and especially you, Kukana, the best nurse anyone could have."

Kukana glanced up briefly before looking down at her soup bowl again. She was going to cry if she looked at him. She might anyway.

Hatch continued. "And Tioni, of course, who with his friends saved my life."

"I only wish we were more faster," Tioni said.

"Better late than never," Akamu proclaimed.

Hatch spoke like a man not used to thanking people, especially for helping him.

"Everyone on Tuva," he went on. "You are all good people."

Hatch raised his wine glass in salute, then took up his soup spoon to indicate he was finished making speeches.

"But why ... ?" Twilla began, before Kamuela cut her off with a wave of his hand.

"He will think about it," Kamuela said.

Hatch rolled his eyes rather comically at Kamuela. The rest of their dinner conversation was inconsequential.

Hatch figured that adequate appreciation and farewells were said last night at the dinner table and would only be belabored by repetition that morning. He woke early and dressed, leaving the house without awakening anyone. It was an hour before sunrise. His pants and shirt, mended and laundered by Twilla, were in the closet, where they had been waiting since his arrival over two months ago. His old clothes felt familiar but odd against his skin, skin that had touched only soft cotton sheets and a lava lava during all that time.

He quietly closed the front door and found his way in the dark, across the yard to the lane running seaward through the row of royal palms. He didn't expect to encounter many people at that hour, but kept to streets on the upper reaches of town before turning down toward the wharf, where he would reach the trail to Kaiwi Point. It felt good to be alone after two months of constant, discomforting attention.

He walked slowly, minding his steps, although there was only a little discomfort remaining – he had known worse. There was a generalized and annoying lassitude, weakness from the long lack of exercise. He was still not used to the lightness of his arms, the casts gone.

When he reached the northern end of town, passing the wharf, he saw the Hard Wind secured at the far end. It was the first time he had seen her, and she was a much larger yacht than he imagined;

probably a waterline length over forty feet, fifty or more overall. What did Kamuela expect Hatch would do with a yacht like that?

The first thing he noticed as he entered the clearing was the hill of trash and junk, and then realized it had been made from the debris that used to be there. It was uncomfortably disorienting, as if a grove of trees had moved ten yards away during the night. He was gone two months; someone must have come out here and cleaned up. But why would anybody do such a thing?

He stopped before the rickety step at the lanai and turned back to look across the lagoon. This had always been a narcotic-like vision for him: the green smooth water in the lagoon stretching out to the whitewater reef, then the expanse of blue blending into the deep purple sea extending to the horizon. There were morning clouds billowing upward, but harboring no rain. It was summer and would not rain again for some weeks.

Calmed by this vision, Hatch pushed open the door and entered his shack.

Even the swept-up clearing around the shack had not prepared him for the cleanliness inside. He felt personally invaded. Someone had not only cleaned, but had moved things around, thrown things out, washed his clothes and bed sheet. Even made the bed. In more than ten years, that bed had never been made so neatly.

He noticed his outboard motor leaning against the railing, the propeller he had traded a shovel for in Napuku, properly installed. Maybe that person did the rest of it? But he couldn't imagine Tioni doing something like that.

"Oh, what the fuck," he muttered to the clean room, and went to retrieve a bottle of Suntory whisky from the storage cabinet below the tin sink. He took a glass, it was clean, and plopped on the sagging cushions of the wicker sofa. He took a long and much welcome drink, then lit a cigarette, also much welcome, and tossed the match onto the floor.

The ensuing days passed uneasily, with a plodding, immeasurable pace for Kukana.

She missed her patient terribly, sometimes making her sick to her stomach when she tried to eat, the pain of his absence flooding from her mind into her belly. She had never felt love like this before, so different from loving her father, her mother, her brother, her aunt, her friends. She had also ached miserably for a long time after her mother died. Even that was not an ache like this one.

When her father was out of the house, sometimes Kukana would go into his bedroom, pull close to the bed the chair she had sat on everyday for two months, and lay her head on the sheet, the way she had done when Hatch was in that bed. But he was not there, and when she lay her arm out, there was nothing to touch but the tapa cover.

No one had seen Hatch after he left the Makani house. Everyone on the island knew by now that Hatch had refused everything, choosing instead to return to his derelict shack and do whatever it was he did out there all by himself. The odd result being that by refusing all his deserved rewards, his heroic stature among Tuvans increased, as did a new round of *Hatch Stories*.

Rumors about him circulated throughout the town. People questioned anyone who had ever spent time with Hatch; there weren't many. One of the Lotus girls, who had occasionally in the past visited Hatch's shack, had nothing to say about him, except that he was a quiet and nice man. She said she would like to visit him again, but he had not invited her for many months.

I thought Hatch was, in spite of spending quite a few evenings in Papa Jack's with him, very nearly a phantom, and I wasn't sure that his presence on our small island was all that comforting, hero or not.

Kukana's girlfriends wanted to know everything, and she wanted to talk about him, but her feelings were private. She could rarely think of anything to say that didn't feel invasive. Although, in secret talks after swimming at Hua Pala beach, Pia Niu, Kukana's closest friend, asked for the specific details no one else would dare to ask. Kukana told Pia that she was in love with Hatch, and she also confessed to Pia's persistent questioning that no, she had never seen him entirely. Her father and Akamu bathed him, sending her from the room. Pia thought everything about it was wonderful and exciting, such a romantic adventure, except, of course, the sadness of separation that now clouded Kukana's typically open and friendly face.

Hatch returned to his world. When not asleep or passed out, he walked in the jungle, worked on his fishing gear, dove for shells, and fished the fifty fathom ledge beyond the reef.

Some days all he did was prowl the interior of his shack with a Suntory bottle in one hand, trailing cigarette butts to mark his passage between the two small rooms. He was often foul with liquor, maybe now even more than before. The scratching in his notebooks became nearly illegible during these weeks.

He ate some of the fish he caught, as well as barnacle-like crustaceans he picked from the pilings of the destroyed jetty. There were guavas and mangoes from trees behind the shack. These trees produced so prolifically that most of the fruit fell to the ground and rotted there. He had a crate of soda crackers, and he made fish sandwiches with them.

He did not begin each day sad and morose. That condition arrived on the whisky tsunami. He had to get drunk to sleep, and he usually started getting ready to sleep at midday. Regardless, no matter how much he drank, there did not seem to be enough to moderate his nightmares.

It appeared that there was some distant sanctuary he hoped to reach. When he had drunk so much that he passed into unconsciousness, a state like death, he supposed, dreamless and dark, where there was no time or space, nowhere thought could exist, no place for dreams, no memories, in there he found the peace of a pseudo death.

12

The new magistrate of police house rose inexorably from the slope between the Makani house and Ho'okahi church, in spite of the fact there was no magistrate to live there.

The house still lacked roof finishes, rain gutters, and interior paint, but was otherwise complete. Having neither skills nor tools for cutting glass, the work crew cut the window openings to fit an odd assortment of existent window glass taken from two different abandoned buildings, so those on one side were slightly larger than the ones on the other, while one of the windows in front was actually a set of French doors, and all the ones in back were jalousie slat.

Because Hatch was unwilling to state any sort of preference, Kamuela decided to paint the walls white – there was a lot of white paint in town – and trim the porch, doors, and window shutters in red, matching the roof tiles. That would give the house an *official* look.

Kamuela spent much of his day at the site, insuring that work followed his plan, and that the men didn't spend too many hours napping or talking with the group of women who continued to picnic on the lawn.

Sooner or later, Kamuela believed, Hatch's curiosity would compel him to at least look at the house, and when he saw how marvelous it was, he would not be able to continue living in that shack, hardly worthy of keeping chickens. He would accept the house, then one thing would follow another, and the hero of Tuva would assume his proper position in island life.

Kamuela had always believed in the lessons of his senses, the evidence offered in full scale by the environment. Like the reef, that great mausoleum formed from the limestone skeletons of enumerable coral polyps heaping themselves, one upon the other, in their multitudes, Kamuela knew that men were their accumulated experiences, which inevitably compelled each man to follow the pathway to the destiny established by his history. Hatch would come to see his pathway and follow it.

Regardless, it might be wise, Kamuela supposed, to give the man a nudge in the right direction.

The location of Hatch's shack was no mystery to Kamuela. In his youth, Kaiwi Point was a special place, where he had courted Emma, where they first made love, where Kamuela believed their son, Tioni, began his journey to the light, the land, the air, the sea.

Kamuela had not been to Kaiwi Point since Emma's death. He was surprised at how overgrown the path had become. Few people used that trail because it went nowhere beyond Hatch's shack. He was not prepared for the dereliction when he came into the clearing. Nor was he prepared for the condition in which he found the hero of Tuva.

From some distance away, Kamuela thought Hatch was hurt, or worse. He was lying face down on the narrow beach, among the flotsam, his feet almost in the water. Kamuela reached down and turned him over. The hero of Tuva wasn't hurt or dead, he was drunk, sound asleep. There was an empty whisky bottle under him, and vomit on the sand not far away.

It was impossible to fully rouse him, so, muttering sarcastically, "the hero of Tuva," Kamuela hoisted Hatch over his shoulder and carried him to the shack like a sack of copra, where he unceremoniously dumped him onto the disheveled cot. Kamuela did not know his daughter had come to clean, and anyway, there was now little evidence remaining of Kukana's visit.

Kamuela pulled a chair close and sat staring at the man passed out before him. What happened to the man who showed such strength against the evil men? Where in that derelict was the one who risked his life for a girl he did not know? The man who never once complained of the pain? The man with such intense pride that he accepted no reward or honors? "What is the demon chasing you?" Kamuela said to the unconscious man.

Kamuela knew where to find at least one demon. He got up and went through the shack, pouring the contents of every liquor bottle onto the ground outside the kitchen window. The lack of decent food was appalling: a bit of fruit, some of it rotting, a half-gone box of soda crackers, a rancid chunk of skipjack tuna laying like excrement at the bottom of the sink, a few cans of cooked beans. What did the man eat?

After searching through the place, Kamuela realized that he had no choice but to leave Hatch there and return to town for supplies. He didn't like leaving the man alone in such a state, but since the liquor was all gone and he was completely asleep, it would probably be safe to leave him.

He laughed at himself: of course, Hatch had survived out here alone like this for ten years.

Kamuela walked back to town and found one of his cousins – he had very many – and told him to get another of their cousins and meet him at Mr. Lee's Emporium. Then he continued to his house to get Twilla.

"Find a box for ice," he told her, "and things you will need for cooking."

"For cooking? What things? To cook what?"

"How do I know? You are the cook? What you need for cooking."

"What am I going to cook? It would help to know."

"Meals. More than one. Things that can be kept

on ice for another time. Fish, pig, vegetables, opihi."

"Where I am going to cook these meals?"

"Hatch's house," quickly adding, "at Kaiwi Point," in case she might think he meant the magistrate's house. "Bring all these things to Mr. Lee's. Akamu will help you carry. I will be waiting there."

Returning to the emporium, Kamuela sent his cousin to Papa Jack's with orders to fill the insulated box with ice, then, with Mr. Lee's amiable help, he gathered some canned goods from the shelves.

Two hours after Kamuela left Hatch's shack, the caravan headed back: Kamuela, Twilla, Akamu, and two cousins, all carrying boxes of food and the ice chest.

When they reached the clearing where the shack revealed itself among the high grass and thick vegetation, Kamuela had the men place the boxes on the lanai; he thanked them and sent them back to town, adding that each should help himself to two beers at Papa Jack's, on his account. Then he and Twilla took the boxes inside.

He *lives* here?" Twilla asked. She followed Kamuela into the kitchen space, shaking her head at the sight of it.

"I will thank you, Twilla Pihi, to never speak of what you saw here, not even to your sister."

"What happened to him?" Twilla saw Hatch still passed out on the bed where Kamuela left him.

"He is drunk."

"So what I am to do now? Cook?"

"Yes. That is why you are here."

"I am to cook using what?"

"Is that not a stove?"

Twilla inspected the tiny countertop cook stove, then looked to find some way to prime and light it.

Kamuela left the kitchen to her. Hatch had not moved during those hours, except that Kamuela had left him lying on his back and now he was on his stomach. Kamuela pulled close a chair and sat watching.

"White men," he muttered. He poked Hatch's shoulder and said, "Wake up."

Hatch opened his eyes, squinting as if into a bright light. He tried to turn and lift his head. When he saw Kamuela, he thought he was still in the Makani house, until he recognized his own raw, unpainted, ragged plank walls.

"You have pain?"

Hatch turned onto his side, then managed to sit up, holding his forehead as if to keep his brains from leaking out through his eyes. He was in pain, all right. He reached toward the floor for the bottle that was not there.

"Pau," Kamuela said.

"What?" Hatch put both hands at the side of his head and squeezed.

"Pau. Gone. No more," Kamuela said. "Liquor all pau from here."

"Well, ain't that the shits," Hatch groaned. How, he wondered, had he managed to drink all the booze in the place? No wonder he felt like crap.

"Cigarettes?" Hatch wondered.

Kamuela looked around on the floor by the bed and saw a crumpled pack. He took a cigarette out and handed it to Hatch.

"Thanks. My mouth tastes like raw shark liver soaked in fuel oil."

Kamuela laughed. He struck a match and lit Hatch's cigarette.

"What did I do?" Hatch wondered. He sat up straighter then swung his legs over the side of the bed.

"Got drunk, I would say," Kamuela answered.

"Hope that's all." Hatch rose unsteadily to his feet, standing still to get his bearings hoping the room would stop swaying beneath his feet.

There were noises from the other room.

"Soon there will be something to eat," Kamuela

said.

"Eat? Who's here?"

"Twilla Pihi. She is making the food. First we eat, then we talk."

Food odors drifted in from the kitchen, the compelling smell of strong black tea.

"This is quite a roaring good dream I'm having," Hatch said.

A dream into which he was about to throw up. Bile rushed into his throat. He swallowed it back, then raced to the porch railing and spewed the contents of his stomach onto the sand below.

Kamuela approached after.

Hatch turned and leaned back against the railing. "I don't get many guests," he said, wiping his mouth with his hand. "You honor me."

"I did not come as a guest. You have no food here. How do you survive? On guavas and whisky?"

"I happen to like guavas and whisky," Hatch smiled. "But I make out all right. The sea is full of good things to eat. Sometimes Mr. Lee's clerk brings some things out. What is Twilla doing?"

"Making something for you to eat."

"I might skip that for a while today."

"You will eat. If you cannot hold that in your stomach, you will eat again."

Hatch shrugged. He already knew how impossible it was to argue with Kamuela Makani.

Twilla appeared in the doorway, surveyed Hatch's dishevelment, and said, "Do you eat on the floor?"

"Pardon?" Hatch squinted his eyes trying to focus on Twilla, who stood half in and half out the door. "Hello, Twilla."

"Do you have plates? Do you eat from a table? There is no table here."

"Plates? I don't know. Let me have a look." He leaned up from the rail, still unsteady.

"Just tell me," Twilla said, holding out her hand to stop him.

"I'm sure I do. Somewhere."

Twilla threw up her arms in exasperation and disappeared back inside the shack. Hatch followed.

A fat pot steamed on the propane stove, the odor of fish broiled in lime and garlic filled the room. There were yams. The strong odor of black tea. Sliced fruit on wax paper on the counter, which was simply a wide wooden plank Hatch had scrounged and secured to the wall. That counter was also his table.

"Plates," Twilla reminded him.

Hatch had two or three tin plates, two or three plastic bowls, and a large wood platter. He found all these things and set them on the counter.

Hatch had at first wondered if it was Twilla who cleaned the shack while he was laid up in the Makani house? But if it were her, wouldn't she know where to find things? If not Twilla?

Twilla served the food and made a setting at one end of the counter. She went to the porch and told Kamuela, "There is what there is. I have other work to do." She looked back and gave Hatch a caustic look, then went carefully down the broken steps.

"Mahalo," Kamuela thanked her.

"Yes, mahalo," Hatch added, still confused about all of this.

They went into the kitchen and ate. Hatch dragged over a packing crate to sit on, Kamuela brought the chair from the other room. They sat side by side and ate quietly.

"This is good," Hatch said.

"Then eat," Kamuela ordered.

Outside, the omnipresent surf rumbled over the reef.

When they finished, the two men walked to the beach beside the lagoon.

"Turned out to be a nice afternoon," Hatch remarked, "considering the unfortunate start of it."

They stopped at the water's edge.

"It's getting late," Hatch said. "Soon the path will

be dark." Hatch's hint that Kamuela leave was not well-disguised, and was completely ignored.

"I know the way. Do you know the last time I was here?"

"No."

"Ten years ago. About the time you arrived on Tuva. I was there," Kamuela pointed to the place where the beach curved away and disappeared at the spit of land called Kaiwi Point, where there are sacred fish ponds. "I came to make my lamentation."

"Lamentation? For what, may I ask?"

"It is the preacher's word. It was the day I buried Emma, my wife, mother of Tioni and Kukana."

"Oh," Hatch said, only acknowledging that he heard.

"Have you a wife, Hatch?"

"No."

"Ever?"

"No."

"Are you da kine mahu?"

Hatch smiled and shook his head. "I prefer the company of women in that regard."

"Why did you choose this place to live, to build up your house?"

"I don't know. There was nobody here, mainly. It is very quiet. Peaceful. Was it wrong?"

"You may live where you like. And it is a beautiful, and yes, empty place. Some people think of it as a ... what is da kine for a private, safe place?"

"Sanctuary?"

"Yes. This place on Tuva is a sanctuary. There are sacred pools over there." Kamuela pointed to Kaiwi.

"Yes. If I had known what it meant to you, Kamuela, I could never have presumed to build this piece of shit shack here. Now that I know, I will tear it down and move it somewhere else."

"No." Kamuela put his hand on Hatch's shoulder. "If there was an objection, you would have known ten years ago. I think you chose this place with the guidance of destiny. Maybe this place waited for you, offering itself to no one but you."

Hatch laughed despite himself.

"You laugh?"

"Meaning no disrespect to you, Kamuela. I suppose maybe it's the idea of a place waiting for some man to show up … especially if that man is a fuck up like me. I sure as hell wouldn't wait around for the likes of me. You know, I guess I just don't have much faith in destiny."

"That is sad. We are the path destiny takes us on. What makes a man go on this path or on that path?"

Hatch changed the subject. "I will be glad to walk into town with you, and honored to buy you a drink at Papa Jack's. Considering there isn't anything to offer you here."

"Men drink liquor for as many reasons as there are men, but there is also a same kind about it. Me, I drink liquor sometimes, and I get drunk sometimes. I like the taste of some, although some of it also tastes like paint."

"Have you drunk paint before?"

"You think to joke, but yes, when I was a boy I tasted from a can of paint. It tastes like gin, which is why you never see me drinking gin. I prefer whisky and Foster's."

"Same here," Hatch said.

They turned and walked back toward the shack.

"I will get Twilla's things. She will need them."

"I'll help, and we can stop at Papa Jack's on the way."

They filled a box with the cooking tools Twilla brought, then sat on the porch as the sun began to blend with the distant horizon.

"I bet it took a long time for that paint to wear off your tongue," Hatch remarked as they watched the sun hover, it trembling an inch above the horizon, about to melt into the ocean. "A magnificent thing to see," Hatch remarked about the sunset.

"And we get to see it everyday."

"Do you believe," Kamuela asked Hatch, "as I have been taught, that the sun does not move in the sky? That it is as solid as an island? That the earth spins like a child's toy tossed from a string? If this is true, why does the sea not fly away like water slung from a pan?"

"Believe? Believing is like faith; all beliefs are only a faith of some sort. I am of the opinion that we know nothing, we only believe things, or not. Do I believe what I am told or what I can see? You need to ask someone who thinks he knows. That isn't me."

"So you say nothing is true? There are not facts?"

"What a strange conversation, Kamuela."

"Why strange? You don't think about such things. Ever?"

"Not often. At least not in a very, very long time. I suppose that we really cannot say for certain that the world does not end beyond our sensible experience of it. Things are not what they seem. The appearance of a setting sun is an illusion of the mind."

"Well then, if it is the mind that confuses us, maybe we are better believing what we know in our hearts."

"I don't know what that means, Kamuela. Shall we be off to Papa Jack's?" He stood.

Kamuela also stood and lifted the box, shrugging off Hatch's attempt to take it. They walked toward the path, Kamuela leading.

"In the hearts of our people, you, Hatch, are the hero of Tuva. It is what we know, and you cannot deny what we know you are."

Speaking to Kamuela's back, while they moved onto the dark trail toward town, Hatch said, and quite abruptly, "I don't mean any disrespect to you, and I hope you know how much I appreciate all that you and your family did for me, but for Chrissakes, can't we stop this crazy hero business? I'm pretty sick of it. It has nothing to do with me."

They remained silent the rest of the way. When they reached Papa Jack's, Kamuela sat the box on a bench and they went inside.

"I will be honored to buy a drink for the hero of Tuva," Kamuela announced as they went through the door.

"Shit," Hatch muttered, rolling his eyes.

People moved to make room for them at the bar. Some minutes passed as greetings were exchanged. Finally, with shots and beers, Hatch and Kamuela were left to themselves.

They toasted, downed the shots, and took long drinks from the tall blue cans of beer.

"You say we cannot know truth," Kamuela turned to Hatch and began, as if the conversation had not ended half an hour ago on the trail. "You say facts are what we decide they are. But I know that a man cannot change what he is, be it good or evil, simply by saying he is one or the other. A man is how he acts, not what he tells to others, especially about himself. You may tell to me you do not have the alcohol sickness, but you do have it; it is plain to see. You may say it was nothing important for you to intercede on behalf of my daughter, and at certain risk to your own life you saved hers. You say such, but what you did is the truth of it. You may say you have no need of other people and wish only to be left alone to rot like the guavas around your shack. Don said you told him this. Yet, you come often into town and spend the whole of the night right here in Papa Jack's, even when you already have plenty of alcohol at your shack … ."

"Well, I used to, anyway."

"You come here because you do need life around you. You say no, but then, here you are. Because you can be a selfish man does not mean you cannot also be a heroic man."

"Thank you," Hatch answered, hoping to stop the conversation or change the subject. He took a long, deep drink from the can of beer.

"Why do you dishonor the people of Tuva, where you chose to make your home, by refusing our gifts to you? Don't you know that it is not about you getting da kine, it is about us giving da kine."

"Is that what this is all about? That I don't want the boat, the house, the job? It is not a lack of respect, Kamuela. What would I do with the house you are building. I already have a house, it suits me. And we both know Tuva doesn't need a policeman, and certainly not me." Hatch laughed. "What would a magistrate of police do here? In America, we call this kind of thing a make-work job, a kind of charity."

"What is wrong with charity? The preacher tells us about faith, hope, and charity. It is our way of doing things, to honor our heroes. Your refusal dishonors me."

"But don't you see, Kamuela? Acceptance dishonors me. Stalemate."

"Stalemate?"

"How do we proceed from opposite positions."

"Ah. We do it by turning around and facing one another, man to man."

"In my world, when men turn away from their walls to stand face to face, it is usually to fight it out."

"You don't want to fight. I would win."

Hatch laughed. "Of that, there is no doubt."

"But I do understand you better now, Hatch. There is honor in your refusal to accept our rewards, even if we have disappointment by it. Yes, you are right. A man should make his own choice where to live, he should choose his own work. But the boat is different. The boat is yours by right. You cannot refuse it because it is already yours … you know, because it already is."

"I think you mean by default."

"What I mean is, because of what happened, according to our laws, the boat is already yours. You may sell it or give it away or sink it, but you cannot refuse what you already possess."

"In what way does that yacht belong to me by rights?"

"It is a prize from war, that is our tradition and also our law. The victim's payment from the criminal."

"Believe me," Hatch said wryly, "that was no war."

"It is your boat. Do with it what you wish. Let it sink and make a home for fish. Let it rot. Give it to Hattie and she can entertain her friends there. Make a playground for children. At least, on Tuva, a man cannot deny the responsibility of his property."

"All right, Kamuela. I'll take the damn boat."

"Good."

Kamuela told Dennis Lindsay to bring them two more shots and beers.

Hatch had never seen Kamuela drunk. It took three of his cousins to get him up the steep slope to his house, like trying to move a sleeping bear.

Hatch then went across the street and sat on one of the docking bollards. Passersby greeted him; Hatch returned a wave. The pier fishermen watched, then went back to their fish. At his back, the Cheoy Lee ketch bumped against the tire fenders in the soft night swells that eased their way across the bay. He stared at her.

There was only a single dim light on a tall pole at the end of the wharf, but Hatch could also see by the flickering reflection from the torches lining the beach, across from Papa Jack's. He made his way along the deck, and even in the dark he could see what a beautiful boat she was: a raised main cabin, teak decks, polished mahogany hatch covers, brass ports, stainless steel winches. He ran his hand along the safety line, walking forward to the bow railing. Sitting on the bow pulpit railing, he looked back over the fifty feet to the stern, which was almost swallowed in darkness. Then his eye followed the foremast upward.

The feel, the smell, the look of the boat, reminded Hatch of the yacht he joined in Singapore, some weeks after he had limped his way out of the Laotian jungle. It was also a Cheoy Lee design; she took him to Jakarta. From there he crewed another yacht to Port Moresby. For a while he worked as a deckhand on a marlin boat out of Cairns. A year after that he got a job helping deliver a luxury motor yacht from Sydney back to Singapore. After working six months as bodyguard to a British banker, he signed on with an American schooner bound for Tahiti. Then Tuva.

13

I happened to be standing in the shadows near the head of the wharf and noticed Hatch walking along the deck. It had taken no time at all for the word to get out that he had accepted the boat. I watched, having a last smoke before going home – I had chosen not to smoke in the house around my daughters. He walked aft again, slid back the cover to the main cabin, and went below.

Kukana startled me, I was so focused watching Hatch.

"Good evening, Kukana," I said, when she appeared beside me.

Her attention was also directed toward the man on the boat.

"Good evening, sir."

A light appeared, shining through the main cabin ports.

"Is that him?" she asked.

"Yes. I suppose you know your father talked him into taking the boat?"

The main cabin light went off.

"Maybe that isn't so good a thing?"

"Why might that be?"

We both saw the flare of a match through one of the cabin ports; he must have lit a cigarette.

"Maybe he will take the boat and sail away from Tuva."

"I rather doubt it, Kukana. He has lived here for a long time, and I have never heard him once mention leaving."

"Now he has a way."

She had a point, and I could not miss the wistfulness in her voice.

"May I ask you a question?"

"Of course."

"You are an American."

"I've been on Tuva so long now, Kukana, that my nationality might be up for debate. But yes, go on."

"What do you think of Hatch? I mean, do you think he is a good man?"

"I have no reason to believe otherwise. Why do you ask?" By then I already suspected why she asked. I had seen her on three occasions tending Hatch, sitting at his bedside, once with her head on the edge of the bed next to him, both sleeping. And now standing here beside me in the twilight, the purple evening sky offering a planet, the first star or two, the pulsing glow from the tip of Hatch's cigarette just visible through one of the portholes, I saw her eyes fixated on the yacht at the wharf's end, and heard that soft, naïve voice of hers asking me if I think Hatch is a good man – Kukana was in love with him, for Chrissakes.

I turned toward her and put my hand on her shoulder. "Kukana, let me give you some advice, which I presume you will ignore, just like my own girls do. But I feel compelled to have my say. Whether or not Hatch is a good man, he is not the man for you."

"I have heard this before, but thank you for offering me your advice."

Her eyes had not once left the boat.

"Well, then," I said. "If you will excuse me. My stomach proclaims the call of supper."

"Thank you, sir. Please say hello to Mia for me."

"I will. And Kukana, be careful."

As I turned to leave, I saw the cabin light come on again, his shadowed image moving from aft forward through the cabin, his form flashing by each porthole. When I looked back, Kukana was still staring at the Hard Wind, taking no notice of the street torches being snuffed along the road behind her.

Hatch fell asleep aboard that night. He had crawled into the forward cabin, after going through the entire yacht to see if anything personal from the crew remained. He found nothing to indicate that four men had lived aboard her.

Awakened by sunlight streaming through one of the forward portholes, darting over his eyes, he turned away from the glare, but it was too late, his sleep already broken. He had slept well, one of the rare nights without one or another version of that same nightmare; the cabin air tainted by his musty sleep odor.

He had slept late, already an hour after sunrise. He became aware of the usual harbor noises as fishing skiffs headed outbound. He opened the portholes on opposing sides to get some cross ventilation.

He went to the cockpit and slipped out of his shorts and tee-shirt, then dove into the bay for a swim. He stopped after a short distance and looked back at the yacht. Her name and hailing port were painted across her stern: *Hard Wind / San Diego*.

After the morning swim, he decided to go back to his shack and go fishing.

He went through the boat securing the ports, then flipped off the power switches. He closed the hatches and double-checked the docking lines as he stepped onto the pier. Then he walked the length of the wharf and turned onto the path to his shack.

Kukana did not know if Hatch would go back to his house, stay on the boat, or sail away. That morning, awakening even before the sun had opened Hatch's eyes in the Hard Wind's forward cabin, Kukana quickly dressed, then walked down the long sloping yard, along the wide path through the royal palms, alongside the banana grove – where after all these months she still could not cast her eyes in the direction of the tool shed – around the back of Ho'okahi Church, the full length of Alii Street through the center of town, to the head of the wharf, where she paused for a moment to look for any sign of life aboard the ketch docked at the end, relieved to see the boat still there, then took the path through the jungle leading to Kaiwi Point, where she planned to go for a swim.

Later, she stood in the lagoon, water to her waist, her back to the beach, and did not notice the man who just came from the path onto the sand. Her wet black hair so long that it fanned out and floated on the surface like the shadow from a patch of water lilies. Her hands floated in front of her, a pose of nonchalance. She was nude.

Hatch stopped the moment he saw her. In that instant he was no longer on the island of Tuva; the world reshaped itself before his startled gaze and he was on the bank of the thin, shallow river running beside the Laotian village of Toulan. Hatch no longer heard the whitewater waves striking the reef, the irrepressible surf, but instead the chatter of birds, the thud of cooking mallets striking wooden platters, the lyrical gossip of the village's old women as they beat their clothes on logs along the riverbank. He did not smell the salt-laden air or the pungent rotting fruit behind his shack, but instead the scent of a wood fire, rice cooking in fish sauce, the steaming urine-scented smell so near the piss pit, mixed with the rich fishy odor from the river.

In that moment, Hatch felt his hand close around the bar of soap he was bringing to Mai, who waited for him waist deep in the river, where she had gone to bathe, her luxuriant black hair streaming out on the water's surface. He called out to her: "Mai?"

Kukana spun around to the sound of his voice, her arms rising across her breasts.

Years of memories sparked through his mind in an instant, and he felt like he was exploding. His hands flew up in front of his face and he saw blood dripping from his fingers down his palms and wrists; he shoved his hands beneath his armpits as if a sudden cold wind crashed through the foliage.

He bolted into his shack, not pausing to close the door behind him.

Kukana said later that the sound that emerged after Hatch ran into his shack was not human, not a scream. It was a howl she heard. Then again, that word: *my* ... . The same word he always cried out in his nightmares when she tended him in her father's bed.

She pushed through the water back to the beach and took her clothes from the net-drying line where she had left them.

The shack was silent.

She stood looking at that derelict old wreck of a house for a minute. Should she leave? Should she go see if maybe he was hurt?

He had seen her without her clothes. But she had probably wanted him to see her in the lagoon, why else did she go to swim there? But that cry! What did it mean? He must be in pain. It was good she happened to be there, if he was sick. That was what she told herself as she walked up to the house.

Looking into the interior darkness from the whitewashed afternoon sunlight, she couldn't see anything. As she stepped closer to the doorway, a plank screeched.

Hatch turned toward the sound. He was on his knees, his hands over his stomach as if keeping his intestines in.

"Hello?" Kukana called out from the lanai.

"It's open." Hatch stood quickly. He lit a cigarette and went back to the main room. A retinal image of Kukana standing in the lagoon flashed through his mind.

Of course, he had previously noticed how much Kamuela's daughter resembled Mai: they were about the same age, that long, long black hair smelling of coconut oil, both tall, both with skin the soft tan color of light milk chocolate, those oversized black eyes set widely apart in their oval faces. He had noticed, but forced himself to ignore it – and her.

When Kukana stepped into the room, backlit in the open doorway, her damp silken hair in aura from the glare behind her, Hatch could not separate Mai from Kukana.

"I'm sorry," Kukana said, moving out of the bright glare. "Are you mad with me?"

"No, why would I be?"

Hatch was still caught in the shrinking space between the two young women. He stepped closer to Kukana and gestured for her to come in, and then it was her in front of him, Kukana. Mai receded into the caves of nightmare.

"Let me get you a chair," he offered.

"Thank you. I am all right here."

Hatch shrugged, blew smoke from the cigarette, and sat on the arm of the dilapidated sofa.

Kukana looked around and saw that all her housekeeping efforts were wasted. "This place gets messy pretty fast," she observed. "Maybe because you live by yourself."

"When were you here … ?" Then Hatch figured it out. "So, it was you who did all this," his arm swept around the room.

Kukana lowered her eyes modestly.

"When?"

"When you were hurt."

"Why?"

"You were hurt. You couldn't do it yourself."

"Well, as you probably noticed. I don't do a lot of housekeeping chores much, healthy or not."

"I saw this."

"I thought it was Twilla at first."

"I like to keep a house, and I like to cook, also," Kukana blurted out rather defensively.

"You can sit if you want to."

Kukana sat down on the sofa at the opposite end,

but turned sideways to face him.

"How old are you, Kukana?"

"Eighteen. Almost, I mean. In only one month."

"You are seventeen."

"Eighteen in one month. May I ask you something?"

"If you like." He put the cigarette out on the floor and Kukana groaned. "Sorry you did all this work for nothing. I just don't think about it. But it really did look nice when I came back; almost like some decent human being might live here. Thank you. Now what did you want to ask?"

"What do you dream about?"

"I don't know. What do you mean?"

"You talk when you sleep."

"Oh yeah? Your father told me. Do I say something, I mean, do I talk?"

"It is hard to understand. Sometimes just sounds that I don't think are words, or maybe words in some language I never heard. Sometimes you keep saying the same word over and over and over."

"What word is that?"

"The same one you said outside, when you saw me. It sounds like *my*, but you never finish, you never say my *what*?"

And then she came out of the cave of memory and stood before him again. Hatch felt like the walls were collapsing around him. He stood abruptly and said, "Let's go outside, where it is cooler."

Kukana followed him.

"Don't you need to go home? Would you like for me to walk you back to town?"

"Do you want me to go now?"

"I didn't mean it that way, exactly. It's up to you."

"I can stay."

There was a log Hatch had split and set nailed to two stumps, like a bench, where he would sit when tending his nets. They walked there; Hatch sat and Kukana remained standing.

"You don't know the answer for my question?" Kukana asked.

"What that word means?" Hatch stood. "Can I get you something? I'm going to have a drink, if you don't mind."

"I can get it for you," Kukana offered.

Hatch smiled. "Well, since a visit from your father not long ago, I have taken to hiding my replacement bottles outside."

Kukana shook her head, she didn't understand.

"I will have what you are drinking," Kukana said.

Hatch arched his eyebrows, then turned and got a bottle of whisky from a patch of high grass next to the lanai. He went inside and returned with two glasses.

"Are you sure?" Hatch asked, starting to pour whisky into her glass.

"I have had this before. Papa likes it."

Hatch poured less than an inch into her glass, and filled his half full. "Do *you* like it?"

"Not really."

They both laughed and clinked their glasses before drinking.

"Why don't you sit down, Kukana. Please."

She did, holding the glass in both hands in front of her, arms resting on her knees.

Hatch sat beside her, both of them facing the lagoon and not one another.

Hatch was going to tell a story that had been burning through his core for fifteen years.

"I am going to tell you *my what*. It is a long story from a very long time ago and I have never told anyone this, ever. But I want to tell you."

When he said that, Kukana fell so much more deeply in love with him that she almost cried from the absolute power of it.

14

"This is a long time ago, but I have forgotten none of it, not a moment, not a vision, and believe me, I have tried. I am still trying.

"There were six of us. We came in and out of the village often, over a period of months, ten months from the first time. We used Toulan as a base ... that's really not the right word. Toulan was the place from where we came and went. It is a village in a country called Laos. We needed a place in that part of the country and Toulan was it. The military reason for this is irrelevant now ... it was never actually relevant.

"Many days might pass when we hardly left the immediate area, then we could be away for a week, sometimes longer. Everyone knew we weren't like other soldiers. We didn't wear uniforms or any insignia; we dressed like villagers, more or less."

"You were a soldier there?"

"Again, more or less. That's not important anyway. Mai lived there. It is her name you heard. M-a-i, not m-y." He spelled the difference.

"Oh yes," Kukana said. "I have a friend with a name like, but spelled M-i-a."

Hatch nodded to indicate he had heard her, then continued.

"She was my girlfriend. Oh, I think that's a stupid way to put it. But what else can I say?

"There were six of us, the Americans: Lieutenant Bo Harper – we called him Guns; Sergeant Mike Richards; three other men – Lobo, Snake, and Jim. We were Team Two of a covert operation designated: Prairie Fire."

Kukana turned and looked at him questioningly.

"Covert means it was all supposed to be secret. I

was a captain, their leader, and they called me Hatch because my last name is Hatcher.

"That day I kissed her goodbye while we were still inside the hut, Mai's mother and grandmother remaining discreetly outside. When it was time to go, I stroked Mai's long hair – exactly like yours, Kukana – and smiled at her obvious delaying tactics. I had to step away from her. I said, 'I love you, Mai;' she understood these words in English, but few others. 'Be good,' I added, patting her large belly, for she was very pregnant."

Kukana inhaled audibly, looking momentarily at him, before returning her gaze toward the jungle wall, her eyes now damp. It was probably killing her to hear this.

"I know she believed – no matter what I said – that one day I would go into the jungle and never come back. She wanted me to never leave the village, she wanted me to be a farmer or a fisherman. I always laughed out loud about this, but I did think it was a pleasant fantasy.

"Then I had to go, we had to go. Our mission, maybe better called a task, only required us to be away one night. At the door, before we went out into the morning, I told Mai I would see her tomorrow. She gripped my forearms tightly and said she had a sense of impending doom; she said this in Lao, which I used to be able to speak reasonably well; maybe those are the foreign sounding words you heard. I touched her belly for luck and told her not to worry.

"Mai was seventeen, seven years younger than I was then, and had been carrying our child in her womb for almost eight months.

"We were only five that morning. Guns Harper had gone to Vientiane – that's the capital of Laos – and was not due back for a week. Once gathered, we five walked out of the village clearing and were swallowed in the mystery that the people of Toulan enjoyed talking about so much.

"We were gone maybe two hours when a large group of raiders from the north entered Toulan. Her mother said Mai was cooking when they broke the door and found some of my American things. They pulled Mai across the room by her hair, spilling the caldron of fish soup, which left a dark stain across the bamboo floor. I saw it later."

"Stop!"

"No. I'm not going to stop now."

"Please stop."

"You can leave, Kukana. I'm not keeping you."

"I can't hear it."

"I'm going to tell this now, even if only the sea listens."

Kukana bent over and put her head on her knees, her hands clutching her head, but she stayed.

"We had freely passed that way often, yet we walked right into it. One moment the jungle was quiet, the same, then Lobo hit the trip wire, setting off two Claymores. Although he turned to the clicks and shouted a warning, it was too late. For all of us.

"I heard the boom and felt the hot blast of dirt, grass, mud, bones and blood, and found myself knocked completely off the trail. Wiggling on my belly like a lizard, I moved deeper into the underbrush. Then I was hit. Bullets tore up the earth and the brush all around. I knew it was one in the leg and one in the back, like being hit with a hammer."

"Those scars," Kukana said, without looking up.

Hatch ignored her; he was in Laos, not on the beach at Kaiwi Point.

"I rolled over and fired off rounds from my shotgun until it was empty; dropped that and kept firing with my pistol until it was also empty. Then there was nothing to do but wait to be finished off. I scooted further back. Everything was wet. That's what I remember – wet vines, wet high grass, the warm sticky wet on my clothes. And the bitter tang of cordite.

"Suddenly it was quiet again. The artificial fog of the firefight drifted through the trees on the silence, clinging to the wetness all over me.

"Then voices, Lao voices, coming from the trail; I could feel their vibrations walking nearby. I heard Pete's South Carolina voice, moaning, then an odd cry for a medic. A pistol shot ended that. There was nothing I could do, just wait to be found. I suppose at that point I lost consciousness. I suppose they left me because they thought I was dead.

"Later, I found out it was those same men who entered Toulan a short time later. Mai's mother told me what happened then. She said Mai would not give them the satisfaction of seeing her cry, but if they tried to do anything that threatened the life growing inside her, she would weep or beg or lick mud from their feet, anything if they would not harm her baby ... our baby.

"They jerked out great handfuls of her hair, kicked her hard, threw her to the ground. They dragged her down to the mud by the washing stream. Suan and Sisana were already there; they had also lain with Americans.

"One man jammed his rifle butt into Mai's head and she blacked out, that short sanctuary of no consciousness. It ended with a bucket of river water thrown into her face, bringing her back to the horrible pain.

"She pulled her hands up from her stomach to protect her face, and the next rifle butt broke her thumb as it smashed into her.

"She cried out for her father, who had left the village two years before to fight with the Royals.

"Other screams, terrible screams, pierced the darkening air by the river. Mai screamed. She knew what was going to happen. She felt her legs being shoved apart; she cried out, protesting, begging, naming her obvious pregnancy.

"Two men tied her feet to stakes spread wide in

the mud. They had torn away her clothes. They jerked her arms apart and tied her wrists to stakes. Her body left the mark of an X there.

"'Why am I being punished?' Mai pleaded. 'I am no soldier. I am only a girl who carries a baby inside her body.'

"The man to whom Mai directed these questions had a disinterested face, her mother said. She said he looked like he came from the Meo people. The only response he gave to Mai was a curse, then he put his boot down hard against her face, breaking her nose.

"It grew dark. Quickly, just as it does here. A man came near, holding a flaming torch. Mai could see in that light the thing he held dangling by its long tail.

"Mai must have known then. Everyone had heard the stories, the rumors, examples made of women in other villages in the south. But she did not live to know it was going to happen to her. A rifle butt smashed into her forehead and she died."

"Oh God, oh God," Kukana cried out, but did not lift her head. She repeated the prayer three more times.

"The Meo man knelt beside Mai's swollen belly and cut her open. The other man, the one with the torch, dropped the implant into her. Then the Meo crudely sewed closed his cut with twine, like you'd use to mend a net."

Kukana had not moved, had not raised her head that whole time. But her body quivered as if she had chilblains. Hatch paused. He lay his hand on her upper back. Evening was also coming to Kaiwi Point, like the evening frozen in Hatch's mind.

Then Kukana spoke, although she still did not raise her head. "What implant means?"

"It was a rat."

Kukana stumbled forward, dropped to her knees on the sand, bending over double, as if she was going to vomit.

Hatch went to her and knelt there, putting his hand on her back again. He was afraid to turn her over, to look at her; a bicameral consciousness kept him trapped within two worlds and two times. Suddenly Kukana turned, lifted herself magically, and pressed her body so tightly against him that from an even short distance they appeared to be a lump, a single mound of unrecognizable substance.

He put his arm around Kukana's quaking shoulders, and she instantly put her arms around his neck, her head leaning against his chest, her tears leaving fat drops on his khaki shirt. He ran his fingers through her hair, his eyes watching the white water rumble at the reef, his mind neither here nor there, trapped in the void between the two.

"I didn't tell you to horrify you or to make you sad," he whispered. He didn't know why he had felt this sudden compulsion to explain to this girl why he stayed out here and why he was a lost cause, a burned out loser. Was it the only way he might apologize and ask for forgiveness from her twin, who, had she lived would now be thirty-three years old, and their son now almost sixteen, only two years younger than the girl crying on his chest?

Kukana lifted her head and turned her face toward his. The kiss came inevitably. As did everything that followed.

When eventually they lay apart on the sand, bodies bright and gleaming in the low-angled light of the setting sun, Kukana put her fingers lightly against the side of Hatch's face.

"I'm sorry," he said.

"I am not."

"You never did this before?"

"I waited for a man I could honor."

"I wish I was that man."

"I know that you are."

She put her head on his shoulder, her hair splayed over his chest.

Hatch knew it was a mistake, that it had been wrong, and whatever else happened next, one thing he knew for certain – he was not going to hurt this girl.

"Can we do it again?" Kukana whispered into his ear.

"I am going to walk you home," Hatch said, getting to his feet and reaching down to help her up. Like children caught, they did not look at each other, not even after they were dressed.

15

They didn't speak while walking back to town from Kaiwi Point. His guilt separated them like a wall. She wanted him to know that it was all right, that he had done nothing wrong; she wanted to tell him how much she had desired this, that it was her only dream. But she sensed that it would only deepen his guilt and thicken the wall.

The path was seldom wide enough for them to walk side by side. Hatch led and Kukana followed, staying close. What she wanted was to press herself against his broad back, never to be separated from him again.

"Will you be all right now?" Hatch asked when they reached the end of the path and came out onto the beginning of Alii Street.

"I am not a child."

"Of course not."

He still would not look at her.

"I love you," she said for the first time.

Hatch shook his head, more in sadness than frustration.

"Maybe you are infatuated."

"I don't know that word, but unless it is the same as love, then it is not true I am fatuated."

"It's something that feels like love but really isn't."

"Then it is a dumb word. What feels like something without being that something? I love you, and I know what that feels like."

"You are seventeen, and I am ... ."

"Eighteen, almost."

"Okay, almost eighteen, and I am forty; more than twenty years older. Old enough to be your father. That makes what I did, what I allowed to happen today, so much worse." He shook his head as if that would cancel everything. How could he explain to her that he had been enmeshed in a memory? That he had made love to someone else, someone long, long dead.

Kukana began to cry. They were standing at the foot of Alii Street, the wharf stretching out to the right. Kukana lay her head on Hatch's shoulder and cried.

Kaavanuii and Pono passed, carrying long fishing poles over their shoulders, each with a bucket in his hand; they greeted Hatch politely, normally, as if to see the daughter of Kamuela Makani with her head on his shoulder, crying desperately, was no more unusual than having no fish in their buckets.

"I see you had no luck today," Hatch said.

"Tomorrow will be better," Pono announced, and they continued toward Papa Jack's.

When they had passed, Hatch gently pushed Kukana back.

"Please, don't cry," he said. "I am so, so sorry."

Kukana took a long swipe at her cheeks to knock away the tears and choke off the crying.

"Do not feel guilty," she said. "I do not care if at this moment I remind you of her, from that other long ago time. I promise this to you. No matter what you might decide about me, I will be your woman forever. I will not look in the direction of another man for the rest of my life. I will always take care of you, we will have many babies if that is what you want, I will fix everything that is broken, and I will bring back to you all that was lost; if you want to go to America, I will go, and if you want to stay on Tuva, I will stay. If you want to go to the moon, I will hold your hand and follow."

"Stop!" Hatch said.

"I will do anything you tell me."

"Then I am telling you to go home."

"I will kiss you first, then I will do what you say."

Without waiting for his response, Kukana lunged forward and gave him a quick kiss. Then she stepped away, turned, and walked briskly down the street toward her home. He could not watch: In his mind at that moment, there was no difference between Mai and Kukana; Mai, who had returned to the living in the form of that young girl walking away, bringing night horror into the light.

Shaking his head in dismay, stunned by what he had done, and even more by the odd and awkward and very likely misplaced tenderness he felt about that girl, Hatch walked to Papa Jack's, but at the door changed his mind and turned back toward his shack at Kaiwi Point.

An hour before dawn, Hatch finished his preparations to leave the island. There was nothing worth taking from his shack. In a cracker tin, he had a little cash in American and Australian dollars. All his clothes fit into a duffel bag. In a smaller canvas bag, he put his K-bar knife, the book he was reading, his journals wrapped in oilcloth, and essential fishing gear. Not much to take toward a new life, but easy enough to carry.

He would later admit that he hadn't thought any of this out carefully, not even to consider whether or not he could handle a fifty-foot, cutter-rigged ketch alone. The fake passport he bought in Singapore had an expiration six years past. No, he had not thought through any of these problems, he just knew he had to go.

He carried the duffel bag slung over his shoulder and walked to the end of the wharf, where the Hard Wind waited.

He started the engine and cast off lines, then eased the yacht away from the pier. He did not look back once after pointing her bow toward the reef passage.

Pono and Kaavanuii, perched in darkness on the other side of the wharf, looked up from fishing to watch. Hattie ambled out of her room behind Papa Jack's in time to see the ketch motoring out of the harbor.

Later, as they came onto the lanai for breakfast, Kamuela and Kukana noticed Akamu Palani running up the lawn, yelling something.

By then the Hard Wind was outside the reef, sails up, on a northwesterly beat in a light breeze.

Nobody could say what happened to Hatch and the boat. Only the two old fishermen claimed to have seen him, and all they said was that the hero of Tuva came to the boat before the sun. He had a big bag and a small bag. Then the boat went away with only Hatch on it. Hattie said that she saw the yacht motoring away, and she added that maybe it wasn't Hatch, maybe somebody was stealing it.

But Hatch was indeed gone, and rumors quickly proliferated in the bars.

Kukana took to her room and did not come down, even to eat, telling Twilla she wasn't hungry. Twilla brought in a tray and ordered Kukana to eat or she would tie her to the chair and stuff it into her mouth, the same way she had done with Hatch. That memory made her cry again. And still she did not eat.

She could see the wharf from her window, the spot at the end of it as empty as her hopes. She sat all day in the fan-back wicker chair by the window, staring blankly toward town, even after the shadows preceding night rushed across the lawn, after it became too dark to see even the row of royal palms defining the lane. Hunger made her stomach ache, and she relished it, wanting it to hurt even more.

Mr. Jolly held forth in Papa Jack's. People came to him, and to me as well, asking to explain the kind of crazy white man who can be a hero and a coward at the same time?

"He is an American," Mr. Jolly said. Then turned to me and added, "No offense, Don."

"Well, I don't think this has much to do with

nationality," I responded.

"You are right. I stand corrected," Mr. Jolly said quickly. "On the other hand, it has been my experience that they are undependable people. Never trust one."

"And would that include me, Mr. Jolly?"

"You are Tuvan, Don. Everybody thinks so."

"I am as much, or as little, American as you are Australian."

"That's not my point. But let's have another drink. I'm buying this round." Mr. Jolly patted my shoulder with one hand and ordered drinks with the other, waving at Dennis with his fingers in a V, so he could be asking for two drinks or declaring victory.

After a few more drinks, Mr. Jolly had changed course and started defending Hatch against the wilder stories making the rounds.

"I have heard," one said, "he has a wife and many children on Rangiroa."

"Did you know he found pearls in the lagoon at Kaiwi Point and sailed away a rich man?"

"Who needs pearls?" another suggested. "The boat he took is worth a fortune."

One woman, wisely confining her tale to a whispered voice, told her neighbor – "I have heard Kukana is with child by the American who raped her."

"On no," her neighbor exclaimed.

"Oh yes. I would not be the one who says this, but I have heard from others."

"They were seen only two days ago; Kukana crying like a child and he was holding her. So maybe you are right."

"Do you think he ran away because he could not be father to another man's baby?"

Such stories roamed the smoky room with the speed of drinks crossing the bar.

Pono and Kaavanuii took no part in the gossip, nor did they answer any questions about Hatch's departure, except to repeat what they had seen: he carried one large bag and one small bag and he left the harbor with the motor, and the sails went up beyond the reef. He was alone, unless someone or some others had been hiding on the boat all this time.

After a while, Pono and Kaavanuii went back to the wharf to fish by torchlight, a light they knew would also make a guiding beacon when the hero of Tuva came home, as they knew he would.

16

Sitting in the large cockpit, looking astern, Hatch watched glowing plankton spreading out in the wake. Mesmerized. A thoughtless way to occupy himself on a clear, moon-slivered night, stars forming intricate, dusty patterns above his head, the sparkling phosphorescence rolling away atop the dark water, the ketch's clean, sharply-angled bow sluicing through the sea as she surfed down the following swells, trying to wallow against the rudder. The only sounds came from the sea pushing away from the hull in a low rumble, and the incongruous, occasional luffing pop in the mainsail.

Hard Wind was a John Alden-designed, Cheoy Lee-built, cutter-rigged, ketch, maintained well enough to look brand-new. She was a lot of boat to handle for one man. Although the breeze was light, Hatch had run up only the jib and main, on a broad-reach running before the wind, but she was still making decent headway south, plowing down the long swells in the giant dark sea like a big toy.

Headway to where?

At first, after sitting down at the chart table to remind himself what was out there, he thought of making his way south, into the vast emptiness beyond the Tuamotu Islands, where Tuva lay at the southern extreme. After Hereheretue, there would be nothing until the sparse atolls of the Australes. Then what? There's nothing after the Australes to the ice of Antarctica. He had no papers, not even proof of ownership of the yacht, so he could forget anywhere like New Zealand or Australia, although he wouldn't mind seeing Cairns, fish the Great Barrier Reef again. But he would have to stay among the far-flung, often uninhabited, atolls. And live how? Or does that matter now?

He had sailed south barely two hours before coming about onto a close-hauled port tack, heading for French Polynesia, Tahiti. He raised the mizzen sail and soon the yacht was heeled twenty degrees, the downwind rail awash.

What would he do in Tahiti? He had last seen Papeete more than ten years ago on the voyage that ended for him in Tuva. He remembered buzzing motor scooters, taxi horns blaring off-key, the crush of people by the harbor. The food he remembered best, food that tempted him more than anything else to linger a while.

He had stayed in the capital of Tahiti only a few days. His last night, a woman he talked with for a while in Quinn's, took him to her bed in an apartment near the harbor, a bed that did not sway. He forgot her name. She was French, from Lyon. She suggested, or at least hinted, that it would be all right if he wanted to stay for a while.

Once, not long after he walked out of the war, he had stayed for a while. When he was deckhand on the fishing boat out of Cairns. She was a hooker, but Hatch hadn't minded that. He never minded anything after Laos.

In those days, two years before Tuva, he lived aboard the fishing cruiser, getting to use the forward cabin in return for keeping an eye on the boat and the fishing gear. Evenings, he spent in a waterfront fishermen's bar called The Lure. There was a trophy black marlin mounted on the wall behind the bar.

Her name was Rose Chamberlain, her second married name. They had known each other from the bar for some months before it became something more. It was not a bar where tourists went, in a bad area of the docks. That was its appeal.

Sitting on stools beside one another one especially empty night, Rose wondered why Hatch didn't hang out with the boat's clients, who would probably stand

him to drinks all night if they'd had a good day out
beyond the reef.

"When you have to fish with them all day," Hatch
answered, "it's not appealing to drink with them at
night."

"Hah," Rose said. "You think fishing with 'em's
bad, try what I do to pay the rent."

"You got a point. Can I buy you another?"

"You are such a gentleman, Hatch."

They clinked their glasses, Rose adjusted herself
on the stool, the slit in her dress falling apart, offering
her awfully nice legs to his gaze. "So, how's it
going?"

"It's all right, Rose. Let's see, I'm more or less
broke, the boat goes out of service tomorrow for a
week in dry dock, I'm working for a captain whose
brains are in his prick … ."

She laughed. "Tell me about it, dude."

"I guess I'm outta here," Hatch said, downing the
last of his whisky.

"God, I'm wired tonight," Rose said. "How do
you like my dress?"

Hatch had stood; he looked at her reflected in the
mirror behind the bar. Her long auburn hair made a
sort of picture frame as it curled around her head and
face, a narrow, freckled face, maybe a too skinny face.
He thought she was well-kept for what, forty-
something? Her breasts were crushed together and
spilling like bags of Jello from the deep opening in the
yellow dress, her skin glistened with sweat. She
looked into the mirror and watched what he watched.

"It's a helluva dress, Rose."

"Sisyphus bought it for me at the mall."

"Sisyphus? That's his name?"

Rose stretched up and whispered conspiratorially
into Hatch's ear: "Because every time he gets it up, it
comes right back down."

They laughed loudly enough to call attention to
themselves along the bar. She laughed like a man,

Hatch thought, with a voice that comes out as if it rolled over boulders in her throat.

"Save me, Hatch. I'm going to freak out in here?" Rose touched his arm and left her hand there. "Whaddaya say, mate? You in the salvation mood tonight?"

Hatch rubbed an abstract pattern in the condensation moisture on the bar. "Sure. I'd like it if you want to come with me."

"Walk all the way out to the dock? To the boat, you mean?"

"I'm afraid that's all I've got to offer."

"Let's go to my place."

A bed that isn't moving, Hatch thought.

Walking to Rose's apartment, Hatch felt the five whiskies he put away at The Lure, on top of the six pack of beer he drink after the charter, while cleaning the boat. It was the first time he had left the bar with Rose; would he be her next Sisyphus? Rose put her arm through his as they walked along. She was telling jokes.

"Know what a Polish lesbian likes?" Rose asked.

"No, what?"

"Men." Rose laughed. Hatch thought she was silly, certainly drunk; he laughed to be polite.

She stopped on the sidewalk and turned to face him. "Pretend this is a sack," she said, encircling her arms in front of her chest.

"A sack? What kind of sack?"

Exasperated, "it doesn't matter what kind of sack. Just a sack sack. A sack, damn it! A fucking bag. Now pretend this is a sack and put your hand in it."

"Put my hand between your arms?"

"Jesus X. Christos! This is going to take so long I'll forget the punch line."

"One hand, or both?"

"It doesn't matter. Jeez!"

Hatch put his hand through the opening.

"Well?" Rose probed.

"Well what? What am I supposed to do?"

"I knew if I ever got you in the sack you wouldn't know what to do." She laughed so hard she gripped his shoulders to hold herself up.

"Where do you get all these, Rose?"

"Funny, huh? You gotta laugh so you don't cry, know what I mean?"

She turned and put her arm under his again, and they continued to her apartment. It started to rain and they went in wet.

"It's nice," Hatch said, looking around and waiting for her to bring a towel. He thought it was tiny, hardly larger than the cabin on the boat where he slept.

"Compared to the trailer where I lived in my married days ... . Let me get us a drink," she said, tossing him a towel and rubbing her hair with another one.

"I didn't know you were married." He spread his towel on the sofa and sat down; it pulled out to become her bed. Rose went to the kitchen, a section of the same large room.

"Shit, Hatch. Everybody's been married at least once. Me twice."

"Then you did it once for me, because I never have."

"I wish you had done your own, then. Because my second was a disaster. He was a fucking American Marine. Never marry a Marine, Hatch."

"I hadn't planned on it."

She brought two whiskies in coffee cups. "Want some coke?" she asked.

"I guess not," Hatch said, taking a quick drink.

"Things go better with coke," she said in a sing-song voice. Before she got the lines up to her nose, Hatch stopped her hand.

"Do you really need that?"

"You can really be quite a prude, my friend." She took his hand off her forearm and brought the rolled bill back to her nose. She sniffed hard through both nostrils. "I suppose you want to inspect my arms," she said.

"Not really."

"It's just candy," she said. "Nose candy."

"Candy rots your teeth, ruins your skin, overdoses your glands, and makes you fat."

"Well, then, this is lots better than candy then, and you are what … ? Billy fucking Graham?"

She lay her head back on the sofa. "Mercy," she said. "Oh, baby."

Rose opened the slit in her dress wider, exposing her legs all the way up. Hatch looked at her, then over at the window above the kitchen sink. The street lights were yellow, coloring the night air like spilled, thinned-out egg yolks. Music came from somewhere, faint but distinct. Rose stood and pulled him up. "Help me with this," she said, and they turned the sofa into a bed.

In the morning, Rose came into the tiny bathroom and stood behind him, her hand touching the scars on his back.

"How'd you get these?"

"It's boring," Hatch answered, then continued brushing his teeth with her toothbrush.

"I bet it's not."

Her breasts without the wondrous bra were smashed against his back.

"I'll listen when you want to tell me," she said, and went back into the other room.

Hatch wondered if he was supposed to leave something, if not money, at least something? He didn't know the protocol was when you accepted a whore's invitation.

Hatch returned the following night, and stayed there for two months; he never did tell her about those scars. He did give her a little payback once. She said a john was stalking her, so Hatch found the man and discussed it with him; when the fellow got out of the hospital, he left Queensland on the fast bus.

When Hatch sailed away on the yacht that took him back to Southeast Asia, where he would sign on with another yacht that eventually took him to Tuva, he was no longer living in Rose's apartment and they were no longer having sex, but they were friends, and when she overdosed that Christmas Eve, he went to her funeral and almost cried.

He might have stayed in Cairns, he might even have maybe married Rose, according to his journal.

Close-hauled, the ketch's bow no longer sluiced, it smashed into the on-coming swells and shuddered like a smacked dog, sending warm, salty spray over the cabin top and into the wide cockpit where Hatch sat with both hands on the wheel.

The wind had come up. Along the dark horizon, lightning occasionally exploded within otherwise unseen clouds. Hatch lifted the bottle from a holder on the cockpit bench and took another drink. In spite of his desire to stay awake, he eventually set the autopilot and closed his eyes, letting the sound of the ocean, the rumbling thunder from the distant flashes, the wind in his face, take him dreaming into the jungles, a conglomeration of all the jungles he had seen: Panama, Dominican Republic, Congo, Southeast Asia. Jungles that sounded like a death rattle, smelled like mold and rot, all heat and oppressive wetness. Those dark dreams always ended up in the same place – *he grabs the rat by its tail and jerks it through the gapping hole in Mai's distended belly, it snapping madly at the fingers holding its tail, until the K-bar blade severs its head; it had been a boy, the side of his head, its well-formed ear, chewed like rejected candy, blood everywhere ... .*

He had had this dream in Rose's bed sometimes. She shook him awake, telling him it's all right, that he's with her; she would put her hand on his cheek and stroke his skin. She always asked if he remembered the dream, and he always told her that he did not. She told him that was probably a good thing, and he agreed.

Sometimes after that, she would make love to him, then he could fall asleep again. With Rose, Hatch sometimes wished there still existed within him, the ability to love someone. He wished he could love Rose. He might have married her regardless. Maybe he would have saved her. Maybe she could have saved him.

He slept curled up on the cockpit bench, the Hard Wind crashing through quartering seas, until dawn's first light found his eyes.

When the rain finally began, it fell straight down in widely-spaced, fat, distinctly individual drops splattering on the teak deck like exploding marbles. The only warning came as a sudden stillness in the air, the odd sensation that the earth had stopped turning. The wind flattened, and the waves lost their shape. The Hard Wind wallowed in the troughs, the sails flapping like dry laundry on a line. Everything was still, the sea flattened under the weight of the heavy air. The planet seemed to have reached a point of abeyance. The first heavy drop fell, then another, and others. As if cued, as if a signal flag had dropped, the Hard Wind stopped moving forward. Thunder rumbled ponderously over the sea and reverberated off the circular horizon.

Hatch sat in the rain. What difference did it make? Everything was wet. He wasn't going anywhere until the center of this depression passed over him and he got the wind from the back side.

He thought about Kukana, even when he tried to distract himself. Alone in the rain, on the undulating water, he could not banish thoughts of her. Vignettes came and went, tumbling and reforming like a kaleidoscope of film frames: at the time he was barely conscious, he had still been aware of her chewing something that she pushed into his mouth, keeping her hand softly over his lips until the sweet mush slid down his throat; awakening from a dream and seeing her leaning over him, her hands on his temples, her fingers stroking the side of his face; opening his eyes to see the top of her head lying on the bedside, she sound asleep with her hand resting on his upper arm above the cast; reading to him from *Lord Jim*, which she said was her second favorite book, and he not thinking to ask which one was her favorite. Now, that was something he wanted to know. Now, he wanted to ask her all the questions that did not occur to him before.

Too late, he thought.

17

Hatch sailed for days, bypassing islands where he figured someone would ask questions, demand papers. Food was not yet a problem; he caught fish by trolling a line off the stern, and there were canned stores in the galley. Fresh water would be, and he may run out in less than a week. Sooner or later, he would have to dock somewhere, or die dehydrated, surrounded by thousands of squares miles of water – another Flying Dutchman.

Concurrently, a few hundred nautical miles east-southeast of the Hard Wind, the two surviving members of her previous crew were being rescued off Palm Reef by far-ranging fishermen from an island on the southern central fringe of the Tuamotus.

Mel Usher was separated from the other three just hours after they were tossed overboard; they never saw him again and presumed he drowned. Bill Byron's younger brother, David, was torn up tumbling over the coral surrounding Palm Reef; he died with a feverish, raging infection seven days later, in spite of his older brother's attempts to keep the cuts clean with sterile coconut water.

Only Bill Byron and Guns Harper were alive to be picked up by the fishermen, who saw smoke from a signal fire. They had survived on coconut water and meat, crabs they could catch, and rain water held in palm fronds.

Had the wandering Tuamotuans not found them, Bill might not have lasted another week. He had dysentery for the past three days and was already severely dehydrated.

Only Guns Harper seemed little the worse for it; he even joked about finally getting back down to his fighting weight.

They were taken to the main village of Rotoava, on the island of Fakarava, and the next day evacuated by seaplane to Tahiti.

That very day, Hatch had taken the Hard Wind to within a hundred and fifty miles southeast of Tahiti. Conceivably he could have noticed the seaplane on its way into Papeete. He did not intend to stop in Tahiti, where the authorities were certain to ask questions he could not answer, demand papers he could not produce, but thought he might try Tetiaroa. He had heard that the actor Marlon Brando bought the island. If not there, possibly one of the motus reaching to the west in the Iles Sous Le Vent.

He passed near Tahiti after sunset, the lights of Papeete glowing against the sky like an auroral phantom. A jetliner on approach to Faa'a, as loud and large as building, passed over. Within it another world, on its way to another world; Hatch the alien.

Sometime that night, after Tahiti lay off the port side, now as bright as a city in the desert, Hatch put the helm over and set his course for Tuva.

The only life he had was there. Somewhere in the night, with Tahiti compelling, he must have finally understood that.

18

When Kukana awoke, the morning of the tenth day following Hatch's disappearance, she went, as always, directly to the window.

"He's back!" she cried out loudly enough to wake the house. In her haste to get dressed, she knocked over a chair.

Kamuela appeared at her door.

"I can see his boat, Papa. He's back."

She pulled a muumuu over her head.

Kamuela blocked the doorway.

"Leave him be," he told his daughter.

"Papa! Please. Maybe he will go away again. I need to talk to him. Please."

"No. Leave him be. Leave him to come here if that is what he wants. It is for him to decide. You cannot chase him; when you chase a man, he runs away. Men do not trust what comes to them too easily."

Kukana knew her father was right, but she was desperate to see Hatch. She knew that she must have done something wrong, something that made him run away from her. She knew that she must apologize immediately, or he could leave again.

She righted the chair and put it by the window, then sat down, looking out. Kamuela nodded his approval and closed the door behind him. He would later admit that he feared Hatch would not come. What would his daughter do then? If Hatch broke his daughter's heart, he would be forced to kill the hero of Tuva.

The night that Hatch disappeared, Kukana told her father Hatch's story of the horror in his war. It explained things that Kamuela thought needed to be understood, but it also brought worries – what do such horrors leave inside a man? Is the sickness of war incurable?

Only an hour passed. Kukana, sitting in the same chair, still staring out the window, saw Hatch turn up the lane and walk along the row of royal palms. She gasped. Should she run out to meet him? He could be coming for her, or he could be coming to take his leave of her.

Akamu asked Hatch to take a seat on the lanai while he accounced his presence to Kamuela.

Kukana heard Akamu knock on her father's door to tell him Hatch was waiting on the lanai, then she heard their footsteps in the hall and on the stairs. She could not see the lanai from her room because of the overhanging roof. She sat and waited to find out if she would live or if she would die that day.

Kamuela greeted Hatch with a customary hug and they sat beside one another at the glass table. They did not speak immediately. Kamuela gazed across the lawn toward the back of the church; Hatch studied the rich grain in the koa wood lanai floor.

"Tea?" Kamuela offered, breaking the awkward silence.

"No, thank you, Kamuela."

"Something stronger?"

"I don't think so, but thank you."

Was it a good omen or a bad one that Hatch turned down a drink? Kamuela wondered.

Hatch took a package of cigarettes from his pocket and offered one to Kamuela.

"Smoke?"

Kamuela accepted the cigarette and Hatch lit both with a match. They smoked quietly for a moment, apparently rehearsing what to say next.

Finally Kamuela broke the silence, "How was the test of your boat?"

"She sails well, but maybe too much for a man alone."

"There are some things that are too much for a man to handle alone, I would say."

"And I would agree."

"The sea teaches us many lessons for a man alone."

"Yes, that is also true."

"On the sea," Kamuela continued, "a man alone has an opportunity to bond with the God who makes the guiding stars, who formed the sea itself, who created the great guide Mano. If he does that, then a man is no longer alone."

"I did not meet God, any of them. Or maybe they did not want to meet me. What I found was fear, Kamuela."

"It must be a discovery of great importance if a warrior finds fear in a such a small and simple thing."

Hatch looked up curiously at the word warrior.

"Kukana told me your story. Don't think badly of this. You speak of fear, Kukana was afraid she had done something to make you leave. She told me your story because she was afraid."

"I'm sorry she was afraid. I didn't mean that to happen. I don't know what to say." The embarrassment was a big stone to carry.

"It is not good for a man to hide something like this in his past life, my friend. The demons appear in the darkness of hiding. They cannot pursue in the light of knowing."

"That's quite philosophical, Kamuela."

"Did you sail away to escape the darkness or the light?"

"What else did Kukana tell you?"

"She is my daughter. Even if she does not say and thinks to keep a secret, she tells me everything, just by a look, a way she moves, or in something she will not speak about. Do you know that my daughter is in love with you? I think you must."

Hatch stared at the lawn. "It is possible she thinks she is."

"This is not big news, Hatch. Everyone saw it when she was caring for you in this house all those weeks. Everyone saw it but you. Well, and me. I came late to this understanding myself."

"It is possible she is confusing pity with love."

"It is. Yes. But it is also possible what Kukana feels is love. We will see. Love endures, the less passes. But now, Hatch, what fear did you find alone on the sea?"

"Every man at some point must face and answer the only important question of our lives: to live or to die. Is living worth the effort, or is it not?"

"You are not dead, I see."

Hatch nodded.

"Did you find while alone on the sea the answer you were searching for?"

"Yes, I think I did."

"Then it was a useful journey."

"You should know, Kamuela, that when I left Tuva, my intention was … ."

"That is of no concern to me. Welcome back to your home."

"Maybe I would like a drink, if you don't mind."

"Twilla!" Kamuela called out.

When Twilla appeared, Kamuela asked her to find the bottle of old brandy that he believed was in the back of the liquor cupboard; bring it and two crystal glasses.

When they had toasted to one another's health, Hatch began. "Kamuela, I want to start again, with my life. And with Kukana. I know everything that is wrong about this. But I want your permission to see Kukana sometimes. I don't know what to call it. I want to be the kind of man honorable enough to do the right thing. If she does love me, I want to be the kind of man who deserves it. I would like your permission to see her. I know I am much older and … well, we both know I am not … ."

Kamuela reached over and clasped Hatch's

shoulders in both hands.

"Do you love my daughter? That is my only question."

"I cannot say that now, because I think first I have to relearn how to do that. I will say that I want find the true answer to your question."

"You have given a wise answer. Of course you have my permission, but Kukana is now eighteen years old; she can make these decisions for herself. She is a woman now."

19

Almost everyone on the island attended the wedding festival. If the island were floating, so much weight gathered on one side would have tipped it over like a plate.

Hatch had a tolerable hangover, residue from the Tuvan version of a bachelor party, and somewhat accentuated by the garland of vines in a tight wreath around his head, but he forgot the headache entirely when he saw Kukana that bright midday on the lawn beside Ho'okahi Church.

Kukana appeared with her entourage, lead by Jenny Makani, taking the place of her mother. Jenny wore a white muumuu, dimly decorated with entwined silver vines and pale plumeria blossoms. The party walked regally out from the church and onto the soft green lawn, down an aisle formed by throngs of islanders. Outside, because not even a tenth of those attending could have fit inside the old church.

Kukana's oiled body was wrapped from waist to ankles in a red and white flowered lava-lava, and, as customary, bare above the waist. Her long black hair cascaded over her shoulders and down her back like a silk waterfall. A halo of fragrant yellow-white plumeria ringed her head.

Hatch weakened as she approached, holding his breath, as if to exhale would make her disappear. To have come so far, to have seen and lived the events of his past, and now to be standing before this vision, to finally be this happy … even though he still believed it was completely undeserved, unearned. He was going to earn the honor that girl gave him.

Kukana smiled deeply at Hatch, then they turned together to face Apalama and the Reverend Mr. Brel.

The ceremony was short, considering how long it took to prepare for it. The minister offered the usual

Christian pretenses, then Apalama blessed them in the island way, giving Hatch an islander's name – A'e Loa, meaning *of the wind*. His wife was now Kukana Pele Makani A'e Loa.

Kamuela hugged them both in his expansive grasp, then uttered the cry to begin the celebration. Kukana was immediately pulled away by a group of women, and Hatch, handed a ceremonial bowl of spirits, was dragged away by a group of men, led by his new brother-in-law, Tioni Makani.

The next time Hatch saw his bride, she had changed into an holoku', a long white dress covering her primly from neck to ankles. They hardly had time to exchange smiles before being pulled in separate directions to dance with others. The music, mostly drumming and a couple of slack-key guitars, was compelling in that way. Even I felt energized enough to try a few steps, dancing with each of my daughters, even my youngest baby, Lily, who was two years old then, giggling as I spun her 'round and 'round in my arms.

Hatch ended up next to Mr. Jolly, who was quite tipsy and playfully teasing his houseboy, Keolo. Hatch asked Mr. Jolly how long he was required to stay at the wedding feast?

"Nobody told you, mate? Why no time at all. You could have left hours ago. It is presumed you will leave when you are ready for the marriage bed," he snickered. "Of course, if the marriage bed is not so new a thing, some men might stay a long time just for the drink. Although I must say that you look very ready, Hatch A'e Loa."

Hatch turned to look for his father-in-law.

His name now: Hatch A'e Loa. The wedding ceremony was a death and rebirth, something like the baptismal act. That day Franklin Jefferson Hatcher was finally able to die, and Hatch A'e Loa, a Tuvan, was born into a fresh, brand-new world.

Hatch found Kamuela happily hugging everyone

who came near, draining every cup put into his hand. Seeing Hatch approach, he shooed the others away.

"I guess we'll leave now, Kamuela, if that's all right." He was embarrassed. After all, he was leaving to take this man's daughter to bed, something he had not done again after that first, awkward time on his beach almost a year ago.

"You know you are to stay in the house tonight," Kamuela said.

"I thought we would stay on the boat and avoid the long walk back to Kaiwi."

"That shack of yours?" Kamuela scoffed.

"You mean *your* house?"

"Of course. It is the way for a young couple to spend the first night of all their life together in the house of the father who has given her. It is only this one night, and do not worry, I will not be there." He laughed. "My duty is to keep this celebration going until the sun returns, and that is an easy duty."

"If that's the way, then that's the way." Hatch was too embarrassed to stand there pursuing it any further. He thanked Kamuela again and accepted another bear hug, before going to find his wife.

His wife.

Undaunted by the girlish giggling of Kukana's friends, Hatch took her hand and led her away. He expected to be followed by the usual catcalls, but as soon as they walked away they were completely ignored.

"What happened?"

"Until tomorrow when comes the sun," Kukana explained, holding tightly to his arm, "we can no longer be seen. We are ... how do you say it? Invisible."

"You mean that if I stopped right here and made love to you, no one would see?"

Kukana laughed. "Well, at least they would pretend not to see." She put her arm around his waist. "I like it when you are silly."

Hatch was uncomfortable enough spending the night in Kamuela's house, but when Kukana told him that they were also to sleep in his bed, Hatch protested.

"But it is the way," Kukana insisted.

"Let's just mess up the sheets and sleep somewhere else. This makes me very uncomfortable. Who would know?"

"I would know. It would be a bad omen for us to begin our life in the wrong way. We cannot begin the first day of our lives with a lie."

"It is the first day of our lives," Hatch said, stunned by what it meant – he had survived the certainty of his slow-motion suicide, and was now reborn. He would say later this was the closest to a religious experience he ever had, the closest he was likely to ever come to redemption.

Kukana sat on the side of the big bed and placed her hands in her lap, waiting. Hatch looked out the window, then came and sat beside her. Suddenly he laughed.

"What is funny?"

"Your dress."

"It was my mother's marriage dress."

"I didn't mean it in a bad way, because it is the most beautiful dress I have ever seen. It's just that in America a bride would wear a dress like this during the wedding, and a lot less after. Here you are half naked during the wedding, but modestly dressed for the honeymoon. In America … ," he stopped. He did not want to remember the times he used to say that to the young woman who was so much like this young woman, in his old life.

"It is for you to take it off from me."

"There are a lot of buttons on this."

"Is the prize not worth the effort?"

The more buttons he opened, the more the front of the holoku' opened to the smooth shadows formed by her breasts. Kukana reached over and tugged off

Hatch's lava-lava.

"I am not patient enough for this," Hatch said, pulling the dress off her shoulders, then easing her back so he could pull it down over her hips and off.

"I love you, Hatch A'e Loa."

Hatch realized that Kukana did not even know his name, his full name. In a world far away, she had just become Mrs. Franklin Jefferson Hatcher and didn't know it. Nor did it matter. For Hatch had also stopped being that man a few hours ago. Now he was Hatch A'e Loa. Now he was free to love this girl, his wife.

Hatch and Kukana spent their first night in the Makani house, as custom demanded. Sometime before they awakened, Twilla Pihi came in and left a tray of food for them. Hatch found the table set up on the lanai when he stepped outside to smoke. He flopped hard into a chair and bit into a mango slice and a piece of toast. Birds fought and played, the sea rumbled, a breeze rustled palm fronds and stirred high grass, and Hatch was a married man. He wanted very much to be good at it; every moment of the rest of his life would be dedicated to being a man good enough to be Kukana's husband.

Kukana appeared, carrying a tray with cups and a carafe of tea. She put it on the table between their chairs and bent over to kiss her husband.

"What are you thinking?" she asked.

"I was just wondering if we might be the only people who went to bed last night."

"We had more fun," Kukana said. She peeled back a banana and took an erotically-charged bite from the end of it, then licked her lips.

Hatch laughed. Her wide-eyed innocence was more cute than erotic.

"So you think I am funny, huh?" She mocked him with a fake laugh. "Is this funny?" She hooked her thumbs into the elastic band of her sleeping shorts and pushed them down. Then she ripped the halter top over her head.

142

"There is a God, after all," Hatch said.

"Of course there is. Many gods. And one of them is asking why do you wear so many clothes?"

Hatch laughed. He was wearing only a lava-lava wrapped around his waist.

Kukana pulled it open and put one leg over his lap to straddle him. She slid forward and eased herself down until he was inside.

"Living with you is going to kill me," Hatch teased, but soon gave in to her rhythm.

"I am the happiest girl in the world," Kukana said, tears coming to her eyes. "The hero of Tuva, my hero, loves me."

20

Hatch wondered if it were some kind of natural law, like falling on ice; once your feet let go, the rest of your body was bound to follow in a certain progression, until you were flat on your back.

Within a week, he was married, had moved from his beach shack into the new house on the hillside behind the church, and accepted a salaried position of four hundred dollars in cash, per month, as Tuva's magistrate of police. He was the de facto owner of a fifty-foot ketch, which was making him into a budding entrepreneur.

Hatch and I struck a deal to refurbish the ketch and turn her into a cargo vessel for direct exports to the copra distribution center on Olowalu.

"Next thing you know," he joked with me, "I'll be running around here in white shorts and knee socks, like some Aussie bureaucrat."

"Kamuela believes that you are the future of Tuva," I told Hatch over lunch at Papa Jack's. "You, and the children you and Kukana will have."

He smiled. "I have almost begun to believe in possibilities.

Dennis Lindsay brought two cans of cold beer and pork sandwiches.

"But," Hatch continued, "I don't think that the future of Tuva should be the same as that of Tahiti, or even Olowalu."

"Few Tuvans want that, but there is more money for the island in tourism, certainly more than in copra," I continued. "Although I am sure that Tuvans are not prepared for the destruction tourists always bring with them."

Kukana came into Papa Jack's, kissed the top of

Hatch's head, then took the chair across from her husband, her hand falling naturally to his thigh. "What are you two talking about in here all this time?"

"Ways to improve the life of Tuvans," Hatch said. "Do you want a sandwich, a Coke?"

"I ate something only a little while ago, with Pia Niu. Her baby is trying to walk. It is so beautiful to watch her. But what is wrong with our life that you want to *improve* it?"

"Ah," Hatch said. "My wife is smarter than both of us."

"Put together," I smiled.

Kukana scoffed in a glance, then reached over and took a drink from Hatch's can of beer.

I continued, "Mr. Jolly says tourists would make Tuva a rich island, to the benefit of us all."

"That may be," Hatch answered, then paused, obviously wondering if his argument against promoting tourism on Tuva was merely self-protection.

"I don't understand why it is so bad now that we need to change something," Kukana said.

"Well, we have the perspective of sitting here with that beautiful view out the window, eating fresh pork sandwiches and drinking cold beer," Hatch answered. "A question such as this ought to be put to all Tuvans."

"Papa is the voice of all Tuvans."

"That would be interesting?" I noted. "They've have never done anything like this before."

"Why not?" Hatch asked.

"Because Papa is the chief." Kukana answered.

"In the meantime," Hatch changed the subject, "Don and I have spoken about the copra. By converting the Hard Wind to have the capacity for carrying cargo, she could haul five tons or more of copra. Instead of piling it up and waiting for the government freighter, we could take it to market ourselves, pocketing all the profits instead of having to share a percentage unfavorable to Tuva in the extreme."

"This is a good idea, but profits for the copra company," Kukana pointed out, glancing at me.

"We would probably be able to employ more people, at least," I spoke maybe a little defensively.

"I will give the boat to the people of Tuva, so each family can share in the profits she produces. That would provide a little cash to supplement the usual bartering. Once she is rigged as a cargo vessel, we can charter her to the outer islands and take a percentage."

"You would be the captain?" Kukana wondered. "I will never step on that boat. Ever," she emphasized.

"I know, darling. But I wouldn't be the captain. I am already magistrate of police," Hatch pointed out with a sarcastic smile, rolling his eyes. "That is more than enough for me. No, I think Tioni should be the captain. He is a much better seaman than I am, and he has experience with large sailboats from when he worked for Island Packet Charters in Olowalu. By the way, I have already talked with Tioni about this, and he is willing."

"Tourists would be exciting," Kukana said. "If we get rich, would you want to go to America and see your home again?"

"Tuva is my home, honey."

We finished lunch, chatting inconsequentially, then Hatch and Kukana walked back to their house.

The magistrate of police's house was small but beautiful, in a colonial-tropical style; a smaller, one-story version of the Makani house a few hundred yards up the steep hillside. The wooden walls were whitewashed, the shutters and tile roof bright red, the lanai long and wide, with wicker furniture provided from a rejected Sears consignment that was stored for the last two years in Mr. Lee's warehouse. The house had five rooms: an interior bathroom serviced by pipes from a rainwater cistern, which flushed into the new septic tank; a kitchen with a propane oven and refrigerator; a living room – the largest room in the house, covering its entire width; a bedroom; finally an office where the magistrate of police had a desk, a sofa, a file cabinet (still empty), and a bookcase holding the books from Hatch's shack, along with the few Mr. Jolly had given Kukana over the years, the ones that had not mildewed beyond saving. The office furnishings were taken from an unused office in the government house.

They went into the kitchen and Hatch sat down at the dining table. Kukana stopped behind him and massaged his shoulders.

"Kukana, we won't ever go to America," Hatch said.

Kukana came around to sit across from him.

"It is your home. You never want to see it again? You talk about America sometimes, and I can hear in your voice that you miss it. You know this is true."

"It is true that I miss some things. Regardless, I can't go back."

"I don't understand. Maybe I would like one day to see America, your home. You say never?"

"I can't go. It's really that simple. I'm sorry if you want to see America, but if you do, you will have to go without me."

"I would never go anywhere without you. I still don't understand."

"Honey, I can hardly even leave Tuva. I cannot be the Hard Wind's captain because I cannot set foot on any other island if I had to produce identification. I don't even have a passport."

"Why do you need some passport?"

"When you went to Australia with your father, even though you were a child, you had a passport, or you were at least included on your father's passport. It is an official document allowing people to travel to other countries. Tuvans probably have, or can get, an Australian passport because you are Australian citizens.

147

"But you are an American, and you said you traveled to many different countries."

"I don't want to make this more complicated," Hatch continued patiently. "But I cannot prove I am an American citizen. The passport I used when I came to Tuva was fake, not a real one. I can't even still use it because the expiration date in it passed years ago."

"This is not complicated? I am more confused. Why did you need a fake passport?"

"You remember the story I told you that day on the beach, about what happened in the war?"

Hatch stood and got a glass of water from the tap, draining it before turning back to face Kukana.

"I will never forget. Do you have something more to tell me than this? This way of talking is making me afraid."

"I'm sorry, I don't mean to frighten you."

"Then stop talking like this. You make me afraid of losing you." Kukana stood and rushed into Hatch's arms.

"You aren't ever going to lose me, Kukana."

"That is all I need to know. You can quit talking on these other things. I don't care about anything except you. Let's go to bed."

21

Being magistrate of police was not without its moments. Problems that were previously handled within the family, or, if important enough, through the intervention of Kamuela Makani, began finding their way to Hatch. Simple things at first: Kale Manu had not paid his bar bill for some months, Rosie Lau's son was skipping school to go fishing with older boys, Keiki Nui knocked out Hupo Mahina's front tooth in a fight over Momona Kalaka.

After a while Hatch could hardly walk through town without being stopped by someone with "one beeg problem for da kine magister police."

Who had dealt with all this stuff before? Hatch wondered. Tuva always seemed wonderfully peaceful to him when it didn't have a policeman. If this kept up, Hatch feared he would be spending more of his time with these suddenly appearing police matters than on fishing and harvesting shells, which he would much rather do.

One night Hatch sat down with Mr. Jolly in Papa Jack's and offered to buy him a drink if the old bureaucrat would offer some advice on how to deal with all the trivial police work.

They took an empty table in back, hoping to be undisturbed in the darkness.

"This police stuff is driving me crazy," Hatch told Mr. Jolly, who smiled and nodded knowingly. "What in God's name did these people *do* before Kamuela got this bright idea?"

Hattie brought their drinks.

"So," Mr. Jolly said. "Sounds like you are managing to stay busy." He did not try to disguise a quick laugh.

"Busy? This afternoon I spent more than an hour trying to make Kahu Pomaikai understand that it's not nice to borrow Makavaana's skiff without getting his permission first."

Mr. Jolly laughed so briskly that his breath blew out the lamp between them.

"I don't see what's so funny about it."

"It's rather amazing what you see when you are forced to look." Mr. Jolly took a match and relit the lamp. "I'm sorry, mate. It's just … well, I just find it funny." He held up his hand to get Hattie's attention to refresh their drinks.

Hattie's bulk blocked them from the rest of the room as though a wall suddenly appeared. She placed the tall, sweating glasses on the table, then dragged a chair over to sit next to Hatch. Leaning toward him conspiratorially, she said, "You gotta help me, Mister Magister. Dis one beeg kine tang, beeg, beeg, beeg. Need da kine police attention right now."

Hatch rolled his eyes so only Mr. Jolly could see, then propped his chin in a cupped hand and feigned attention in Hattie's direction.

Hattie leaned her body so close that their shoulders touched. "Dis beeg tang, same like when you save Kukana, now you wife, from da kolohe kanes."

"What exactly is the big problem, Hattie?"

"Beeg problem is him, dat kane," Hattie said, twisting her enormity slightly and raising a ham hock arm to point toward Kaavanuii, who sat at the bar. "Dat kanaka dere."

"Kaavanuii?" Hatch looked at the old pier fisherman who was carefully nursing the same beer he'd started an hour ago.

"Da same."

"You can stop pointing now, Hattie. I see who you mean. What did Kaavanuii do?"

Hattie dropped her arm with a thud and twisted back to lean into Hatch again. "Dat guy come my room last night, him say he wanna make wit me da fuck."

Hatch smiled. "Excuse me if I seem slow to catch on here, Hattie, and I don't mean any disrespect, but, I mean, isn't that sort of what you do?"

Mr. Jolly took a drink to muffle a laugh.

"Sure, Mister Magister. Dat my kine tang sometime. See? Problem be dat kanaka come to make da fuck wit me, den after he do it, he say he want holo-holo kine."

"Ah," Hatch understood. "He didn't want to pay."

"Yes. Holo-holo. He doan wan' pay Hattie for her service wit him."

Mr. Jolly was losing control and had to turn halfway around to face the wall, unable to contain his laughter any longer.

"I see," Hatch said, unable to stifle his own laugh.

"You go and put him in da jail."

"We don't have a jail, Hattie. But instead of arresting him, wouldn't it be better if I saw to it that Kaavanuii paid for … what he owes? You did tell him before that there was a price? You agreed on it?"

"Sure I tole him. Hattie don't fuck holo-holo."

"What exactly did you tell him?"

"What I exact tole him is, I say, 'Kaavanuii, you wan' fuck wit Hattie, you gotta pay one half dollar Australian; you want Hattie suck you worm, you gotta pay one whole dollar.' Dat's what I tole him."

Hatch looked across at Mr. Jolly and silently mouthed the words, *you worm*? It was all they could take. Hatch dropped his face into his crossed arms and heaved with laughter. Mr. Jolly's head banged against the wall as he howled.

"Hey, hey!" Hattie shoved so hard against Hatch's shoulder than she nearly knocked him out of his chair.

Hatch coughed back his laughter. "I'm sorry, Hattie. I wasn't laughing at you, really."

Hattie crossed her arms over her gigantic chest and looked skeptical.

"Listen," Hatch said. "Tell me how much Kaavanuii owes you. I'll talk to him."

"Dat old man owe me one dollar and one half dollar."

Hatch spun away and beat his hands against the flimsy bamboo wall, knocking askew a framed picture of a young Queen Elizabeth. Mr. Jolly, having laughed himself sick, put his head on the table and moaned in pain. Hattie stood with her hands on her dangerous hips, her arms like curved trees growing out of basketballs.

Finally Hatch managed to compose himself enough to tell Hattie that he would speak with Kaavanuii and get her money. Satisfied, Hattie returned to her station at the far end of the bar. Hatch excused himself from Mr. Jolly, who was trying to swallow the acid he had laughed into his throat, and walked over to have a talk with Kaavanuii.

Hatch took an empty stool beside the old fisherman and leaned on the bar with both elbows, shaking his head when Dennis Lindsay came over to see if wanted a drink.

"Kaavanuii, it has come to my attention that you owe Hattie some money for … well, you know."

Kaavanuii looked at Hatch with the pride of an old man caught in the backseat with a cheerleader. He nodded and said with gusto, "One dollar *and* one half dollar."

"Well, if you knew, why didn't you pay her?"

"I got no dollar."

"Did you know you had no money before you accepted her price?"

Kaavanuii nodded.

"How were you going to pay her?"

"Wit fish."

"Did Hattie agree to accept fish in payment?"

Kaavanuii shook his head. "She tole me she already got plenty kine."

"How did you pay for this beer?"

"Pono buy for me," Kaavanuii indicated his fishing buddy on the opposite stool.

"I see." Hatch pondered that for a moment. "So," he continued, putting his hand on the old man's pointed shoulder, "how about if I buy some fish from you, then you take that money and pay your debt to Hattie? Would you agree to that?"

"If you say do it, Hatch A'e Loa, then I do it."

"It's not just what I say, Kaavanuii. It is doing the right thing. Hattie did something for you, and you have to pay her. I have not had time to fish for myself lately and could use some fresh opakapaka for the table." Hatch dug into his pocket and found two dollar bills but no change. He handed the money to the old man and said, "Here, take this and pay Hattie. Pay her right now so I see you do it. Use the change to buy a beer for Pono."

Kaavanuii accepted the money and nodded his head in thanks. "I will bring you fish tomorrow before the sunset. The fish will be clean and ready for table, so you new wife she will be so much happy. You know what means it when wife is happy." Kaavanuii giggled.

Hatch extended his arm the rest of the way around the old man's shoulders. "And if you need to see Hattie again and don't have money to pay her, I might be in the market for more cleaned fish."

Kaavanuii nodded happily. "You da best kine magister ever."

"Well, Kaavanuii, I am the only magister ever."

After Kaavanuii went to pay his bill to Hattie, Mr. Jolly approached Hatch at the bar and said, "We should vacate this den of iniquity before you are accosted again."

"Fine idea," Hatch agreed, ordering a pint bottle of Suntory Scotch and a couple of beers.

They walked slowly in the warm night air toward the wharf, Mr. Jolly's right arm looped through Hatch's left.

"Want to sit a while?" Mr. Jolly suggested.

"If we drink this, we'll be better off sitting."

They continued to the end of the wharf, Mr. Jolly sitting atop a fat black bollard, Hatch squatting on his haunches next to it. Hatch pulled the tab on a can of Foster's, drank half of it in two gulps, then poured whisky into the can through the hole.

"Ugh," Mr. Jolly proclaimed. "I will have mine straight and in a glass, although since I am without a glass at this moment … ," he took the bottle and drank straight from it.

Hatch got tired of squatting and sat down on the wooden pilings, leaning back on his elbows. They drank in silence for a couple of minutes. A turnbuckle clanked on the Hard Wind's mast. The ketch tugged gently at her mooring lines from the soft swells inside the bay; there were a dozen skiffs moored nearby, and outriggers pulled onto the sand.

"I need to foul wrap that halyard to stop it banging in the wind," Hatch said.

"How fares your beautiful bride?"

"Well. Happy, I think."

"Kukana is a good girl. She has a quiet, almost melancholic side, but has always been my favorite young lady on this beautiful piece of volcano. She reads books, you know?"

"Yes, she often reads to fall asleep. And you're right, she does have a melancholic side. I think it is because she feels things so seriously. She has a lot of questions about why things happen? Usually questions that have no answer."

"You, Hatch? Are you also happy?"

"Except for this police pretense, yes, I am happy. That is something of a miracle, I think. Completely unearned."

"Good to hear. But don't sell yourself short."

Mr. Jolly drank from the bottle, then passed it over to Hatch, who poured more into his beer can. A gull cried. Both men looked up and watched it swoop low over their heads, hoping for a handout.

Finally Mr. Jolly blurted it out: "I know about your past."

"What do you know?" Hatch asked, a fatalistic tone in his voice.

"Kamuela told me … Kukana told him."

Hatch stared into the darkness. The pier torches were snuffed out for the night and there was only a sliver of moon.

"Good thing we don't have a newspaper here, else everybody on the island would know by now."

"Don't blame Kukana, because she was worried about you. It was when you went away that time. She loves you rather enormously, you know? She naturally turned to her father when she feared for you, and he naturally to me – a white man with knowledge of the ways of white men, one supposes."

"It's all right. It's not important now." Hatch looked up at the stars, multitudinous without a distracting moon or ground light. "You can't fight destiny, Kamuela always says."

"Rest assured," Mr. Jolly continued," Kamuela would guard your secrets with his life, such is his affection for you. As for me, I will never speak of it again."

"I doubt that it really matters anymore," Hatch said. "It was a long time ago, and a very long way from here. I doubt if there is anybody who even cares what happened in some jungle in another life. In a way, having you know is a kind of relief. What I don't understand is why Kukana was so worried?"

"She only wants to protect you, if it comes to that. All this talk about tourists coming to Tuva – which is a capital idea in my book. She is afraid something might happen and you would be taken away. And that is why Kamuela told me. Make no mistake, Kamuela runs this island lock, stock, and barrel. But I am the government representative here; official inquiries always come first to me, and I am answerable to my superiors ... more or less, at least when they happen to remember that I am here.

"The reason Kamuela told me," Mr. Jolly went on, "is that I was preparing to submit a request to Canberra naming you magistrate of police, and to arrange a method for your salary disbursement. I asked Kamuela if he had any name for you other than Hatch, and he wanted to know why. That's what started it all.

"You don't actually have a passport, do you?"

"No."

"Well, no matter. We don't need to belabor this. With a last name like A'e Loa, we won't have much trouble passing you off as a Tuvan, at least until somebody sees you and sees how bloody American you look. Only recently have we begun having official birth certificates here. I submit documentation verifying a person was born on Tuva, on such and such a date, if known, and is a Tuvan citizen. Then Canberra issues a passport. We're going to get you made official. You're going to be a bleedin' Aussie. Hatch, which is quite a step up for an American."

Hatch laughed and nodded agreement.

"Why is this even necessary? I'm not going anywhere, and this could get you in trouble."

"It is necessary if you are to be magistrate of police and receive your *lavish* salary."

"Maybe that's a good way to get me out of this ridiculous job."

"Not likely. Kamuela wants you to be Tuva's cop and you will damn well be Tuva's cop."

"That's what I figured. I'll probably need a salary to subsidize Kaavanuii's visits with Hattie."

They laughed, then were quiet for a few minutes, lost in private thoughts.

Then Mr. Jolly asked Hatch if he wouldn't mind telling him how it ended, that story he told Kukana? Why didn't he die? Why wasn't he killed with the others?

Hatch told Mr. Jolly that a small group of Recon Marine LURPs – Long Range Reconnaissance Patrol – had come over the border with Vietnam chasing a VC communications detachment and heard the firefight. It was the Marines who found him. He didn't know why the attackers left him alive. Probably because he was unconscious, they thought he was dead. There was a Navy corpsman, he patched his wounds, more or less, and they carried him back to Toulan on a jerry-rigged stretcher, while one of the Marines with the same blood type dripped his blood into Hatch's arm through a direct tube.

That's when they found what had happened in the village, when Hatch found Mai.

Hatch spoke to the darkness. Mr. Jolly turned his head away, but continued to listen, horribly fascinated.

"I couldn't stand, but I knelt next to Mai's body and pulled out the twine holding her abdomen closed; I jerked out the rat and decapitated it. Our child would have been a boy."

"Oh dear God! There cannot be such evil in the world. I refuse to believe such horrors can exist."

"Take my word for it." Hatch's tone carried more than enough weight.

"What about those Marines?" Mr. Jolly asked.

"They stood back, walled off, I suppose, by the horror of it. The Gunny tried to pull me up and take me back to 'Nam with them, but I refused. I said I would kill any man who attempted to make me leave. Before morning light, they moved back into the trees and ghosted east, back over the border.

"I buried Mai and our son then. I couldn't stand much at all, so I dug the grave lying on my side. The corpsman had made a crude splint for my leg, but I couldn't really stand on it. I couldn't go deep enough lying on my side, but I went as deep as I could. Then Mai's mother and grandmother finished the grave. After that, they squatted beside it and wailed."

"I am hearing things from you, Hatch, that cannot be real. Such things cannot be possible. Even in the books of Mr. Conrad, there are not such horrors."

"I wish. I wish so much, Mr. Jolly."

"What happened?"

"Mai's uncle took me away to a cave in the mountains. People from the village came in and out to tend my wounds and bring food.

"Two days later, men from the private army of a warlord named Prince Phoun Som returned to occupy Toulan, which they would now use as a base in moving his operation southward. The villagers were forced to slash and burn their crops and plant poppies instead."

"And you hid out in that cave the whole time?"

"For months. When I could manage to walk with a stick, I limped my way out of the mountains, across the valleys, out of the jungle, out of the country, out of the war, and out of the way of the civilized world – to here."

22

The season of rain would come soon. Kukana looked back as the island slowly receded in the outrigger's thin wake, watching clouds begin to thicken in the late morning sky. The clouds increased and grew darker week by week, building complex towers in the darker blue velvet sky.

Sea birds went about their hunt more earnestly, dipping and plunging headfirst into the thin, opalescent water where the swells crested and fell.

The ocean rolled, undulating ahead of their outrigger skiff as the small motor drove them laboriously forward. Kukana watched a tern dive into the tumbling top of their wake, then awkwardly lift off with a tubular flying fish in its beak.

To Kukana, it had always seemed that those birds fed in death spirals, gliding over the sea like paper in the wind, then dropping suddenly into the water as if shot by an unseen, unheard gun; when they rose again to flight, it looked like a miraculous rebirth.

Since she started working with her husband, this was the farthest out they had gone. With the rainy season came migration through Tuvan waters of ahi, the powerful yellowfin tuna. Other fishermen reported seeing the great fish feeding on small skipjack tuna near the surface. Men from Napuku caught three yesterday, proudly displaying the new cuts inside their hands as proof of the struggle such fish bring.

The Tuvan word for yellowfin tuna, ahi, meant fire, and the giant tuna was named for the cry of the fisherman who found one hooked to the other end of his hand line: *Ahi!*, he cried, the line burning through his palms.

Hatch sat at the stern and steered. Kukana, in the

center, faced him. She watched the island and Hatch watched the sea. If signs of tuna appeared behind them, she would know. Kukana liked being with her husband in the boat, liked them being alone together, far away from the village and the demands Tuvans placed on him.

For two months they stayed within the lagoon, where Hatch speared fish and Kukana dove for shells. Sometimes they surfaced together, Hatch with a wiggling fish on his spear and Kukana with her net bag of shells. They would hang off the side of the boat and push up their face masks, leaning together for a salty kiss.

But today they were going for ahi. Makavaana's sailing skiff was far ahead of them. Two other outriggers without sails were dots behind. Kukana wondered which was her brother's boat? He was still in the bay when they left. Tioni had taught Kukana to fish from an outrigger when she was still a girl, and now she was excited for him to see her all grown up and fishing with her husband.

It was difficult keeping her attention on the surface of the sea, watching for working birds, looking for the telltale signs of panicked flying fish escaping marauding tuna. Her eyes kept returning to the island, the stark green rise of Kilohana – how different it is all going to be soon, she thought. She glanced down at the new swelling of her breasts, then across her stomach, smiling coyly at her secret. Caught looking down instead of scanning for signs, Hatch said, "I suppose that would be a good technique if this were a glass-bottom boat." Kukana returned her gaze to the sea and sky, smiling anyway.

Everything was prepared for fish, with hope. Hand lines were carefully coiled, one in the bow, one in the stern. Leader lines were rigged, and the thick, stainless steel, Mustad hooks, for which Hatch paid thirty cents each, were already baited with chunks of shad. Kukana had hand-tied bright feathers to disguise the hook, and to offer an alluring flash for the tuna's alert eyes. She tied yellow and red feathers in alternating sections because it would give the appearance of squid in panicked flight. Kukana had also added her own magic, kissing each hook before giving it to Hatch for baiting.

Then the birds appeared, as if from nowhere, suddenly swooping with excitement from the empty sky, over fish still invisible to the human eye, diving into the silver flashes that churned the water ahead.

"Ahi!" Hatch shouted, gunning the motor, pushing the bow up and over the next swell. Kukana turned in time to see the dark birds darting down from the blue, plunging into the sea, defining a single spot on the water, toward which every boat within sight raced at once. She picked up a coil of leader line with a baited hook and made ready.

"You steer," Hatch told Kukana, moving aside to give her room to reach the motor's steering tiller, which she grasped without allowing the motor to lose speed. Hatch moved forward and tossed over the trolling line just as they approached the still unseen tuna.

Spray washed over the low bow and stung Hatch's eyes. He wiped his face with one hand and trailed out line with the other. As the outrigger skiff raced through the frenzied school, Kukana cried out with delight. Theirs was the first boat to reach the tuna. Hatch fed line out alongside the boat as they passed through the feeding fish.

"Mahimahi," he yelled back to Kukana, pointing out the brightly flashing dolphin working along the edges of the bait fish. Hatch hoped the racing dolphin fish would avoid his hook because it would take so long to get the fish in and unhooked that they could lose the chance for an ahi.

Kukana saw the exact moment the big fish took their bait and hooked itself: Hatch grimaced as the line ripped through his hands, before he could throw a loop over the Samson post on the bow to create drag. The line tore around the post and through his hands as if it were attached to a race horse. Kukana could see traces of blood on the line as it slipped around the post and descended into the water. The pull of the fish overwhelmed the power of the small outboard motor; the bow jerked sideways, thrown onto a new course of the ahi's choosing.

"I think it's a big guy," Hatch yelled to Kukana.

Thin puffs of smoke rose from the wooden post as the line frictioned into it.

"Cut the engine," Hatch ordered.

Kukana throttled down and let the engine die from lack of fuel; they lost no momentum as the tuna pulled them like a tow.

"He's diving," Kukana called out when she saw the line's angle increase. Then suddenly the line descended straight down from the bow and the boat stopped. The bow dug into an oncoming swell and drenched Hatch. "Shit," he cried when the salt water hit the rawness on his palm.

In two minutes, the fish found the limit of its strength. The line stopped spinning around the Samson post and Hatch was able to hold it, monitoring a little slippage when the tension became too strong.

"You've got him now," Kukana cried.

The outrigger turned side to the swells as the fish began moving in a great wide circle hundreds of yards below them. Hatch and Kukana were forced to kneel in the bottom to keep from being pitched out by the radical rocking.

Kukana watched Makaavana hook into the school. Then Tioni's boat pulled up short when a fish took his line. But before any of the others reached the quickly moving school, the bait fish had moved away or descended. The birds lifted off the water to resume their search pattern, arcing higher and higher in the pale warm air currents.

Hatch held the fish for ten more minutes before it tired enough to be retrieved, hand over hand, slowly and with great exertion. Kukana crouched behind Hatch and watched as the retrieved line coiled in the bottom of the boat. It took another twenty minutes to bring the fish to the surface, appearing first as a shadow rising from the deep.

"Looks big," Hatch said, not masking his excitement.

Kukana leaned over the side and peered intently into the water where the line disappeared. She could see its shape, its color: silver and deep blue, with long yellow fins. "It is ahi," she said. "A great and beautiful fish."

"She's at least a hundred pounds, I'd say, from the feel of her." Hatch noted, smiling with glorious exhaustion. The fish was close, barely moving, mortally exhausted.

Kukana watched the line coming up, the fish rising at the end of it, and now could see that the ahi had swallowed her bright feathered hook, taken it into the throat instead of the jaw, which explained why it had not fought so long and was no longer capable of even trying to escape. Although easier for the fisherman, Kukana did not like it to end this way. She hated pain. Maybe it was all right if the fish feels the hook in its mouth, but it is not the pain such great fish fight against, it is the control of the line taking their freedom. But not if the hook was swallowed. It would die now, whether it was taken to eat or not.

Hatch looped a half hitch around the post and reached over to wind a second line around the tuna's tail, securing it to the side of the hull and the extended outrigger. "Maybe even a hundred and twenty," he said.

Kukana, who only understood kilos, giggled at what she believed to be an amazing exaggeration. "I think you caught one kohola."

Hatch laughed. "In kilos, fifty maybe."

"Ah, so we have fish, not whale."

She held Hatch's hands and looked at the palms. The new scratches were not so deep; they crisscrossed from the rope, like the weave of a sack. She told him to put them into the saltwater. The sting tightened his lips, but he knew she was right. "More scars," she said.

"But these are good ones," he said. "What a great damn fish she is!"

With the drag of the ahi lashed against the hull, it was all the small outrigger could do to make three knots wide open as they returned to the bay. Kukana handled the outboard motor and Hatch sat in the middle, watching her. He wrapped his hands in brine-soaked cloth.

Kukana stared at him until she could see that her steady gaze was making him uncomfortable, but she did not avert her eyes. From behind, Tioni's outrigger pulled up next to them.

"Did you get fish?" Hatch yelled across the rumble of the two outboard motors next to each other.

"Mahimahi," Tioni answered. He reached down and pulled up one by its scythe tail. In death, the sleek fish had lost its bright electric colors and turned a pale gray. "Three," he added, holding up three fingers. "I see you have one big ahi. You have nothing but luck every day since you marry with my sister."

"Luckiest day of my life," Hatch smiled, then felt a twinge of embarrassment. Even now, he was not used to what it meant to be married, much less married to a girl still a teenager, at least for another month, when she would turn twenty.

"She no longer brings luck for me," Tioni said. "You see the mahimahi got to me first, then ahi all pau. If I had such a good helper as you have ... ." Tioni gunned his motor and pulled away.

"I don't deserve you," Hatch said to Kukana, reaching over to put a rag-wrapped hand on her leg, "and I am the luckiest man who ever lived."

Kukana had intended to tell him that night, when they were in bed and clasped together in love, but she could no longer wait, the joy of this moment was too right.

"If your next helper is not so lucky for you, nobody you can blame but yourself."

"What?"

"Because you will be the maker and you will be the teacher."

"Is this a riddle?"

"It is the father who makes the child and it is the father who teaches his child the ways of the sea and the fish, is it not?"

Such an idea was so far from his thinking that Hatch went through several possibilities before the obvious one appeared.

"Are you ... ? The utter power of the idea prohibited the word from coming to his lips. "Are you ... ?"

Kukana nodded and smiled broadly. "I will miss fishing with you when you are working with your child. I will be jealous."

"You ... we are ... ?"

"We will have a baby even before Christmas. Twilla says maybe Christmas Day." Kukana was flushed with the joy of watching her husband's face go white, then brighten with happiness.

Hatch leaped toward her and Kukana let go of the throttle; the boat squatted to a sudden stop just inside the reef. They tumbled into the bottom kissing until Hatch realized he must be crushing her.

"Oh, I'm sorry," he said, getting up and lifting her back onto her seat. "Did I hurt you? You sit still right there. Don't do anything." He moved around her to take the throttle arm.

"I am not sick, you know?"

"Of course not, I know that. But you have to be careful."

"And what do you know about having a baby?"

"Not one damn thing, obviously. Why didn't you tell me before we went out today? You could have gotten hurt."

Kukana shook her head in exasperation, but never stopped smiling.

Hatch opened the throttle all the way and the outrigger took its time reaching speed because of the drag of the tuna tied to the side. Hatch put his free arm around Kukana's shoulders and squeezed. "I love you so much," he said into her ear, shouting over the roar of the motor. He was thinking, looking at his pregnant wife, that nothing he could do or say could thank her enough for saving his life and showing him how to live like a human being.

He looked down at her stomach, still flat, and shuddered involuntarily from a feral dream, a savage, lurking nightmare – the demon always behind. He almost called her Mai again.

But now, at least, he knew the difference.

23

In this way passed our days, in peace, tranquil; we aged, some of us died, babies came. Hatch and Kukana named their daughter Emma, after her mother.

Hatch was often seen carrying her on his chest in a sort of East Asian sling. He carried her many places – to the beach, along village streets, on walks to Kaiwi Point, the market, up the lane to his father-in-law's house – but never to Papa Jack's or the Lotus.

We met in the bar sometimes, Hatch and I, sans baby Emma, and we shared a few drinks; no one saw him drunk again, not after Emma. I had thought he was an alcoholic, but if so, it must have taken an iron will to still drink but be able to stop short of shit-faced.

Frankly, I was surprised to see Hatch become such a successful family man. It was so abrupt that it made me suspicious it might have been some sort of rouse, or, at best, simply a temporary aberration in his natural character.

But then, who among us knew what Hatch's true character was? I doubt if even Kukana knew. Although Kamuela seemed to never have any doubts about the man he pronounced to be the hero of Tuva. Who knew what his past lives had been, what penalties they claimed from him? What is that saying? A mystery wrapped in an enigma?

But less so, as our days went by, as if whatever life had made of Hatch, or he had made of it himself, had somehow taken on less importance, or value, in the grand light of his new life – husband of Kukana, father of Emma.

Before the feeder line from the electrical generating station was strung to Hatch's house, the house of the Magistrate of Police, there were only kerosene lamps and propane for the stove. In those days, or those nights, Kukana said that her husband spent some hours in the late evening, often after she was in bed and had given up and fallen asleep, at his desk. In the beginning, when she asked what he was doing, he would say work. But what work? Who knew?

Now we know he kept journals, a stack of lined school notebooks. Kukana said he did not hide them, nor did he ever ask her not to look at them. She just did not. She believed that if he wanted her to know something, he would tell her. If he did not say, there was a reason for it, and not a reason for her to worry about.

But how could we not wonder? A man in our confined space like Hatch A'e Loa.

Then a piece of the puzzle came out the sky.

It was particularly hot. No shade on the pier. Wind slackened under the weight of approaching evening, lifting the accumulated heat of the day.

At the copra factory on the lower reaches of Kilohana Mountain, workers shuffled past mounds of drying coconut meat. I was about to leave for the day and paused by the window to gaze out toward the quotidian view of multicolored fishing skiffs and outrigger canoes on their way home, laboring under aging outboard motors. There was an unusual sound.

Inside Papa Jack's, Hattie waddled around the tables, lighting decorative hurricane lamps, anticipating pau hana, when the ever-thirsty copra workers and sea-stained fishermen would demand cold beer to end their work day. Stopping suddenly, a burning match held flickering above a red lamp, Hattie turned her head to the same faint and alien buzz I heard. She would say it sounded to her like the guttural hum of Suji Fukimoto's 1952 Yokohama-model dental drill. Leaving lamp duty, she went out to the plank sidewalk and raised a beefy arm across her forehead, squinting against the fat setting sun.

In the Government House, Mr. Jolly scooted his chair away from the desk and leaned toward the window in order to see around the side of the building to the banyan tree, where Kimo napped. He called out to waken him.

The amphibian aircraft banked hard starboard out of the sun and skimmed over the reef, as if its wingtip were tracing the line of a runway, then climbed again to circle the perimeter of Tuva Bay. By then there were more than forty people gathered on the wharf. The seaplane banked again and under full flaps flared just as it cleared the jagged coral reef, smacking into Tuva Bay and bouncing three times before settling into the foamy green water like a sun-dazzled albatross. I had seen better landings.

As the plane taxied toward the wharf, boys perched on the bollards, ready to dive for coins. Women backed away and held their woven pandanus hats against the wet gale blown back by the props. Two men went to take tether lines.

A door opened on the side behind the high wing and a man dressed in a white shirt with shoulder epaulets stepped onto the pontoon. As Mr. Jolly and I approached, the seaplane disgorged its single passenger, then the pilot, offering a cocky salute, went back into the plane and closed the door. The engines revved, the tethers released, and the plane taxied back into the bay for takeoff.

Turning from the spray, holding their hats and the hands of small children, the crowd on the wharf watched the plane leap from the bay and fly off, back into the setting sun.

As we approached through the crowd, the female passenger began removing her passport from a pocket on her sweat-stained khaki shirt.

"My name is Jolly Malcolm. I am what passes for government here."

"Jan Moss," she said, handing over her passport.

"American," Mr. Jolly observed. He introduced me as a fellow countryman, and I shook her soft hand. I had not seen a white woman this attractive in a very long time. She wore makeup. A Tuvan woman's version of makeup was rubbing on her lips a bit of red from a sea urchin spine. If that.

"I was assured by the Australian embassy that I would not need a visa," she said, using the tip of her index finger to push up her sunglasses, which had slipped along the sweaty bridge of her nose.

"Not for a stay of less than thirty days. More or less."

She nodded and flicked aside a long strand of yellow hair from her forehead.

Mr. Jolly returned the passport and she put it back into her pocket.

May I inquire regarding your business on Tuva?"

Curious Tuvans jostled one another to get closer to the blond haole wahine; children gathered expectantly around her legs. Jan Moss patted a little boy on the shoulder and smiled indulgently.

"Shoo," Mr. Jolly commanded, waving his hand at the children. "Go on now, shoo. Get off the lady's feet, you heathens."

"I don't mind them," Jan said courteously.

"They're your shoes. I see that your ride has left. How long do you intend to visit our little island?"

"Just two days, I'm afraid. That is, if my ride comes back. Although it looks like a beautiful place for a holiday." Jan jerked her foot away when two wrestling boys fell on her toes.

"Momona! Get your bloody heathens off our guest."

She smiled, and I liked the way it softened her face, which was a bit sunburned and freckled.

"So you are not on holiday? The whirlwind tour of the South Pacific?"

She smiled again, adding a short laugh. "Actually, I am looking for someone, an American, said to live here."

Mr. Jolly visibly stiffened, and I probably did, as well. Besides Tioni's wife, only two other Americans had ever lived on Tuva, and I was one of those. "Would that be a woman named Jenny?" Mr. Jolly inquired.

"No. His name is Frank Hatcher; he would be called Hatch, probably."

I cannot imagine now how, or if, we did not show what must have been abject surprise.

"Why did you come all this way to see that particular man?" Mr. Jolly wondered.

"It's personal, if you don't mind."

Naturally, I wondered: Wife? Girlfriend?

"What makes you think this man lives on Tuva?" I asked.

"That is also personal. I'm sorry."

Wife, I decided.

"Maybe it would be best if you waited while I inquire about the man you seek," Mr. Jolly told her.

"Is there a café, a bar?"

"Of course. There are two bars, a restaurant; no cafe, exactly. Papa Jack's is the nicer. There is also a pleasant cabana restaurant on the beach a couple of hundred meters up the street in that direction."

"If you would kindly direct me there, to the bar, I mean. I will have a beer and wait. If your inquiries produce a result, please tell Captain Hatcher that the sister of Boone Buchannan would like very much to see him."

Gobsmacked, as Mr. Jolly might say.

The night was warm, soft, quiet; even the surf rumbled lazily, muffled against the barrier of the reef. Torchlights, illuminating the pier and beach, flickered against the purple backdrop of the dark, sharp mountains; the amber glow of kerosene lamps rendered life to the small houses scattered along the thickly vegetated slopes.

At the end of the pier, Kaavanuii and Pono fished, silhouetted against the evening sky; they, and their long, arching poles gave the night a kind of permanence, captured, as on a charcoal sketch. Occasionally a halyard slapped the main mast on the Hard Wind, anchored in the bay, still in the process of being refitted for cargo. In a moment of time caught between swells breaking on the reef, it was so quiet you could hear, even from the wharf, water lapping against her hull.

Jan Moss sat at a table beside Papa Jack's largest window, its bamboo shutters rarely closed, nursing her third, or was it fourth, Foster's, picking at the remains of a fish burger. She saw the object of her inquiry approaching from the direction of the pier.

Hatch entered the bar and turned immediately toward Jan's table. He paused only a moment, then sat down across from her. She offered her hand first, and Hatch shook it.

"How do you know Boone?"

"I am his sister."

"Janet, of course. That Jan."

"I am."

"I heard Moss."

"I was married for a while."

"I'm surprised. In fact, I am stunned. How did you even find me here?"

"Boone told me, and don't ask me how he knew, because he didn't say."

"I wish he had come himself."

"I'm sure he also wishes that."

"There's a problem?"

"Boone is dying. He has cancer. Pancreatic."

"God damn. Fucking God damn!"

Hattie brought Hatch his usual, a Foster's and a shot of Suntory whisky, shaking her finger at him after putting the beer down.

"What is that about?" Jan asked, when the waitress left.

"I believe that was Hattie's way of letting me know that she knows I'm a married man and you are an attractive young woman who is not the attractive young woman I am married to."

Jan laughed heartily. "That makes me feel better," she said.

"Can I get you something else?" Hatch asked.

"I think I'm already a couple of beers over the line, so better not."

"How bad is it? Boone? I find what you've told me to be the most tragic thing I have heard in a long, long time."

"He's about come to the end of this part of his journey. That's the way he puts it. Boone thinks the next part will be less interesting, but he's curious about it."

"Sounds like Boone. He's right. It would take a lot to be more interesting than the life he's already had. Where is he?"

"Thailand. He never left Southeast Asia. He had a bar in Phuket for a while. For the last, oh, about ten years, he's been farming pearls. He has a Thai girlfriend; she's taking good care of him."

"I can't imagine how Boone knew where to find me, but I am glad he did."

"That's sort of why I'm here."

Hatch looked at her questioningly.

"Maybe one more," she held up the empty Foster's can.

Hatch beckoned Hattie and ordered another for Jan, as well as for himself.

"I may already be a bit tipsy. Which is the girlie way of saying plastered," Jan announced. "I was waiting a long time."

"Sorry about that."

"You don't have to apologize."

Jan leaned back into her chair. She was obviously wobbling a bit. "I'm sorry," she blurted, then stood abruptly, knocking back the chair, and ran for the door.

When Hatch came out after paying, he found her kneeling on the sidewalk, having already thrown up in the street.

"Oh God," she said. "I am so sorry. Look what I've done. Right on the street."

"Don't worry about it. The street's mostly sand, and your little contribution won't be noticed among all the contents from this bar that preceded you."

She stood and held onto one of the poles supporting the roof overhang.

"Let me take you ... where are you staying?"

"I didn't have a chance ... I don't really know, actually. Is there a hotel, maybe? Jeez, I'm sorry."

"There's not really a hotel. I'll take you to my house. There's a sofa. I'm sorry, but it's not really uncomfortable, I think."

"I don't know if ... ."

"There aren't any decent choices."

Hatch put his arm around her waist for support and guided her along Alii Street.

"I'm sorry there is only one bedroom," Hatch said, as they crossed the veranda and he held the door open for her. "But the main room is kind of huge, and there is an office behind it. The sofa in there is long enough for you, I'm sure."

"You could plop me in a bed of nails and I wouldn't notice. Thank you."

Hatch led her across the main room and opened his office door, reaching around for the light switch.

"There is also only one toilet, but if you are sick again, that door opens into the kitchen. And of course there's plenty of nature around here."

"I pray not. Nice office. Looks very official. Your house is lovely." She pronounced it luffly.

"I'll get you a sheet and pillow."

"I don't want to disturb your wife. I'm okay."

"We have a baby; she is probably sleeping now. You may hear her. She keeps early hours and gets hungry very, very often."

"A baby. That's nice. You don't have to do this ... but do you mind if I just lay here for a little while?"

"I'll get that sheet."

"Thank you. You are a nice man. Boone said you were a good man. I can see that. You really are a nice, nice man. Well, really, nice might not have been the word. But I thank you very much for ... you don't even know me, and here I am already on my knees puking in front of you, and crashing in your house; oh God, I guess I'm chattering like a bird." Jan kicked out of her sandals and fell back on the sofa, turning to her side with her back to him.

Hatch covered her with a sheet and put a pillow on the end of the sofa where she could reach it if she wanted. Then he went to the bedroom. Kukana was asleep, as was Emma in her crib, both sleeping curled in the fetal position.

He went to the veranda for a cigarette.

24

"Wake up," Kukana touched Hatch's shoulder. He turned over and opened his eyes. "There is a naked woman sleeping on the sofa in there."

"Naked? Are you sure? She wasn't in that condition when I put her there."

"You put her there? Who is this haole wahine?"

"Her name is Jan, she is the sister of a very old friend of mine, from the Army. She doesn't have anything on?"

"There's a sheet, but it's on the floor. Don't change the subject. What is she doing in our house?"

"Don't raise your voice, you'll wake Emma."

"Emma is already awake. She is in the kitchen for her bath."

"You didn't leave her in the sink?" Hatch swung his legs off the bed and stood.

"You lolo haole kanaka! What do you think?"

"Calm down, give me ten seconds to wake up. Where did you leave Emma?"

"In her high chair. You want to keep changing the subject. Why is that woman, why is that *naked* woman, sleeping in my house?"

"I'm sorry, I suppose you mean me," Jan said, standing in the open doorway with the sheet wrapped around her.

"See?" Kukana said, hands on her hips.

"I'm just searching for the toilet. I'm sorry. I thought Captain Hatcher might have told you."

"Down the hall on the right, it's the last door," Hatch said.

Jan grimaced and bit her lower lip in embarrassment, then turned and went down the hall.

"Told me what?" Kukana said. "That my husband brought his naked girlfriend home and left her on the sofa in his wife's house, where she is sleeping with their little baby girl? Told me that?"

They heard Emma fussing. "I know, I hear her." Kukana said.

They went to the kitchen.

Kukana took the baby from the high chair and put her to a breast. Hatch warmed bath water in the sink.

"I didn't tell you last night because you were asleep, you were exhausted and I didn't think it was worth waking you up for. And I don't like you jumping to stupid conclusions, either. You can stop acting like a teenager."

That cut Kukana where it hurt, because now she was twenty. She sat at the breakfast table, her bare feet tapping nervously on the floor, and squeezed her breast to increase the flow. She made it a point not to look at Hatch, shutting him out.

"Like I said," Hatch continued, adding more warm water from the faucet, "she is the sister of a man I knew in the Army, one of my best friends. She came here looking for me, because her brother is sick, he is dying. You know there's not a decent place for her to stay in the village, so I offered the sofa to her. She did have too much to drink. But when I left, she was completely dressed and very much asleep. That's it."

"How did she know to find you here on Tuva?"

"That's a good question. We didn't get around to that before she got sick."

"I don't like this thing, but I am sorry about her brother, who is your friend."

"I am so sorry," Jan interrupted, now dressed, standing in the open doorway of the kitchen. "Oops," she noticed Kukana breastfeeding. "I'll come back later."

"No," Kukana stopped her. "Please, come in. It is not our way to treat a guest such ... what is the word?" She looked to Hatch for an answer.

"Rude?"

"Yes, in such a rude way. I am sorry. Please sit

down. Hatch, will you make tea for us." To Jan, she added, "Juice? I will make breakfast when Emma finishes hers. You can watch my husband give her a bath. It's like a comedy show."

"You are very sweet." Jan came in and sat at the table opposite Kukana. "I can't begin to imagine what would be going through my mind in your situation. Your baby ... Emma? She is really beautiful. A Gerber baby."

Kukana thanked her, but looked puzzled.

"A Gerber baby," Hatch explained, "comes from an American baby food company that always had pictures of cute babies on the label."

"Ah." To Emma, Kukana said, "Emma A'e Loa, did you hear that? You are the Gerber baby." Emma suckled obliviously. "Nobody eats until Emma eats," Kukana said.

"I envy you such a beautiful baby," Jan said.

"You have no babies?"

"No."

"I'm sorry. On Tuva, girls have many babies. Too many babies I think sometimes. This is number one for us. Emma is named for my mother. When we have a son, he will be Kamuela, after my father."

"Oh God," Hatch rolled his eyes, then began making tea, watching in fascination the odd conversation occurring at the breakfast table in the kitchen of his still-awkward house. Ten minutes ago, Kukana seemed ready to throw him out as a flagrant adulterer, and now she was chatting away with this total stranger as if she were a neighbor. It was so Tuvan, he thought.

Bathing Emma was a show, Jan agreed. She rejected his offer to try her hand at it. Jan volunteered to make breakfast, and worked on that while Hatch finished Emma's bath. Kukana sat at the table and said, "I feel like the queen."

They ate a hearty breakfast and spoke about the not so important things in their lives. While Hatch put

Emma onto a pallet on the floor, then started more tea, Kukana asked Jan how she even knew how to find her husband?

"Do you want to talk about this here, now?" Jan asked Hatch.

"I don't know what it is we're talking about?"

"What I said last night. At least what I think I said last night."

"I have no reason to hide anything from Kukana," Hatch said. "Plus, I have no idea what you're trying to tell me."

Kukana looked at her husband and smiled. He smiled back and leaned over to kiss her hair as he refilled her teacup. Then he refilled Jan's cup. She thanked him, rubbing her temples and wincing.

"You're paying the piper," Hatch told her.

"Paying the piper?" Kukana wondered.

"Our guest seems to have a mighty and well-deserved hangover."

"Ah, this is something you know well," Kukana told Hatch.

"I'm afraid I do."

"And I'm afraid he is right," Jan said to Kukana. "But I'll survive."

Emma flipped onto her stomach and inched her way off the pallet; Hatch got up and put her back in the center of it, offering her a toy boat made of koa wood, which she immediately tried to get inside her mouth.

"I would like to know how you found my husband here?" Kukana asked in a worried tone.

"It's kind of a long story," Jan said "My brother, Boone, heard a rumor that Captain Franklin Hatcher was alive and living on this atoll. He says the source was Guns Harper."

Hatch looked surprised. "I'm pretty sure Harper must be dead. Do you know what happened here?"

"Boone told me that Harper was aboard a yacht that docked here, and that he and the other members of that crew ended up tossed into the ocean."

"That's pretty much what happened. So, they survived?"

"Not all of them. Only Harper and another one, the boat's owner, I believe. They washed up on some atoll and were found by fishermen. Boone didn't know whether to believe the story or not. He thought all this time you were dead. Thus … here I am."

"If you came to see if I'm alive, you've seen me."

"Not just that."

"Is Boone in contact with Harper? How did this rumor get to him?"

"I don't know. Boone has always had his hand in things, even after he retired … if he ever actually retired. I'm sure you know what I mean."

"Who is this Boone?" Kukana asked. "Why would he want to find you? I don't understand any of this. It makes me afraid."

She reached down and picked up Emma, who was fussing again, and rocked her on her lap.

"I don't mean to make you afraid," Jan said.

"Boone Buchannan, her brother, and I were friends a long time ago," Hatch explained. Then he turned to Jan and asked why she came to Tuva, rather, why Boone sent her to Tuva.

"He wants to see you, Captain Hatcher."

"Let's stick with Hatch."

"All right. I came here hoping you would return to Thailand with me, to see Boone."

"That's pretty much what I thought," Hatch said. "Otherwise, it makes no sense, you coming all this way just to tell me Boone's … sick."

"Not just sick. He's dying."

"Did she say she wants you to go to Thailand with her?" Kukana interrupted.

"Yes," Jan confirmed.

"Where is Thailand?"

"In Southeast Asia," Hatch answered.

"Why would you go there?"

"I don't know why," Jan answered. "It's very important for my brother to see your husband. He wouldn't tell me, but I know it's very important. So I came to find your husband and to ask him to return to Thailand with me."

Hatch had remained silent, his eyes indicating that his attention was not in the kitchen any longer.

Kukana suddenly realized exactly what the pretty haole woman had said – that two of the men who had assaulted her did not die in the ocean. She grabbed Hatch's forearm.

"Two of those men are alive? Is that what she said?"

"Yes," Jan answered for Hatch. "The one who knew your husband from the war, and the one who owned the boat they came here on. They must have done something pretty horrendous to get tossed into the ocean and left to drown."

"They did," Hatch said.

Abruptly, Kukana stood so forcefully that she knocked the chair over. Emma began crying. Kukana, now also crying, took Emma and rushed out of the room.

"Gosh, I'm sorry. I don't understand what … ."

"It's not your fault; you're just the messenger."

"I should tell you that I don't have the kind of money for a trip like this. I also have a dubious Australian passport. Which, by the way, states that my name is Hatch A'e Loa, and that I was born here, on Tuva. I've never tried using it. It would surprise me if it works."

"I can't do anything about your passport, but money isn't the issue. In fact, I already have your air ticket to Bangkok."

"That's fairly presumptuous."

"Well, not of me. Boone said he knew you would come."

"If you will excuse me for a moment, I need to see about my wife."

"Of course. Should I wait here?"

"If you want."

Apparently Hatch made the decision to go with Jan Moss sometime that evening. He had already left with her by the time Kukana told me she wanted her husband to find and kill the two men from the Hard Wind who had survived.

I wondered how Kamuela would take this news?

25

Hatch and Jan Moss flew by seaplane to Papeete, and from there a UTA flight to Bangkok. In Tahiti, no one questioned Hatch's passport; he thought it would have been a different story had they gone through Sydney.

In Bangkok, they spent the night in adjoining rooms at a small hotel on a narrow street behind the klong near Jim Thompson's house. Hatch had encountered Thompson in 1964, at a bar on Phya Thai Road. Thompson, the sometime spy who created the Thai silk industry, secured for Hatch his first job after he walked out of the war: bodyguard for the family of a Chinese banker in Singapore. When Hatch went around to the house to say hello, he found out that Thompson disappeared on a trip to Malaysia in 1967, and had not been heard from since. His house, filled with antiques and expensive Thai art, was turned into a museum.

He knew that nothing was going to be the same.

Boone Buchanan's house was near Karon Beach, not all that far from a Club Med. It sat on the beach just beyond the high tide line. A tangle of jungle completely enclosed the back of the house. In front, a rickety plank pier extended all the way from the veranda out a hundred feet into the bay. A holding tank, made from sticks tied with hemp, floated in the calm black water at the end of the pier. Chunks of rotting Styrofoam kept the tank afloat against the weight of hundreds of large oysters held inside. Oysters impregnated, as it were, with mother-of-pearl beads planted into the mantle tissue as irritants, and which were now halfway through a four-year gestation. Dim, bare, light bulbs vaguely illuminated the end of the pier and each end of the holding tank.

A small dark silhouette of a man dressed in black silk pajama-like clothes squatted in the shadows on a floating platform beneath the end of the pier. On his lap lay an automatic rifle with a collapsible metal stock.

As they approached the house, Hatch first noticed the man as the swelling and falling red glow from the tip of his cigarette. The guard was only a dark profile against the black water, then Hatch noticed the weapon in his lap. He put his hand out and stopped Jan.

"They're holding tank for the pearl beds," Jan said. "It's guarded, but he knows me."

They could easily hear water from the bay lapping over the top of the holding tank frame. Faintly, far away, more a feeling than a sound, Hatch noticed a thumping musical bass beat, probably coming from the bars at Karon Beach, from where they had just walked along the road that became a path, until reaching Boone's house.

"Your brother must not get many unannounced visitors."

"None, I would guess."

A burst of laughter came from the tile-roofed house. Then the front screen door, which opened onto the veranda, banged open, and the shadowy stick figure of a man appeared. He took a cigarette from his mouth and flicked it in a high arc toward the water; it disappeared like a miniature meteor. The guard suddenly stood attentively. A woman's voice called out something in Thai from inside the house, and another light came on. The man on the veranda walked down the pier and said something to the guard. The woman appeared in the doorway, silhouetted from the light inside the house. She was topless, wearing a sarong, hands on her hips.

"Poo-oon," she called out in a plaintive singsong tone, giving the word two syllables and heavily accenting the first.

"That's Boone's girlfriend. Her name is Linn."

Jan then called out to her brother as they walked up to the veranda.

"Well, fuck me in the ear! You were surely dead, brother"

"Not yet, Boone. Not yet."

Boone's thinning black hair was slicked back over his wide scalp, he wore thin flip-flops, a pair of baggy khaki shorts, and a ragged gray tee-shirt with the faded logo of Harvard University loose over his chest.

The two men fell into a hug, slapping each other's back. Like schoolboys, Hatch and Boone broke from the hug throwing fake punches at one another, which clearly exhausted Boone. Jan started into the house; Boone put his hand on her shoulder and thanked her.

"My pleasure. Your friend lives on a beautiful island" Jan said, disappearing inside.

"God *damn,* I'm happy to see your fine ass."

"Poo-oon," came Linn's high voice from inside.

"You just got to love hearing a damn near naked girl call you 'poon,' Boone smiled, adding, "she can't say B, so it comes out P."

"Coming, Lotus Blossom," Boone sang in a cartoon tone, looking back at the open door. "Christ a-mighty, Linn, cover thyself, you heathen lovely." Then he put one arm around Hatch's shoulders to lead him inside.

Linn, whose name was actually Khunying, pulled open the screen door for her lover and the foreigner. When they stepped inside, Boone introduced her to Hatch.

"Linn is *not* a Phuket girl," Boone said, patting her butt.

Linn pulled the sarong higher on her gamin body.

"She's a mainlander, a Bangkok chick. Phuket girls don't have a sense of humor, do they, Lotus Blossom?"

"Phuket girls' pussies dry up like old durian,

185

smell same," Linn said.

"I'd glad I'm not a Phuket girl," Jan said from the hallway, returning from getting rid of her suitcase.

Boone shrugged hopelessly and sent Linn into the kitchen for a bucket of ice, then excused himself to go to the bar for a bottle of gin. "We'll toast our reunion with some fizzes."

"Are you living here, too?" Hatch asked Jan.

"Oh no, God forbid. I live in San Francisco. I just came out when Boone … . I was here only a few days before going to deliver his message to you."

"More a request than message."

"Yes, I suppose so."

Hatch noticed that the room was virtually a museum. Every space filled with acquisitions reflecting Boone's interests and his thirty-two years in Indochina. There were many antique weapons, tribal masks, authentic shrunken heads. Just the collection of East Indian woodcarvings and statues alone was worth hundreds of thousands of dollars. Hatch was inspecting more closely one of the shrunken heads when Boone returned with the makings for gin fizz.

"From a tribe near Morobe, New Guinea. A chief killed in battle. That head is seventy-four years old, and even now if the tribe knew where to find it, they'd have my head on a pole."

"You mean people were still shrinking heads seventy years ago?" Jan asked.

"My dear, they were shrinking heads in the mountains of New Guinea last week." Boone let out a bone-rattling laugh, which descended into a hacking cough, then he called out something in Linn in the kitchen.

Boone made their drinks and Linn brought fresh pineapple spears, shrimp crackers, and fillets of spicy lime-marinated raw fish. While they ate, Boone regaled them with the story of selling his bar and massage parlor in Patong Beach and retiring to this house and pearl farm. Linn flirted flagrantly with

Hatch, which Jan, to her confusion and dismay, found infuriating. At least Hatch seemed only polite and not interested.

"Up off your pretty butt, my little bubble," Boone said to Linn. "A room for our guest. Wiki wiki! Chop chop!" He clapped his hands like a potentate.

"I'll help," Jan said, standing and leaving with Linn.

Hatch noticed that Boone stood from the armchair with some effort. He was maybe a hundred pounds lighter than the last time Hatch saw him, in their other life. In those days, Boone's nickname was Buffalo, and he was about as big and strong as one. Hatch shook his head and said, essentially to himself, "Buffalo Boone Buchanan."

"Maybe a bit more gazelle these days," Boone smiled wanly, reaching down for the gin bottle. He poured two fingers into each of their glasses. They clinked glasses. "To our old friends, among whose number we alone remain," Boone toasted.

"We, and Guns."

"Let's not include that motherfucker in this category, shall we?"

"Isn't that why I'm here?"

"Among other things, my friend. In good time. I want to wallow in your presence." He laughed again.

Boone asked Hatch to fill him in on the time since he walked out of the Laotian jungle, but Hatch skipped to his arrival in Tuva, the trauma with Guns Harper and the yacht's crew, up to Jan appearing.

"That fucking Harper. He's the fucking devil incarnate, snakes slither away from him in terror."

"Then obviously he hasn't changed?"

"Maybe gotten worse."

"Is he why I'm here, Boone?"

"As you can see, after I heard that you were alive, I wanted to say goodbye to an old friend. That's part of why I asked you to come. There's also something I'm glad I can get off my soul before I go find out what actually happens to one's soul. And because I owe you a warning. How about another little fizz?"

"Sure, Boone." Hatch handed over his glass.

Humidity increased during the night as clouds from the marine layer hugged the coastline, trapping the day's heat and the sea's salty moisture. Even with the ceiling fan on high, Jan lay nude on top of the damp, warm sheet, and now understood Linn's aversion to even a sarong. The mosquito netting around the bed mitigated the fan's effect. Although she was drowsy, she could not fall asleep.

She folded the pillow behind her neck and looked down over her body, which glistened with sweat in the soft yellow light from an occasional moon. Her bedroom was at the front, with French doors overlooking the veranda and the pier. She felt something erotic in the heat, the wild distant noises of birds and animals, the glistening skin of the body she worked so hard to maintain, maybe intensified by the feeling of anonymity.

She tried to block those thoughts and go to sleep, but they would not go away. Even above the swishing blades of the ceiling fan, she could hear water lapping over the pearl bed holding tanks, reminding her of the steady rhythms inside her own body.

She gave up on sleep and decided to go out to the veranda, hoping the open air would cool her skin a little. The house was quiet. Her weight made the floorboards creak as she walked to the French doors, which were already open. She pulled on a pair of shorts and a tee-shirt and went outside, hoping Linn's father would not shoot her. She could see his dark form at the end of the pier and thought of waving or making some sign, but maybe it would be better not to call attention to herself. She strolled quietly to the far end of the veranda, nearest the water, where maybe it would be cooler; there was a table with a pair of wicker rocking chairs. The far end of the veranda was dark and she had to feel her way along the railing. When she reached down to probe for a chair, her hand touched warm flesh.

"Just me," Hatch said, leaning forward until his face met a tiny strip of moonlight at the edge of the veranda overhang.

"That just about stopped my heart," Jan said breathlessly.

"Light attracts blood suckers; it's better to sit in the dark."

Jan took the chair next to Hatch. Now she could see his outline as her eyes adjusted to the dark, as well as the glint off his watch and the silver ring he wore on the ring finger of his right hand. She had noticed this right away, when he came into the Tuva bar. Her brother wore an identical ring.

"I was trying to be quiet so Linn's father wouldn't take a shot at me," Jan said.

"That's not her father," Hatch said.

"Oh?"

"The guard shift changed about an hour ago. There's a new man out there now."

"Sounds like you've been out here for a while. You know more about this part of the world than I do, but it's hard for me to fathom how Linn's father can sit out there guarding Boone's oyster farm, while his daughter, who is barely an adult, runs around up here half-naked, and sleeping with a man who must be well more than twice her age. If I were Boone I don't think I'd want that girl's father sitting outside my house with a machine gun."

"Linn looks grown to me," Hatch said. "And I am twice Kukana's age."

"I didn't mean … ."

"The Thai are a proud people, strong, moral, religious, brave."

"Well, then?"

"Linn and her father are from Bangkok, which Boone made a point of saying. Bangkok is a city, like

New York or Manila or Paris. Cities anywhere. Money corrupts. Capitalism annihilates moral values."

"A professional soldier who's a communist?" Jan teased.

"Definitely not a communist. Just a realist. And professional soldier is quite a stretch. In answer to your question, fact is, Boone has what is to people like Linn and her father a helluva lot of money. People who have none find ways to get a little. Or die. Communist or not, isn't it obvious that the fuel that feeds capitalism and makes a handful of people obscenely rich is the desire of everybody else to just survive? Don't the rich eat the poor?"

"Odd conversation we're having on the veranda of a pearl farmer's house at the far end of Thailand. But I'm curious, if you don't mind?"

"Give it a try.

"How long have you known my brother?"

"I've known Boone since we were at the JFK Spec War School at Bragg. Boone was good, but the Army wasn't his style. The military held him back. He was too smart and too independent for a career in the Army. He went out on his own about the time our team went into Laos. More than that, you'll have to ask him. Last time I saw Boone was here, in Bangkok I mean, in 1966. A long time ago.   Don't   you know all this?"

The sudden flare of a match jerked their heads toward the pier. The guard had stood and lit a cigarette, the machine gun propped over his shoulder like a worker's shovel. Still illuminated by the match, the guard turned and looked toward the veranda, then shook out the match.

"I am fifteen years younger than my brother. We had another brother between us. He was killed in a car wreck when I was ten. By that time, Boone was already in the army and I rarely saw him. In fact, I hadn't seen him for seven or eight years when he called me two weeks ago."

"You came."

"Wouldn't you?"

"I'm here."

"Can I ask you a question?"

"Another one?"

She smiled and sort of shrugged. "One of the first things I noticed when you came into the bar was your ring. Boone has an identical one. But I guess you know that. I never asked him about it, but now, seeing that you have the same one, I'm a little curious. It doesn't look like a military thing."

Hatch looked at the silver signet ring on his left hand, where a wedding band would usually be.

"Back at Bragg in 1962, there were some special operations recon teams formed."

"Boone was a part of this?"

"Yes, he was. Eventually five such teams were formed, seven men each. One of these teams was placed in a small Laotian highland village from where we ran recon patrols and performed the odd political nullification."

"Is that a cute term for what I assume were assassinations?"

Hatch nodded. "I don't know how much you know about what your brother did ... ?"

"Almost nothing. It was so long ago and we've never talked about it. I just knew he was among the first of the Green Berets after JFK authorized the special forces. I still have his first beret. It's in my flat in San Francisco."

"Those five teams went a bit beyond the Green Berets. We became what was at the time known as the Black Star Mobile Training Forces. Even within the special forces world we were known as the ghosts, or the spooks. We were essentially independent from anything that could be called the military infrastructure. We didn't wear symbols of rank or unit, we had no direct lines of accountability outside the circle of Black Star. You could chopper drop us into the middle of any jungle, anywhere in the world, day or night, and inside an hour we would know our way around."

"By we, you mean you and Boone."

Hatch nodded again. "And about forty others."

"It's hard to imagine my brother like this."

"That's one of the reasons he was good at it."

"What does this have to do with the rings you wear?"

"Early on during our training cycle, it turned out that every member of our team were Scots by ancestry. It wasn't long before men in the other teams were calling us the Scotties.

"Anyway, the rings. Boone had seven identical rings made up by a jeweler in Raleigh; paid for them with his own money. He gave each man in the team one of those rings the day we shipped out. This one," Hatch rolled the ring around his finger, and the one Boone wears, are the last two on living fingers."

They heard Boone coughing again. Twice in the past hour they had heard him moving around inside the house.

"I expected it to be worse, he'd be bald, or something like that," Hatch said.

"Did he tell you? He rejected treatments. He knows this kind of cancer is a death sentence, sooner rather than later, and he doesn't see the point in making himself sick as a dog the last weeks of his life."

"Does he have weeks?"

"I don't know. I hope so. Months would be even better. You see how weak he is, how much weight he's lost. In some ways, it's hard to see if this has effected him at all. He was always … ."

Jan lowered her chin to her chest and clutched her hands together in her lap.

Hatch stood and put his hand on Jan's shoulder.

"I'll say goodnight."

Then he disappeared back into the house.

26

Hatch awoke first, still dark, no one else about. He drank some juice, rinsed the glass and left it in the sink, then went out the kitchen door and walked around the house to the pier. The sun was well above the trees and the morning bay mist had risen to form the first layer of what later in the day would become towering, rolling stratocumulus clouds to drop a few inches of rain over the inland mountains.

Divers worked the oyster beds. A sampan skiff was tied up at the end of the pier; on the far side of the holding tank was a narrow boat, not unlike a *hang yao* – the thirty foot motorized canal boats, commonly called long-tails in Bangkok. The night guard had been replaced by a new man, who guarded with the same Chinese K-50M, as if there was only the one weapon and they passed it from guard to guard as the shift changed. Hatch made his presence known, stepping loudly onto the pier. He thought it unwise to surprise a man holding a submachine gun.

At the end of the pier, Hatch approached the guard and pantomimed that he was going for a swim. The guard waved him off and said, "Mai chai. No swim."

"Okay," Hatch said. "Ti nai?" Where?

The guard pointed across the spit of land on which the house sat and said in Thai that there was a swimming beach over there.

Around the point Hatch found a narrow, sparkling white beach, behind which tall coconut palms arched toward the water, and a young banyan tree offered shade. Hatch left his shirt over one of the banyan's lower limps and walked into the bay, which was as warm as a bath and flat as a pond in a calm. He dug in with his arms and stroked ahead with no sense of destination.

The swimming and the solitude gave him time to think, to focus his attention on what he now saw as the inexorability of his return to Indochina.

When Hatch returned to the house, Boone told him they were going to Wat Pratong, a temple a dozen miles north of Phuket City.

After removing their shoes, Hatch and Boone entered the temple and stood before the Enlightened One's gilded statue. Watching Boone standing there with his eyes focused on the complacent Buddha image, Hatch felt weighted by sadness, enough to sink him. He stopped to compose himself before speaking.

"Interesting statue," Hatch said "What happened to the rest of it?" The bottom half of the Buddha was missing.

"Somewhere in Burma there are people worshipping a pair of crossed legs and a golden butt," Boone laughed.

Hatch thought the laugh was muffled, respectful, although he had not known Boone to be particularly respectful about anything that had not clearly demonstrated being worthy of it.

"According to local legend," Boone went on, "a boy working in the fields tied his water buffalo to this strange rod sticking out of the ground. He went off for a nap and was later found dead, the buffalo was also dead. Trying to remove the buffalo from the spike, the villagers began digging around it. What they uncovered was a gold-plated Buddha, this one. They worked and worked and worked, trying to dig the thing up, but to no avail. So, I mean, what would you do? They built this temple around the statue they couldn't unearth."

"What happened to the bottom half of it?"

"So the story goes, some Burmese tried to steal it for the gold. They didn't have enough men to carry the whole thing, so they cut it in half. They were discovered coming back for the top and were killed. Which means there was no one left to say where the bottom half went."

"Interesting," Hatch said. "So instead of a reclining Buddha, somewhere in Burma there's the Wat of the golden legs."

Boone smiled. They moved aside for a group of worshippers. Boone gestured and Hatch followed him outside.

"Let's find some shade," Boone said, leading Hatch to a grove of trees at the side of the temple. Nearby, a group of local women swept and raked a stone garden with bamboo implements. A teenage boy on a moped bike showed off for his girlfriend by spraying her in a shower of pea gravel spun from his back tire. Boone sat down and leaned back against a tree trunk. Hatch squatted Asian-style next to him.

"I've lived in the East too long," Boone said, his expression placid.

"How do you mean?"

"This stuff's starting to make a little sense to me."

"Stuff?"

"All this spiritual mumbo jumbo."

"Like Buddhism?"

"The lot of it. There's not much of a barrier between these Asian spiritual philosophies. We've got them all in this neighborhood: Buddhists, Hindus, Muslims, Animists, assorted Christians, and even a few Jews. The space between Buddhism and Animism is pretty narrow here. Did you happen to notice that spirit house at the edge of my veranda?"

"I did."

"Things were happening in my house, weird things, stuff going missing, things broken, people getting sick ... ."

Hatch nodded and waited for Boone to continue.

"So I put up the spirit house, and another one at the edge of my property on the jungle side. You never can tell."

"You are right about that, my friend. You never can tell."

For more than two minutes they quietly watched the scene around Wat Pratong. Clouds were building towers in the distance to the east. It would likely rain in a couple of hours as the clouds backed up to the coast. It would not be a long or hard rain, it was still a month away to the monsoons.

"Do you ever wonder what death is like?" Boone asked after a while.

"From time to time, I suppose. It's not easy to avoid thinking about it now and then."

"What do you think?"

"I don't think I have a useful opinion. I guess I don't think there's anything that endures beyond death, for people, for anything. Even if it is a mental impossibility to imagine nothingness. Whatever nothingness is, that's what we end up with – nothing."

"I don't want to find out," Boone smiled. "I want to stay here forever with this body ... well, maybe a better body, with my friends, and lovers, and my house, and all my things; everything staying the way it is now forever."

"You don't mean that."

"Actually, I do. But for plan B, I'll take coming back. Reincarnation."

"With memories?"

"Exactly. With my memories intact."

"Me," Hatch said, "I'll take a pass on keeping the memories."

"Well, in your case ... ." Boone laughed. Then he asked, "Are you afraid of dying?"

"To a certain degree, I suppose so. Are you surprised?"

"A little."

"Maybe afraid is the wrong word, Boone. A better way to put it is, now I have something I want to live for."

"Well, scares the shit out of me, my old friend.

Does that make me less a man, you think?"

"I've never known anyone more a man. But you sure made some odd choices for somebody afraid of dying."

"So I did. As did you."

"Damn, Boone. This is some really morbid shit."

Boone let go with a belly laugh that plastered his back to the tree and squeezed his face so tight it looked like a grimace. The laughter was infectious and in a moment Hatch had tumbled to his side, laughing as hard as Boone.

Two boys and a dog stopped to watch the two strange old farangs laughing together like children.

They left the temple and walked a short distance down the road to an outdoor bar. They took a back table and ordered beers.

"How did you know how to find me?" Hatch asked, the question that had stalked them all day.

"I wanted to see you for two reasons. After getting over the shock of you being alive, that is. One for my soul, the other to honor our friendship. It's not a short story. I'm glad I'm getting the chance to tell it face to face."

27

Hatch mostly listened to Boone's monologue. The questions could wait. It took Boone a long time to say what he wanted to say, and very many bottles of beer. After a while, he began:

"I was the reason Guns was in Vientiane that day, the day your team was ambushed, the day ... ," he paused hard, as if he would stop, then continued. "When the bandits went into Toulan. But I promise you on my honor that I did not know what Guns was up to; our meeting was about something else entirely; I don't even remember what. He used me. I didn't know it at the time, but he sure as shit did. Something I am not these days very proud of. Had I known, it would never have happened. I promise you that. And when I did figure it out, I would have killed Guns had I ever seen him again. But that didn't happen. I didn't find out from Guns, anyway. It was first a rumor passing around within the community; it was many years later I figured out what actually happened, what Guns had done that day. What he allowed to happen that day.

"Guns was pretty deft at playing both sides, staying active in the league while at the same time batting on Prince Som's team. He used the meeting with me to avoid being anywhere near the ambush, an alibi, you could say, although why would he need one? It wasn't your fault, I hope that at least you understand that now. You know it would never have happened without Som's little army having the information Guns supplied to them. Until that odd happenstance when Guns showed up on your island, everybody, and that includes me, believed you were long dead. MIA/KIA."

Hatch raised his hand to stop Boone, who seemed to welcome the break.

"Why, Boone?"

"The universal why: Money. You can have no idea how rich Guns became. Not only him. There was this whole little criminal clique in the community that did pretty damn well for themselves. You remember Welch?

"Colonel Welch?"

"Now Major General Welch. Did you know his aide, Captain Whitman?"

"Of him."

"Now Congressman Whitman of North Carolina."

Boone finished his beer and gestured for two more.

"I suppose," Hatch said, "I sort of knew, at least I had the feeling that some people in our dark little world were making deals with drug lords like Prince Som. I figured they were probably using the funds to finance some of the adventures that needed to be kept out of the political processes."

"Es verdad, mi amigo. That was the community within the community. But Lieutenant Harper, Colonel Welch, and Captain Whitman, were way past that. I guess you could say they were the community within the community within the community." Boone smiled and took a long drink. "They kept the money. And believe me, Hatch, it was a shit pot full of money."

"What did our team have to do with any of that? Why was that necessary?"

"Som was moving into the south, he needed Toulan to expand his poppy production. Team Two was there and in the way. It ought to be more, I know, but that's pretty much it, Hatch."

"It wasn't just the team who died … ."

"I know. Believe me, Hatch. If that had happened to me, to someone I loved, I would have self-destructed too."

"Captain Frank Hatcher died that day, Boone."

"I know."

"A big part of him is still dead."

"That I can see. And I wish that part of your past could stay dead and buried. It would be better for you and yours."

"What does that mean?"

"How do you think I knew where to find you?"

"How did you?"

"Our little community was never very big. Once in it, you're never out ... unless you die. Guns finding you alive sent a pretty big ripple through the pond, such a big ripple that it even passed my way. There are people who want to know how much you knew about what happened in those days in Laos. There are treasures and powerful positions, the existence and continuity of which depend on what you might know ... and could reveal."

"All I know is what you just told me."

"I see that now. How ironic. On the other hand, now you do indeed have information that threatens them. Whether you had this information before, or not, doesn't matter now. All they had to do was have the question."

"What are you getting at?"

"You are not safe on your island anymore, Hatch. Also not anyone you are close enough to, who you might have talked to."

"That's the warning?"

Boone nodded.

"You're telling me Guns Harper, maybe others, would come to Tuva to kill me?"

"No doubt about it."

"What the fuck am I doing here, Boone? I should be there."

"If you aren't there, they can't get to you. That's why I brought you here. I don't have very long, and I owe you. You're here because I am leaving everything I have, and it's a damn helluva lot, my friend, to you.

You can stay here … ."

"Stop. What the fuck! I have a wife, a child. You think I'd leave them? I think this disease has gone to your brain, Boone?"

"I didn't know about them before you arrived. I assumed you were alone there."

"Well, I'm not."

"We can get them out, bring them here."

"Jesus fucking Christ, Boone! How do I know Guns isn't already on his way to Tuva, or already there?"

"I know where Guns is. I mean, I know he's still around DC. He has a house in northern Virginia. I make it my business now to know where he is and where he goes."

Hatch stood abruptly, the chair fell back and he bent over to pick it up. Boone also stood, fishing in his wallet to pay for the beers.

"You don't owe me anything, Boone. But I do need one favor."

"We can agree to disagree about that, but name your favor."

"I don't have any money."

"That's easy to fix."

"No, that's not what I mean. I want an air ticket back to Tuva, and I want it on the next flight I can get out of Bangkok."

28

As we now know, Boone Buchannan was wrong about the location of Beauregard Guns Harper. The day Boone took Hatch to Wat Pratong, Guns Harper was in an Irish Pub in the beach town of Coronado, California, sharing a pint with Bill Byron, waiting for a third man to join them.

Scotty Bates arrived at Paddy's a little late. A hangout for SEALs and other Naval Special Warfare people from the nearby amphibious base, Bates knew most of the people there; Richie, the bartender, was an old friend.

Richie saw Bates when he came in and began pulling his usual draft Guinness.

"How's it, Scotty boy," Richie said, setting the dark mug on the bar as Bates looped one leg over a stool.

"It's hanging," Bates said. He picked up the beer mug and told Richie he was meeting a couple of guys.

"Those your friends over there?" Richie cocked his head toward the two men seated at the farthest corner table, near the fireplace.

"Looks like it," Bates said, nodding to Byron and Guns, who nodded back.

Bates ordered another round for the three of them and walked over to the table.

"Scotty Bates," he introduced himself and they all shook hands.

"Bill Byron."

"Guns Harper."

"Why Guns?" Bates asked, taking a seat.

"My nick from the Black Star days in Laos. I had something of a rep with an M-60; it just stuck."

Bates looked back toward the bar to get Richie's

attention. "I got stouts coming," Bates explained.

"Good man," Byron said.

"Black Star," Bates went on. "You're the first alive and in-person dude I ever met who was in that game."

"Somebody had to do the fun stuff," Guns smiled sardonically.

After Richie went back to the bar, after they watched the brown foam diminish into the black beer, they raised their glasses. "To revenge," Bill Byron toasted.

"To revenge," Guns repeated.

"I'm not one for beating around the bush," Byron began. "If you want to come along on our little soiree, then besides the three of us sitting here, there's one more, Jim Kenyon. Maybe you know him?"

Bates shook his head. "Don't think I've had the pleasure."

"It doesn't matter. He's independent now. But maybe you remember that thing in Little Creek a few years back?"

"The toilet bowl event?"

Byron nodded. "Jim was one of them. So he *decided* to retire early and start working for a living."

"Been there, done that."

"Ain't we all," Byron agreed. "Here's the deal," he continued. "I'm paying expenses and fringes. Plus, you and Jim will get ten grand each; half before, half after."

"What's the time frame?"

"A week, tops."

"Whew. Lot of time for a little money."

"But a lot of fun. Here's the dilemma. The best way to get to this place with the equipment we need is by boat, a private boat. We can't move these items by commercial airliner, of course. We'll fly into Oz, round up the equipment, and then charter a flight up to Tahiti."

"The ten grand carved in stone?" Bates asked.

"That's what it pays, man. You can take it or leave it. I'm not a Tijuana street hustler doing a little bargaining."

"Just checking. What's the mission?" Bates asked.

"It's personal and I can afford it. But all will be revealed on a need to know."

"I'm in. Sounds like fun. But now if you gentlemen will excuse me, I'm going to go float a boat." Scotty Bates got up and headed for the toilet.

"You sure about this guy?" Guns asked Byron.

"What about you?"

"Well, he does seem a bit ragged around the edges, but hey, we're not going to marry him."

Byron laughed out loud and held up his empty glass to get Richie's attention.

"Okay. We fly to Sydney on Saturday." Guns said.

They clunked their beer mugs and drained them dramatically.

That night from a room in the Hotel Del Coronado, Guns Harper placed a call to a memorized number in Prospect Hill, Virginia. When the connection was completed, Guns said simply: "General? Harper."

"Go," came the reply.

"Saturday, to Sydney, then Papeete."

"This time he *will* be dead."

"He was dead. They were all dead."

"So you say, and so you've said before."

"Yes sir. All I had to go on was what Som's men told me. I didn't have eyes on it, you know."

"You were responsible."

"Yes sir. You've got my word. If I'm not dead, Captain Hatcher will be."

"I'm not going to take your word for it this time, Lieutenant. And I'll take that deal. If he's alive, you better not be."

"I understand."

"And you better be the only one of you four little

commandoes who leaves that fucking rock alive."

"I know. I will be."

General Welch hung up.

Guns Harper replaced the receiver, waited ten seconds, then lifted it again and called for room service to bring up a bottle of Glenlivet, a bucket of ice, and a tall glass.

29

Bill Byron sat at the forward edge of the cabin top of the motor yacht *Fortune's Lady* with an M-16 across his lap, the lumbering rumble of the twin diesel engines tingling through the soles of his bare feet. Scotty Bates lay at the end of the foredeck with a sack of empty cans and bottles beside him. Every once in a while, without warning, Bates threw one of the cans high into the air. Byron swung the rifle up and fired a burst that shredded the can. The rifle fire sounded like close thunder.

Below deck, Guns Harper lay on the settee in a sweat, trying to nap, unable to escape the stupid noise of the M-16. At least below he didn't have to watch Bill Byron's Annie Oakley show. Between random bursts of automatic rifle fire, Guns tried to concentrate on a paperback novel about a supertanker running down a sailing yacht; maybe not the best reading choice, considering.

Jim Kenyon, short, dark, bull-like, sat on the flying bridge, cleaning an H & K MP5 with an oily rag. He was at the wheel, but since the gleaming white motor yacht was on autopilot, there wasn't much to watch.

A solitary porpoise appeared off the port bow, racing in the wake. The porpoise eyed the boat, then darted to the other side. Its movements attracted Bates's attention and he leaned over to throw a bottle at it, missing by a good five meters. The porpoise, undaunted, made a complete circuit around the long hull, then raced along near the port quarter.

Byron flicked his M-16 to full automatic and went to the port rail. The porpoise lazed along with one eye gazing up curiously at the two men above. Bill lowered the barrel and fired off half a clip. The water exploded in blood, flesh, and foam, pieces of the porpoise churning in the blood-slick sea and spreading outward from the hull like a stain.

Bates leaned over and looked down. "Good shooting," he said sarcastically. "You can hit a large stationary object twenty-five feet away with a fucking M-16."

A thin, black powder haze hung in the air. Byron leaned back against the front of the main cabin and propped the rifle upright against his hip.

Guns, drawn up by the roar of the rifle on auto, stuck his head through the hatchway and said, "What the fuck was that all about?"

"Billy boy here just killed Flipper," Bates answered.

Jim Kenyon shook his head, leaned over the top and shouted above the engine noise, "You fuckers are crazy."

Guns looked over the side and saw the blood patch receding in the wake.

"The blood ought to bring around some sharks," Bill said. "How about you bring up a fresh clip?" he asked Guns.

"I've got a better idea. Why don't we put away our toys, crank up the speed a bit, and get the fuck on our way."

"We'll need the fuel … which I have already told your ass about a hundred times. So stop bellyaching and get me two fresh clips."

"Get 'em your own fucking self," Guns replied. His head disappeared back into the cabin.

"Here sharky, sharky, sharky," Bill called out, standing up and looking over the side.

Guns picked up his book. He was thinking how he had come damn close to killing Bill Byron when they were stranded on the atoll, and wishing he had. Byron was the epitome of a pure asshole. The guy just didn't know how to keep his mouth shut, his ego was oceanic. But then, Bill was paying for all this – the weapons, the boat, the air tickets, all of it. Killing him later would be good enough.

There was no moon. Thick, black clouds obscured the stars. The ocean was calm, the wind still. Jim Kenyon brought the M/V Fortune's Lady as near to the reef as possible, without damaging her or betraying her presence to anyone on the island.

Bill Byron, attracted by the flare of a match, crossed the cockpit and knocked the cigarette from the lips of the man preparing to launch the Avon rubber boat over the stern swim step.

"Damn it, Scotty! See if you can go without a fag for another hour," Byron said angrily.

"Who's gonna be awake on that rock at four in the morning," Bates responded, although it was evident in his tone that he was embarrassed being caught in such an unmilitary act.

"I said no lights, and I mean no lights." Byron's tone carried his authority, the power of his wallet."

"Won't happen again, Billy boy."

Byron gave Bates a pat on the back, then moved along the rail forward.

"No lights, equipment check, launch in three," Guns said, running through a mental checklist of his equipment, relishing the arrival of his old friend – adrenalin. He had been in positions like this so often that it had the familiarity of a walk in the park, even if that life was decades ago.

Jim Kenyon, in charge of leading them over the reef and to shore in the Avon, rehearsed the route. They were not able to take the power boat through the single reef passage and still maintain the element of surprise. After studying the charts, Jim figured that at high tide they could safely pass over the coral reef at a point just beyond the place called Kaiwi Point, which was also supposed to be the location of one of their targets.

One by one the men descended the boarding ladder into the Avon. Kenyon and Bates took up paddles on the left, Byron and Harper on the right. With the tide peaking, they glided easily over the ragged coral heads and entered the lagoon where it narrowed at the point. The only noise came from the slight splash of their paddles. It was so quiet they could easily hear water lapping languidly onto the beach ahead.

They didn't bother hiding the Avon after beaching it. Dawn would reveal the yacht anchored offshore anyway. But by that time, if they kept to Bill's meticulous schedule, the power generating station would be blown and hiding their presence would by then be moot.

Bill had it all figured. In the predawn darkness, with no means of communicating off the island, the natives would panic, and during that chaos the raid could be carried out swiftly; the raiders would be away with their captives before sunrise.

The four men crouched on the beach, hardly fifty meters from Hatch's old shack, and listened to Byron's final check. First, they would enter the shack just ahead, kill the man in it, then Bates and Kenyon would take the C-4 plastique explosive and work their way past the pier, along the edge of the town, to the generator building fifty meters beyond the government house. Byron and Harper would take the upper road past the church to the Makani house. They clasped hands and headed out.

Bates and Kenyon took up positions on either side of the shack, at the open windows, while Byron and Guns Harper went through the door.

It was empty.

"So, where the fuck is your friend?" Byron asked.

Guns shrugged. Now Hatch could be anywhere, he could even already be dead. Maybe he died from the beating they gave him.

"Maybe we already killed him," Byron supposed.

"That's what I'm thinking, too. We'll find out when we get the others."

Bates and Kenyon had expected to encounter no one at that hour, and were surprised to see two old fishermen walking toward the pier carrying poles and a bucket.

"What the hell are those two old fuckers doing?" Bates wondered.

"Looks like they're going fishing," Kenyon said.

"At four in the fucking morning?"

"They haven't seen us. Let them pass, then we can get on our merry way."

"What if they did? I say we take them out now."

"Oh, let 'em be," Kenyon told Bates.

But Bates was already approaching the two men from the rear.

"Do what you like, but I'm got a mission to blow that generator exactly on schedule, and that's what I'm going to do."

"Go on. I'll catch up."

Bates withdrew his Randall knife from the sheath taped to the webbing across his chest and moved silently along the edge of the pier. The two old men with their backs to the intruder never heard him coming. He sliced through Pono's windpipe with a single, quick motion. Before Kaavanuii could make a sound, the blade slipped under the old man's rib cage and into his heart. He pushed their bodies into the water, then jogged back to catch up with Jim Kenyon.

"Guess you were just in the mood to kill something," Kenyon said sarcastically.

"One less thing to worry about on our way back," Bates answered.

Guns Harper checked his watch. It was already a minute passed zero-four-fifteen. He was in position behind the Makani house. He was thinking that this thing could go fucking belly up really fast. He checked his watch again. Blowing the generator was now two minutes late.

Guns was here for only one reason, to kill Captain Franklin Jefferson Hatcher, if he wasn't already dead, and he had to get it done before the whole clusterfuck revenge scheme crumbled with the ineptness of the half-stoned commando-playing dopers he needed to use. He did smile at the thought of what Byron and the other two were going to do when they got back to the Avon and found it gone, along with the Fortune's Lady, and them trapped on this rock with a whole bunch of really pissed off natives. Guns had personal experience with what that meant.

Then the sky over the treetops to the southwest exploded in a flash of thunder and brilliant yellow light.

Moments after the explosion, Mr. Jolly ran from his apartment in the government house wearing only a bathrobe and, for unknown reasons, carrying his umbrella. He knew immediately from proximity that the explosion came from the generating station. He raced down the street with the bottom of his bathrobe flapping behind him.

The raging fire brightened the sky. Mr. Jolly ran around the corner of the empty open market stalls, and directly into two men wearing military clothes running toward him.

Mr. Jolly was knocked flat on his back before realizing that his legs had been shattered by bullets from the guns those men carried. He was astonished. First the stinging slaps in his legs, then finding himself flat on his back on Alii Street. He looked up at the flecks of ash floating in the air high above, like gray Tasmanian snow. He had been shot. Those men had shot him. It was the most horrible pain he had ever felt.

His eyes were closed and he did not see the two men run by him, but he heard their voices.

"Why did you fucking have to shoot him? Now they know where we are. Idiot."

"Go fuck yourself, Jim-bo. I thought that was a gun."

"Jesus X, dude. It's a fucking umbrella!"

The explosion jolted Kukana from her sleep. She sat up in bed and reached for Hatch, but he was already at the window.

"What is it?" she asked.

Hatch turned back toward her. "I don't know. An explosion somewhere." He was already pulling on his pants and reaching for his shirt. He did know. Guns Harper had arrived.

Kukana rolled off the bed and padded behind him in bare feet. Even before reaching the window she could see the flickering fire glowing against the white walls of the bedroom.

"I think it's the generator building," Hatch said. "Try the lights."

Kukana turned the light switch and nothing happened. "It's not working," she said.

"I'm going down there. I want you to go to your father's house."

The distant but distinct sound of automatic rifle fire stopped him suddenly.

"What was that?" Kukana asked, going to look out the window.

"Stay away from the window," Hatch cried, grabbing her arm and jerking her back.

Hatch knew exactly what it was, no matter how unbelievable such a sound on Tuva.

"Do what I tell you. Now! I want you to take Emma and go to your father's house, and stay there. Don't leave until I come to get you, no matter what. Do you understand?"

"Maybe I can help at the fire."

"No! Don't argue. I mean it, Kukana."

"The way you talk makes me afraid."

"Don't be afraid. I just don't want to take any chance you could be hurt. Now get Emma and do what I tell you."

"Tell Kamuela I'll meet him at the generator building," Hatch shouted back to her, as Kukana, with Emma in her arms, ran up the hill.

Hatch went to his office and got his shotgun.

I also knew what it was. When Hatch returned from Thailand just eight days before, he asked that Mr. Jolly, Kamuela and Tioni, and I, meet at his house, where he told us the whole story; everything, from even before he joined the Army, through his recent visit with his friend, the brother of the woman who came for him.

We considered many options, but in the end we understood there was little we could do but wait. Hatch could not predict what would happen, when it would happen, and how many people, criminals, would come for him. He also couldn't say if it was only him, or if they would be after others, especially others close to him – Kukana, her family.

There were not very many weapons on Tuva. Hatch's shotgun; Kamuela owned a shotgun, a bolt-action hunting rifle, and an antique US Army .45 automatic pistol, for which he had a box of twenty very old cartridges. The rest would be in the category of sharp tools of one sort or another, essentially banana machetes. We decided … rather, Hatch decided, that Kamuela would keep his shotgun, Tioni would take the hunting rifle, and I would get the pistol. Mr. Jolly announced that he had no interest in touching any kind of gun.

I had fired pistols in the long ago past, and knew how to load the magazine. But I was quite doubtful if the cartridges were still viable. Regardless, when the blast woke me, the first thing I did was insert the clip into the pistol, then dressed and ran toward the generator station.

30

Kukana found the front door wide open. She called out for her father but there was no answer. She went into the hall and the only light came from the far end, from the partially open kitchen door. She called out Twilla's name, and again no answer. She wondered, had they run to the fire so quickly that they left open the front door? She hurried toward the kitchen.

When she pushed open the door, a hand grabbed her wrist and jerked her forward so forcefully that she fell face down and Emma spilled out of her arms. As she rolled over and started to get up, a man put his foot on her chest, pointing a gun at her face.

"Hi, honey," he said.

Emma screamed.

It was him. She closed her eyes tight and pleaded, "No, oh please, no." Then she opened her eyes, hoping the nightmare was over.

"I'm still here," Bill Byron said, a leering smile on his face. "Shut that fucking kid up."

Kukana pushed herself away from his foot and began crawling toward her baby, now at the opposite side of the room. She bumped into something that stopped her, a bare leg. It was Twilla Pihi, a black hole like an open bruise in her forehead, her eyes open and staring emptily at the ceiling. A widening pool of dark blood spread out from behind Twilla's head.

Kukana screamed and backed away. Then she saw her father.

Kamuela was in a chair in the corner by the sink, his arms tied behind his back and his feet wrapped in duct tape. There was a rag stuffed into his mouth. Another man held the barrel of a rifle pointed at her father's head.

"Papa," Kukana cried.

Kamuela shook his head and moved his eyes in some signal to Kukana that she did not understand.

"What are you doing to us? Why have you killed Twilla? Oh God, why did you do that to her?"

"Just rig the bitch and let's boogie," Guns said.

"My baby!" Kukana cried.

Bill Byron shoved the baby across the floor with his foot. "God, I can't stand that fucking squalling."

Kamuela lurched his chair sideways into Guns Harper, who jammed the butt of his rifle hard into Kamuela's ribs.

Kukana tried to crawl to Emma, but Bill kicked her hands out from under her.

Guns removed a package from a satchel hanging over his shoulder.

"Just don't forget Hatch," Guns said.

Hearing her husband's name, Kukana said, "He will find you; he will make you cry and beg for mercy; then he will kill you forever."

Byron laughed, then reached down and pulled Kukana to her feet.

"Get the old man up," he told Guns. "Give me the Charlie Four."

Guns handed the package of C-4 explosive to Byron, then he cut through the duct tape binding Kamuela's legs.

Bill unwrapped the paper cover and rolled the clay-like lump into a pencil lead thin tube.

"If either one of them moves, kill the girl," he told Guns. "Do you understand what I said?" he asked Kamuela. "She's nothing to him. He will blow a hole in her pretty little head just like the one he blew in her head," he nodded toward Twilla's body.

Byron wrapped the C-4 tube like a necklace around Kukana's neck and connected the wires of a blasting cap to a pair of longer wires leading to a small hand crank detonator. He told Kukana to stop crying, but she couldn't. Emma howled.

"Do you know what this is?" Byron asked

Kamuela. "If I turn his handle just a little bit, we make a big boom-boom. Capisce? There won't be enough left of your pretty little daughter's head to make hors d'oeuvres for a dog. Are you clear on that, old man?"

Kamuela nodded, his eyes blazing. Kukana reached up toward the explosive necklace around her neck, but Byron slapped it away.

"Now you don't want to go playing with that, my darling girl. At least not while I'm this close." He laughed.

"Where is Hatch?" Guns asked Kukana, knowing now that he was alive.

She shook her head. Her throat was so dry she couldn't speak.

"We've got what we came for," Byron said. "Let's boogie."

"You got what you came for. I still have unfinished business. That's what I came for."

"I think we can count on that fucker finding us."

"Just so long as you know, I'm not leaving until I see that man dead."

"I've certainly got no problem with that."

Guns shoved Kamuela ahead with the barrel of the M-16 hard against his back. Byron pushed Kukana ahead of him and let the slack go out of the detonator wire, staying five meters behind her. "Now try not to fall down, honey."

Finally Kukana urged her voice to work. She said, "Hatch is my husband and she is his baby. He is going to kill you more slowly than a jungle rat; you will suffer so much, you will pray for death. He can do this. I promise."

"His baby?" Byron said to Guns. "Now there's a little bonus for you." Then he said to Kukana, "If you give me any trouble, your baby will be dog food, too."

"Stop this crap about the baby," Guns said, caught in an uncomfortable memory. They could still hear Emma screaming inside the house, where she lay abandoned on the floor beside the body of Twilla Pihi.

The procession left the Makani house and headed down the path around the banana grove, passed the back of the church, and toward town in the direction of Kaiwi Point.

Hatch ran into the main street, surprised to find it empty. People had probably rushed to the fire. He crossed between two houses and turned toward the Government House. It grew lighter by the minute as the sun crept closer to surmounting the peak of Kilohana.

The two men standing between Mr. Lee's Emporium and a storage building saw Hatch come into the street. They were waiting for Bill Byron and Guns Harper to join up with them before heading back to the Avon. They were to provide cover for the retreat.

"That guy look like a native to you?" Kenyon whispered.

"I bet he's the one Guns wants."

"He's armed. You see that?"

"That's gotta be Guns' guy."

"We can't let him go. Guns'll shit."

"Just wound him, then."

Jim Kenyon clicked the safety off and chambered the first round, as he moved around the corner of the storage shed, leading with the barrel of his M-16.

At the snap-click of the bolt, Hatch, reacting on pure instinct, rolled to one side and hit the ground, bringing up the shotgun at the same time. He fired once, then quickly pumped up another shell and fired again. Then he rolled a few feet to the side and stopped behind the trunk of a palm.

Jim Kenyon squeezed off one round at the same moment the blast of double-0 buckshot ripped into his chest, knocking him backward like the slap of a giant fist. Kenyon's only bullet tore through the trunk of the palm above Hatch's head.

Hatch rolled out, jumped to his feet, and raced

across the street to one of the nail barrels in front of Mr. Lee's, guessing that the other man would go around back of the store to come up behind him.

Scotty Bates stepped over Kenyon's body without needing to see if he was dead. Going to full auto, he fired a burst into the wall of Mr. Lee's and into the trunk of the tree Hatch was no longer behind. Then he ducked back into the alleyway and ran toward the back, stumbling straight into a group of ten men, including myself, who had raced toward the sound of gunfire.

Komo Niu grabbed Bates's weapon and jerked it out of his hands before he could insert a fresh clip, and by then the rest of us were all over him. I tried to shoot him, but, as I suspected, the gun jammed. The man we now know as Scotty Bates was beaten to death with clubs, shovels, and his own rifle butt.

Byron and Harper and their two hostages heard the gunfire. "Shotgun," Guns said. "Maybe the only thing you're going to have to check is a body," Byron noted hopefully, having what he wanted tied to the detonator in his hand.

They left the main path and took the upper street toward the far end of town. Kukana walked in front, tethered to the detonator wire. Guns stayed at the rear, his rifle pointed at Kamuela, whose hands remained tied behind his back, the gag still in his mouth.

The sun was just up, although full light had not yet penetrated the thick canopy of trees along the leeward valley slope. They picked up the pace now, continuing to move toward the beach at Kaiwi Point, where they left the Avon. While they were urgent, there was no panic. They had decades of experience in dangerous situations, and this was nothing, especially having the trump card connected to the end of the wire.

We found Hatch at the corner of Mr. Lee's, and in moments the street filled with Tuvans.

Komo Niu and I reached Hatch first. "We killed

one man," Komo said breathlessly. I noticed the shotgun in Hatch's hands. "You killed that one?" I supposed, indicating the dead man in the street behind Hatch. "Are there more?"

"At least one more, that's certain. More, I suspect. Where's Kamuela?"

"He's not with us. I didn't see him; he wasn't at the fire."

Another, smaller, group of men ran up the street from the direction of the pier. Mr. Lee grabbed Hatch's arm and shrieked words in Chinese. When Hatch shook him, Mr. Lee changed to English. "Oh me, oh me. We see body from Kaavanuii, all dead, pau, gone."

Makavaana approached and pushed Mr. Lee aside. "Pono, too. Pau. Ma'ke."

"Where's Kukana?" I asked Hatch.

"I sent her to her father's house. Shit!"

Hatch broke away from the crowd and ran toward the path up the slope to the Makani house. I, and some others, ran after him. Halfway up the hill, we encountered Tioni coming down.

"She is dead, Hatch. She is dead."

You could actually see Hatch feel the horror, his face dying before our eyes. He grabbed Tioni's shoulders. "Who is dead? Tell me."

"Twilla is dead," Tioni answered, his voice cracking. "She is shot right here," he pointed to his forehead.

"Kukana?"

"No Kukana. No Papa. Just Emma is there."

"Is she all right?"

"She is very angry, but yes, she is not hurt. Jenny stays with her."

"Did you search the whole house, the garden?"

"They are gone, Hatch. Everybody gone except Twilla and baby Emma."

"These men," Hatch referred to our group, "say Kamuela was not at the fire. That means he, and probably Kukana, must have been taken by whoever killed Twilla."

"Where do we go, Hatch?" Tioni begged for direction.

"We go find them," Komo said.

"Divide into smaller groups," Hatch said. "We can cover more ground faster. Look, they had to have come here on a boat."

"There is no boat in the bay," Komo said.

"Well, there's a boat somewhere. We have to find it, and there we'll find them. Tioni, take ten men and search every building in town. Don and I will take the copra trail out to Kaiwi Point. A boat might anchor off the point and they could use a dinghy to come into the beach. Be careful. We don't know how many there are and what weapons they have. Now go!"

Byron and Guns and their captives came into the clearing beside Hatch's old beach shack. Byron sat Kukana on the porch step and handed the detonator to Guns.

"What's next in your little clusterfuck?" Guns asked.

"We wait."

"How much you want to bet Bates and Kenyon won't be showing up?"

"You're probably right, because they would have caught up by now. We're not waiting for them. But we'll wait a few more minutes for the third member of our little party."

"That's good, because I'm not going anywhere until I see him dead."

"He'll be here. This is his house. This is his wife. And we left a trail a moron could follow. On the other hand, I could be satisfied with these two. Although I would like to get all of them at once."

"I'm not going until Hatch is dead, certain dead."

"Go, stay, whatever. But I'm taking at least these two back out to the boat in ten minutes."

"Never trust a man blinded by revenge."

"Whatever that means."

"It means I'm not going to die here for your revenge. This is way more important than that."

"And you mean?" Byron said, lighting a cigarette.

Hatch knew we were following their trail. The morning light revealed bits of white cloth stuck to thorny bushes. He knew the cloth came from Kukana's night shirt. He told me we had to pick up the pace.

We were on the direct path to Kaiwi Point. Hatch figured the raiders must have landed a dinghy on the beach there, probably near his shack. No other place, except Tuva Bay, was that easily accessible through the reef, yet still hidden from town.

"Faster," Hatch urged. He was already running and I tried to keep up. But I was soon quite a ways behind. Hatch stopped and told me that he knew they must have come ashore at Kaiwi Point, and I should run back to town and alert the others. "Tell them to come to Kaiwi Point, to my old house. Tell Tioni and his men to head out from the bay in their boats, and come around the point by sea. There has to be a boat there."

That's what I did.

31

Guns felt a creeping exhaustion and chastised himself for having gotten so wired that he didn't sleep much last night. He just wanted this mess over with. It was a botched up bitch from the start. It was supposed to be fast and easy. He'd ice Captain Hatcher, then have a little R & R in Tahiti. Instead, here he was sitting in front of a derelict shack, waiting for a few hundred natives to show up and wax his ass. Wasn't this how Captain Cook bought it in Hawaii?

Distracted, antsy, waiting for something to happen, Guns looked at Kukana. She sat on the top step of the busted old porch with her head buried in folded arms over her knees. She reminded him of another young girl a long time ago, Captain Hatcher's girl in Toulan … what was her name? They could be sisters. Somehow Hatch had obviously survived that ambush and ended up on this goddamn rock in the middle of nowhere. Guns knew that nothing would stop Hatch from coming after this girl. He just had to wait. If Byron tried to leave before that, it would be the last move he ever made.

Bill Byron laughed out loud and Guns turned to see what caused it. Bill was taunting Kamuela with a cigarette ember, touching it to the skin of his chest as the giant old man sat without reacting except to squint his eyes.

"Stop it!" Kukana yelled and started to stand.

Guns grabbed her shoulder and pushed her back down. "Stay put," he warned, showing her the detonator in his hand. "I don't think your daddy wants to stuff your pieces into a coffee can for burying."

Byron flipped the cigarette into the sand and walked back to Kukana. "Keep an eye on pops," he told Guns.

Guns handed Byron the detonator and walked over to a stump next to Kamuela and sat down. Kamuela turned his head away.

"I take it you don't like me much," Guns joked.

Byron grabbed a handful of Kukana's hair and pulled her head back so she had to look at him. Kukana closed her eyes and Bill jerked her hair again. "Look at me!" Kukana opened her eyes defiantly. "That's better." Bill pulled her face down toward his crotch. "How about a quick little blow job, darling? If you can get me off in two minutes I might let you live." Kukana whimpered and closed her eyes tight.

Kamuela lunged at Byron, but fell forward when Guns stuck out his leg and tripped him. Guns planted one foot on the back of Kamuela's neck and held him down.

"Oh, just leave the girl alone," Guns said. "I mean, shit, why make this more difficult?"

"Don't be jealous, man. You can be next."

"Lay off. That's all I'm saying. If you're smart you'll be keeping your attention on her husband. That's what we need to be doing here."

"Yeah, for five more minutes."

Hatch reached the shack and crouched in the tall grass where the trail opened up to the beach. He heard the last exchange between the two men, and saw the coil around Kukana's neck. He knew what it had to be. He recognized the Hard Wind's skipper, and that surprised him. But seeing Guns Harper there, Hatch knew what this was about. Boone was right.

Hidden at the edge of the jungle, Hatch crept toward the shoreline. He could see the Avon now, and the motor yacht anchored outside the reef.

The blond man held a detonator switch, the wire leading to the coil of what was probably C-4 around Kukana's neck. Guns held a rifle inches away from Kamuela's head. With only a shotgun he couldn't get both men close enough together for one of them to either shoot or flip the switch. He should have taken the H&K MP5 from one of the dead men.

Something about this didn't make sense. If that was C-4, there was enough around Kukana's neck to kill everybody within a twenty-five-foot radius. Killing her would be suicide. Maybe it was a bluff? Either way, he didn't want Guns Harper dead, at least not yet.

Hatch pushed through to the edge of the high grass and used his shotgun barrel to open a clearer line of sight.

"Not planning to leave without me, were you?" Hatch called out.

Byron ducked behind a porch pillar and Guns jerked Kamuela around as a body shield. Kukana cried out her husband's name.

"Let's don't anybody get stupid," Hatch said. "You don't shoot me, I won't shoot you."

"Your lady's wired to Charlie Four, man. Shoot anybody and she's fish bait."

"I can see that. What is this, a suicide mission? Don't you need a longer det cord?"

Byron laughed, but he knew Hatch had exposed his bluff, and he was right. If he blew up the girl, he blew up himself with her.

"I'm willing to try if you're willing to spend the rest of your life trying to separate my bits and pieces from her bits and pieces," Byron said.

"You can leave my pieces out of this," Guns said.

"They want to hurt you," Kukana called out.

"Just sit still and don't do anything," Hatch answered. "I'm okay, baby."

"This is just too, too sweet," Bill Byron said, still hiding behind the porch pillar.

Scanning the grass for evidence of Hatch's location, Guns called out, "Guess you recognize me, Captain?"

"Lieutenant Beauregard Harper. You're getting around pretty good for a dead man."

"I could say the same."

"You know what, Guns? I never had a clue what happened there. Not until now. Is that why you're here? You stupid fuck, freaking out over something I didn't know shit about?"

Hatch stalled, trying to figure out his next move.

"Maybe you did, maybe you didn't. But you had a little visit with Buffalo Boone, so it's likely you know more than enough. Now, anyway."

"Well la-de-da," Byron said, "Let me get a kettle on and we can all sit down for a spot of tea and do a little catching up, do us some jaw-boning about the good old days. But pardon me if I'd just as soon deal with the dilemma we got here."

"There doesn't have to be any dilemma," Hatch said. "If you let the girl and her father go, I guarantee you safe passage away from here."

Byron laughed out loud. "Now why would I do that? I've got right here all the guarantee I need." He pulled on the cord attached to Kukana's neck.

"What is that shit? Modeling clay? You don't appear to be the suicidal type to me."

Byron laughed again. Hatch was right, but was he willing to see his girl blown to bits just so he could take him out? Doubling down, he put the barrel of his rifle tight against Kukana's head.

"Mexican standoff," he said.

Guns shoved Kamuela to his knees and put his rifle barrel against the back of Kamuela's head. "You know I can blow his head off before you take a shot, especially with that old scattergun."

"And you know you're a dead man before your finger comes off the trigger," Hatch said.

"So, Captain," Guns said. "Is it worth getting your little family unit killed just so you can get some payback on me for Laos?"

Hatch wasn't close enough for accuracy with a shotgun, and both men had automatic rifles. He also knew that both Kamuela and Kukana would be dead even if he manage to drop the two men. "Isn't this really about me?" Hatch said. "I'm the one you want, and here I am. Let's make a deal where we all get something. Let the girl go and I come out. Me for the girl."

"No fucking deal," Byron answered. We keep the girl and we keep the old man. You, I'd just as soon shoot your ass here and now and be done with it. But for these two, I got special plans."

"I guess that's your answer, Captain."

Hatch realized that half the town ought to be descending on the beach soon, and when that happened he would no longer be able to control what happened in the chaos. If anything happened to Kukana, he would just as soon be dead.

"I suppose I could ask for you word ... never mind. Hold your fire. I'm coming out."

"No," Kukana cried. "They want to kill you."

"I know that, honey." Hatch stood, exposing his position. He tossed the shotgun out in front of him, then raised his arms and stepped out from the tall grass.

"The knife," Guns said.

Hatch reached behind his back and pulled the K-bar from its sheath. He threw it over his head into the grass.

"You poor sucker," Guns smiled. "Women always were your downfall, man. Just like that slope chick in Toulan ... what was her name?"

"You know what, Guns? I have just about enough hate that you could empty a clip into me and I'd still have enough steam to rip your head off."

"Ooo, nasty, nasty," Guns mocked.

"Enough of the fun chat," Byron said." The man's stalling. Is it reasonable to assume that our two companions will not be joining us?'

"Yep. They're as dead as you're soon to be."

"Well, then I suggest we be on our merry way."

Byron pulled Kukana up by her arm. Guns

prodded Kamuela forward with his rifle.

When they reached the Avon, Kamuela was untied and his gag removed. He and Hatch were given paddles. Bill sat in the rear with his rifle barrel tight against Kukana's head. Guns in front of them. They paddled quickly across the quiet, flat lagoon, and skimmed over the reef on a falling tide.

"Tell me something," Hatch asked Guns without trying around to look at him.

"Shoot, Captain."

"Just confirm the sequence for me. It can't make any difference now. I just want to know why the team was set up and ambushed? What was so important? I mean, you're right, I know what Boone said. I would also like to know how you could allow what those animals did in Toulan? How about satisfying my curiosity before killing me."

"I thought you were dead all this time. I've got a few questions for you, too."

"Why don't you boys have old home week some other time," Byron interrupted.

"Go fuck yourself," Guns said. "This is him and me."

"Don't push your luck, cowboy."

"I could say the same."

"How did you get involved with the Pathet Lao? Hatch brought Guns back to the subject.

"Is that what you thought? You thought those were PL's? What the hell would I be doing with a bunch of Commies?"

"Well ... ?"

"It was Prince Phoun Som."

"Yeah, that's what Boone told me. It's the kind of thing criminals do, not soldiers."

"It wasn't about politics or any such shit, Hatch. It was money. Just money. And the money was flat-fucking astounding! Some brass had a political agenda dealing with the Prince, but not me, brother."

"What bothers me most is that I didn't know from

227

the start that you were worth less than a steaming pile
of pig shit."

Guns laughed.

"Tell me, Hatch. You really didn't have a clue?
Not until Boone told you his story? By the way,
Buffalo Boone has sloughed off this mortal
situtation."

"Boone died?"

"Boone, and everybody around him."

"Was his sister still there?"

"I'm afraid she was. A bit of a waste. Pretty girl."

"I don't know how yet, but I am going to kill you,
Guns."

Guns laughed out loud and slapped his thigh.

The yacht rocked bow to stern in the oncoming
swells, tugging at her anchor on the rise. She was only
a short distance ahead now. Hatch sensed that
Kamuela was about to make a move; he nudged his
father-in-law's arm with his elbow, shaking his head.

Hatch and Kamuela faced forward and did not see
that Bill's hand was up Kukana's tee-shirt. Kukana's
eyes were squeezed tightly closed, tears wet her
cheeks.

"Som couldn't use Toulan until you guys were
gone," Guns continued. "That's all."

"You guys? It was us, Guns. We were all
brothers."

"Sure, brothers bold and true. My brothers are all
in my bank account."

Hatch squeezed his paddle so hard he could leave
fingerprints.

"Suan, Sisana, Mai ... the baby. You did that for
money, Guns?"

"Hey now, that wasn't any of my doing. I ain't a
saint among men, but come on. I would have stopped
that. That's just how the Prince makes examples.
Slopes do that kind of shit all the time. They picked
those three because they knew they were fucking
Americans. I won't take the rap for that kind of shit."

Hatch's paddle came out of the water and swung hard to the rear, catching the side of Guns' head before he could raise the rifle from his lap. The crack sounded like a plank splitting. Blood quickly bubbled from a gash above his ear.

"Goddamn it, you motherfucker!" Bill Byron screamed, jerking his hand from under Kukana's shirt. "I'll blow her fucking head off right here, right now." He poked at the side of Kukana's head with the rifle barrel.

"Calm down," Hatch said. "I'm finished."

"Fucking-A straight you're finished. You and Pops move up to the bow. If you even blink in my direction, I'll blow a hole through her skull you could put your arm through."

The Avon had reached the boat at the aft swim step.

Guns held the side of his head with one hand, pointing his rifle at Hatch's head with the other.

"Guess I didn't hit him hard enough," Hatch whispered to Kamuela.

Guns was still dazed. Byron ordered Kamuela to secure the Avon to the boarding ladder rail.

Guns looked at the blood on his hand and said, "You are going to die in a sorry ass way, Hatch. I was going to make it quick and neat, but now, you son of a bitch, it's going to be slow and messy."

"You get aboard first," Byron told Guns. Then I'll send our boys up."

"I'm all right," Guns said. "It's this fucker who isn't." He kicked the back of Hatch's head as he climbed out of the dinghy and onto the swim step.

Kukana cried out and started to move, but Hatch shook his head and told her to be still.

When Guns was on deck with his rifle ready, Bill ordered the others up the boarding ladder. Kamuela first, then Hatch, followed by Kukana, who was still attached to the det cord.

"Remember, boys, if you try anything at all that I

don't like, I pull her chain and let the pieces fall where they may."

"Let's get them locked up," Guns said when they were all in the cockpit.

"Got yourself a little headache, Beauregard?" Hatch teased.

"Enjoy your last few minutes on this planet, dude. Because you are about to run out of lives all at once."

The three prisoners were taken below, to the forward cabin, which Byron had already prepared to hold them securely. After Hatch and Kamuela were inside the cabin, Byron removed the C-4 collar from Kukana's neck and put in on the chart table with the detonator box.

"Didn't think I was going to leave you alone with the Charlie-Four, did you?"

Then he shoved Kukana into the cabin and closed and locked the louvered door.

32

Kukana dropped to her knees beside Hatch and threw her arms around his legs.

"Are you hurt?" Hatch asked.

Kukana shook her head, now sobbing.

"I heard the explosion," Kamuela said. "But before I could leave the house, those men were inside. They had Twilla. The one you call Guns shot Twilla." Kamuela's voice gave off more than sorrow; the stronger emotion was guilt.

"I am so sorry for this, Kamuela. For everything that's happened. They are here because of me."

"That is not true, Hatch A'e Loa." Kamuela insisted. "I gave that man the chance to live. It is a mercy he does not return. It is my fault I did not kill him. He is not doing this because of you; he came for me."

"Maybe, but the other one is here for me. It doesn't matter why they came," Hatch said. "What matters is getting us out of here."

"Are they going to kill us?" Kukana asked.

Hatch and Kamuela ignored the question; the answer obvious and unnecessary to state.

There were noises from the deck above; preparations for getting underway. Hatch began opening lockers, pulling off bunk cushions. Kamuela got up and removed the cushion on his side. "What am I looking for?" Kamuela asked.

"Anything we can use."

Clearly the cabin had been sanitized to hold prisoners. Now the footsteps on deck were directly above the forward cabin. Hatch saw a pair of ankles pass one of the portholes, then heard the anchor windlass engaging. The engine started with a vibrating rumble.

Chain dropping into the locker clanked and banged loudly. They heard the gears engage, the throttle accelerate. They boat began to move ahead. Disguised by the noise of getting underway, Hatch had managed to split a seam between two louver panels in the door.

"I think they will throw us into the sea," Kamuela said. "I heard them speak of this."

"An eye for an eye," Hatch said.

"I think they will cut us for the sharks."

Kukana gasped and covered her face.

"We can't just sit here. We need to keep them from getting too far out, hold them up long enough for Tioni and the others to reach us with their outriggers. I sent Don back to tell Tioni to get the boats."

"Tioni will come," Kamuela said.

"We have to keep them from getting so far out that the outriggers can't catch up."

"I can pretend to be sick," Kukana offered.

Hatch shook his head. "I doubt if they care how you feel. But I do have an idea. Only if it backfires, we'll be in a lot of trouble locked in here."

"Do we not already have plenty da kine?" Kamuela said. "What is this idea?"

"I doubt if they thought of this," Hatch explained, opening the door to the forward cabin's toilet. "This is a pump toilet. These kinds of toilets all have sea cocks, two way valves through the hull for discharge and refill. If I open the sea cock, water will flood into the bilges and eventually sink the boat. The flow of sea water through that opening would be more than bilge pumps could handle. Once they realize the boat is taking on that much water, they'll have no choice but to come into the cabin to close the valve."

"I like this idea, Hatch A'e Loa. We make them open the door."

"It will be dangerous. We will have only one chance to get a weapon."

"Do it," Kamuela said, sitting on the bunk next to

Kukana and putting his arm around her shoulders. "We are ready."

Hatch went into the head and opened the sea cock. Water quickly began filling the bilges. Hatch moved Kukana as far forward as she could go, against the door to the chain locker; Kamuela took a position on one side of the cabin door and Hatch stood on a bunk cushion on the other side.

It didn't take long before the cabin compartment covers started floating upward, and the cabin sole itself went underwater. Hatch could feel the boat slowing under the added weight.

Footsteps descended the ladder into the main cabin. Hatch bent down to peer through the slit in the door and saw Bill Byron dropping to his knees in the center of the cabin to lift one of the sole covers.

"Kill the engines," Byron yelled back toward the cockpit.

The boat slowed instantly and then stopped dead in the water, picking up the motion of the sea pushing against the hull, then beginning to wallow with the swells.

Byron got the compartment cover open, although it was already starting to float up on its own. Guns went aft, telling Byron he was going to check the propeller shaft packing. He saw that the bilges were completely flooded and the pumps were not keeping up.

Byron approached the forward cabin door, Hatch could only see his belt buckle through the cracked slat.

"You goddamn motherfucking prick," Byron cried. "You opened the fucking sea cock! Well, Mr. Ingenuity, did it occur to you that you're trapped in there? You idiots are going to drown like bilge rats."

"Bilge rats don't drown," Hatch said through the door. "They're always the first off a sinking ship. And your ship is sinking."

"So what? It's a rental. Guns and I just take off on

the Avon and you head for Davy Jones' locker."

"Take the Avon where?" Hatch said. "Back to Tuva? Now that would be an interesting welcome. It's a long way to paddle to Tahiti."

"You do present an interesting dilemma," Byron said.

Guns came forward from the engine room and told Byron that it wasn't leaking from the stuffing box.

"Your buddy opened the sea cock in the forward head," he told Guns.

"Shit, we've got to close it. We're fucking sinking!"

Byron held out his arm and stopped Guns from opening the cabin door. "That's exactly what he wants us to do."

"Yeah, but we're fucking sinking."

"So are they, and they are trapped."

The water in the forward cabin was already reaching Kamuela's ankles. In ten minutes or less they would pass the point of no return, and even with the sea cock closed, the boat would be on her way down.

"Be ready," Hatch whispered to Kamuela. "If they don't open the door, they may try to shoot us through it. I think I can take this door down if I can hit it hard enough. It opens out."

Hatch looked at Kukana crouched at the bulkhead and gestured for her to lie down flat.

"What the fuck," Guns said. "Let's just kill them right now." He looked down and watched the bilge water climbing up his shins.

"Might as well do it," Hatch said through the door. "What difference is it to us if we drown, get thrown to the sharks, or you shoot us right now?"

Byron understood then that Hatch was not bluffing. He was right; it didn't make any difference. He stepped closer to the door, his rifle pointed straight ahead. Guns picked up his rifle from the settee and stood behind Byron.

"I'm going to unlock this door," Byron said, "and you come out of there one at a time."

At that moment, when Byron put the rifle under his arm and approached the lock, Hatch moved as far back as he could to gain some momentum, but before he could move, Kamuela stepped in front of Hatch and crashed through the louvered door, his massive body shattering the slats and knocking the entire door off its hinges.

The surprise of the door crashing down and into his chest knocked Bill Byron backwards. He fell into the bilge water, now floating above the cockpit sole, with the remains of the door on top of him. At the same moment, Guns opened up with his M-16. Three slugs ripped through Kamuela's body, but his momentum carried him forward into Guns. They collapsed into the narrow space between the dinette and the galley, with the M-16 wedged across Guns' chest and under Kamuela's weight. Kamuela grabbed Guns' hair and began pounding his head against the cabin sole, each jolt splashing water like a rock thrown into a bucket. Blood from Guns' head spread out in the water.

Hatch grabbed Kukana's hand and jerked her out of the cabin. Byron, still trapped under the door, managed to bring up his rifle and point it toward Hatch. But before he could squeeze off a round, Kamuela rose up like a wall. The bullet aimed at Hatch went through Kamuela's chest, passed through his back, and smashed into Hatch's upper leg. Kamuela fell on top of the door, pinning Bill firmly below it, with the water rising over his face.

Hatch shoved Kukana toward the cockpit ladder.

"Papa," she cried.

"Go, go, go," Hatch screamed at her, forcing her up the ladder.

Kukana, moving by the force and urgency in her husband's voice, ascended the ladder and stepped into the cockpit.

Kamuela had one hand around Gun's throat; Byron could not move from under the weight of Kamuela lying atop the door.

"Go from here now," Kamuela told Hatch, his voice weak, fading. "Do not let my daughter die. Promise me."

Kamuela crushed Guns' windpipe. Bill Byron's head was completely submerged now.

Hatch tried to lift Kamuela. "Come on, let's get out of here."

"Go now," Kamuela said. "Kukana … ."

Kamuela slumped and his eyes closed. Hatch checked his pulse and knew that Kamuela was dead. He touched his cheek, then forced himself to leave.

"Hurry, hurry," he heard Kukana's screaming from above.

Kukana stood frozen at the aft cockpit rail.

"Jump!" Hatch cried.

"Papa?"

"Jump now, Kukana!"

Below deck, Bill Byron was drowning and did not have enough strength to push Kamuela and the door off him. He heard Hatch's voice yelling jump. He stretched his arm toward the settee and let his hand fall heavily over the detonator switch.

There were twenty outriggers in the flotilla heading around Kaiwi Point. The motor yacht lay dead in the water only three hundred yards away. The combination of twenty outboard motors sounded like a massive swarm of bees.

Then the explosion, its concussion wave rocking the outriggers back and forth. The motor yacht shuddered like an object shimmering in a distant heat haze, then a ball of yellow fire roared into the sky as the fuel tanks went, obliterating the boat down to its rapidly sinking shell.

The outriggers bobbed quietly in the soft swells. Slivers of wood, chunks of metal, shattered bits of fiberglass rained over the sea like hail from a black cloud. The smell of fuel arrived, small patches of fire dotted the debris-laden surface.

Tioni Makani and I, in the lead boat, looked into the smoke and across the flaming surface of the sea, offering a prayer to our neglected gods. The boats moved steadily forward now, moving into a search pattern. I rather knew that no one could have survived that blast, but we would look.

Tioni moved to the bow of his outrigger and faced forward, staring at the empty sea, so the men would not see him crying.

33

The large silver seaplane made a full circle around Tuva before arcing wide around Kaiwi Point and settling over the lagoon to land.

The arrival was announced two days before, and Tuvans gathered with anticipation. The pier itself filled with people: brown stringy children scurrying around the legs of their elders, older children waving Australian and American flags on thin sticks, adolescent boys clinging high up palm trees along the bay front, young girls in church dresses giggling anxiously; some men wore the jacket from an old suit, their wives in flowered hats.

Inside Papa Jack's, Dennis Lindsay wiped down the long bar and sipped Japanese brandy, waiting the rush of business sure to follow the main event.

Hattie bustled a broad path to the end of the wharf, wearing her finest hat and waving an American flag in one hand and an Australian flag in the other.

Apalama Makani, now the chief of Tuva, waited with his wife Lahela for Mr. Jolly Malcolm, the Australian government official for Tuva, to be brought from his office. The status of chief had gone to Tioni Makani, but he refused the honor. "I want only to be a fisherman," he said. Regardless of that desire, because his Uncle Apalama lived in a small village on the opposite side of the island from Tuva town, Tuvans were deferring to Tioni in matters that had once gone to his father.

The seaplane taxied slowly over the quiet waters of the lagoon to the brand new disembarkation platform built off the end of the wharf.

The government representative was late; Apalama stood nervously waiting. He was not prepared for such official events, especially involving Americans.

Hatch, Jenny, and I were the only Americans Apalama had ever known. Besides, it was not proper for Mr. Jolly to be missing. He began to fidget and Lahela touched his arm, telling him to be patient.

Finally the double front doors of the government house opened. Two burly men, holding Mr. Jolly's chair between them, emerged. Mr. Jolly, dressed in a fine white jacket, white silk shirt and navy tie, topped with a Panama hat, both empty pant legs folded neatly beneath the stumps above his knees, sat in the chair like a king.

"Let's not make the bloody buggers think we have nothing better to do here but stand around waiting for them," Mr. Jolly said to Apalama, who approached and shook Mr. Jolly's hand.

Apalama fell in step beside the chair, Lahela following discreetly behind, sneaking a couple of last puffs from her Chesterfield, watched the delegation exit the plane. Tioni and Jenny Makani approached and took their places beside Tioni's Uncle Apalama. People, gathered on the pier, parted to let them pass.

Five men exited the aircraft. Two wore uniforms of the Australian Navy, two in uniforms of the American Army, followed by an American dressed in a bush jacket and floppy hat, as if he were going on an African safari. After a short pause, a Polynesian man everyone recognized as the chief of Olowalu, squeezed his bulk through the door.

The chief of Olowalu stepped to the front and shook Mr. Jolly's hand. He said, so that people on the wharf and up to the nearby street could hear, that all Olowalu was proud of Mr. Jolly's bravery and terrible sacrifice.

"Thank you, Chief Kolokane," Mr. Jolly replied. "But it is nothing to what all we Tuvans have lost."

The ranking Australian officer approached, saluted Mr. Jolly, and said, "Please accept the sincere regrets of your government for your loss, sir."

Then the officer introduced the two American

military officers. "I have the pleasure of introducing Major General John Welch of the United States Army, along with his aide, Lieutenant Colonel Alvin Baker."

General Welch indicated the civilian standing behind with a quick glance, and introduced him as Mr. Smith.

Welch leaned close to Mr. Jolly's ear and whispered, "Is there a body?"

"General, please." Mr. Jolly responded formally and rather loudly. "Our tiny home is seldom graced with such distinguished visitors. You must allow us the honor of showing you our hospitality before we visit the resting place of our honored departed."

Welch bowed graciously and stepped back with the others.

The chair bearers lifted Mr. Jolly and turned to lead the way. The others followed to the great lawn beside the government house, in sight of the burned-out hulk of the generator shed. Then the festivities could begin. A throng of Tuvans came up from the wharf, singing the song written to praise the hero of Tuva. Then the dancers, the musicians, the children with flowers, platters laden with food. Loud cheering followed the announcement by the Australian Captain that a team of Royal Navy engineers would arrive day after tomorrow to replace the generator station with a new, much larger one, and install a new radio set in the government house.

It was late in the afternoon before the party wound down to the point where the dignitaries felt comfortable taking their leave, although it was obvious the party would continue probably throughout the night. Mr. Jolly noticed that the American General was distracted and had obviously intended to come and go without all these silly festivities. Mr. Jolly also figured that he knew why.

Following close behind Mr. Jolly and his chair bearers, the two American military men and Mr.

Smith, along with myself, Tioni, Jenny, and Apalama Makani, walked down the center of the main street to the church, then to the cemetery at the rear.

Reaching that place near an ancient banyan tree, the group stopped in front of three new stone markers of equal size and shape, the graves lying side by side.

On the first stone was carved:

Kamuela Pukalani Makani
Husband of Emma, father of Tioni and Kukana
And father of all Tuva.
Beloved by his people.

On the second stone:

Kukana Pele Makani A'e Loa
Daughter of Kamuela and Emma,
Wife of Hatch A'e Loa
A child of all Tuva.

And on the third:

Hatch A'e Loa
A Tuvan
Husband of Kukana
Hero of Tuva

General Welch moved toward the third grave and knelt to study the earth there. He looked up at Mr. Jolly and said, "There were no burials here, this earth has not been turned. Where are the bodies?"

"There were no bodies, General. Here their spirits rest."

"No bodies?" Welch stood. There was sarcasm in his tone.

Tioni took an angry step toward the General, but Mr. Jolly held out his arm to stay him.

Welch stood his ground, and his skeptical demeanor. "You didn't find anything?"

"Nothing was omitted from my official report," Mr. Jolly replied. "The bits and pieces we found I will not mention in this company. These are family members, you know."

"Please forgive my persistence, sir. I do not doubt the honesty of your honorable self or your report, which I read thoroughly. I hope you will understand that the man you called Hatch was Captain Franklin J. Hatcher of the United States Army. He is a war criminal, and he has been listed as killed in action before. Yet obviously he has been living on this atoll for more than ten years. One wonders how many lives he may have?"

I overheard Welch turning to whisper into Lt. Colonel Baker's ear: "I don't believe it. Find out."

"In fairness, General, I should warn you to exercise caution with your words about Hatch A'e Loa, for whom I see not one shred of evidence he was what you claim; but of course I am not calling you a liar." Mr. Jolly smiled in a way to show that indeed that was exactly what he was calling the General. I could not surprise a laugh. "Please forgive me for not saving the bloody scraps we found floating in the sea; oh, if only we had found a finger for you to print. If we could have caught the sharks and emptied their bellies … ."

"I meant no disrespect. I apologize if I come across as blunt or harsh. I am sorry for the lives you lost in his beautiful place, and I apologize for the participation of American citizens in his stupid carnage. There are bad people everywhere. The man you called Hatch was one of the bad people, and those men came here to arrest him, not to harm your people."

Tioni again moved toward Welch, only to be stopped again by Mr. Jolly. I could not help but wonder if this was a task a Major General in the US Army would undertake. Seemed a bit of overkill to me.

"General, that is a lie. I don't know if it is your first lie today, but it is your last, because now no one here will listen to you. Those men came here to kill our beloved chief and his daughter, and in that brutal mission they were successful."

"We are working from different information … ."

"Let me explain one more thing to you, General," Mr. Jolly interrupted. "The man you claim is this Captain Hatcher was a hero to our people. The song you heard at the beginning of the festivities was written in his honor by a people who loved, who even revered him. I will be blunt. The Tuvans believe you came here today to honor Hatch's memory, because he was born an American; to honor his heroism. If they were told otherwise, if they heard the claim you just made, you would not have been allowed to set foot on this island. If you came here intending to stir up some bloody goddamn mischief about Hatch A'e Loa, I promise that your departure, and we all hope it will be soon, will not be nearly as pleasant as your arrival. Do you catch my drift, General?"

Welch nodded, but with a smirk. Then he leaned down close to Mr. Jolly's ear. "I will give the man this. Hatch was the best fighting man I ever had the pleasure of commanding in war. Regardless of what happened in another time and place, I would happily shake his hand before turning him over to a courts-martial."

Mr. Jolly laughed. "I bet it would have given him a laugh him to hear that." Then he gestured for his bearers to lift his chair. "We should return so you can make your flight."

The seaplane with its Australian Air Force markings taxied into the lagoon. A crowd as large as that welcoming the plane had gathered on the pier to watch its departure. Mr. Jolly, perched with dignity in his wicker chair, waited in front of Papa Jack's until the plane lifted off. Then he directed his bearers to take him into the bar.

"The usual," he called out to Dennis.

The bearers put the chair down near the end of the bar, then accepted the beers Mr. Jolly ordered for them.

"Wasn't that a great bloody show," he said.

Those still gathered on the pier waved as the plane became smaller and smaller, finally disappearing into the late afternoon sun.

Jenny Hunt Makani put her arm through her husband's and leaned into him, finally able to once again feel warm and secure. Tioni stared at the plane until it was gone.

"I think Mr. Jolly handled everything quite well, don't you?" Jenny said.

"That he did," Tioni answered. "But I still want to crush the head of that American jellyfish."

Jenny smiled and leaned closer into her husband's side. "I think I would have enjoyed seeing that, but you know what I would rather do?"

They began walking back into town from the pier.

"What do you want to do?"

"I want to go see our niece."

They held hands and walked by the church and along the banana grove to the path leading to the Makani house. Jenny looked at Tioni's face and saw tears.

"What's wrong, my darling?"

"I wish Papa … ."

"So do we all."

They reached the cutoff to the magistrate of police house and walked onto the veranda.

Inside the house Kamuela Makani had built for his daughter and son-in-law, Kukana sat in a soft chair in the bedroom. Her eyes were closed as she drifted through a daydream of things that now would never be. The shoulder strap of her sundress was pulled down to free the breast where Emma suckled.

After the seaplane departed, her husband, Hatch

A'e Loa, came back into the house from the back garden, where he had spent much of the afternoon pulling weeds from his wife's flower bed. He was still limping, and in fact, he always would. He stopped in the doorway and looked in at his wife and child.

Sensing his presence, Kukana opened her eyes.

He looked at his daughter. She was asleep but sucking at the nipple.

"How can she eat and sleep at the same time?" Hatch wondered.

"I do not know," Kukana answered.

When Hatch came over and kissed the top of her head, she began crying again.

Hatch, Kukana, and Emma disappeared from Tuva a few days later. They sailed away on the half-reconstructed Hard Wind.

We met that morning, as he was stacking supplies on the ketch's now open aft cockpit.

"I suppose it's for the best," I told him. "But it still seems wrong, somehow. Unnecessary."

"It is necessary," Hatch replied.

He was right, of course. It wasn't over. Other men would come for him.

But it wasn't just that, I believe. The deaths we suffered on our island were because of him; he knew that, as did we all. Although we did not blame him, he most certainly blamed himself. He could be the cause of an action without being at fault for it. Who is responsible when a storm lashes our island and people die? God is the cause, but are the deaths His fault?

I will leave that question for the philosophers.

www.ingramcontent.com/pod-product-compliance
Lightning Source LLC
Chambersburg PA
CBHW060130130626
46556CB00006B/2299